FROM A PARIS BALCONY

BOOKS BY ELLA CAREY

ELLA CAREY

FROM A PARIS BALCONY

GC

GRAND CENTRAL
PUBLISHING

New York   Boston

Cover design by Elizabeth Connor. Photo compositing by Debra Lill. Cover images: doorway and woman © Lee Avison/Trevillion; balcony and railing © Lee Avison/Arcangel; others from Shutterstock. Cover copyright © 2022 by Hachette Book Group, Inc.

Grand Central Publishing
Hachette Book Group
1290 Avenue of the Americas, New York, NY 10104
grandcentralpublishing.com
twitter.com/grandcentralpub

Originally published by Lake Union Publishing in 2016
Previously published by Bookouture, an imprint of Storyfire Ltd., in 2020
First Grand Central Publishing edition: December 2022

Grand Central Publishing is a division of Hachette Book Group, Inc. The Grand Central Publishing name and logo is a trademark of Hachette Book Group, Inc.

The Hachette Speakers Bureau provides a wide range of authors for speaking events. To find out more, go to www.hachettespeakersbureau.com or call (866) 376-6591.

Library of Congress Control Number: 2021952443

ISBN: 9781538722589 (trade paperback)

Printed in the United States of America

LSC-C

Printing 1, 2022

Chapter One

Boston, 2015

The small green chest was concealed at the back of the wardrobe. Its hinges were made of brass that must have shone once, but now it was roughened with amorphous black spots. A key was bound to the lid, almost endearingly, Sarah thought, with layers of old sticky tape whose edges curled under a canopy of dust. Sarah had no idea how long the chest had lain there, wedged underneath a pile of her father's moth-eaten sweaters, alongside his other hoarded treasures—the pipes that he used to sneak out into the garden to smoke and the stained yellow tobacco tins that he always reused for fishing hooks. Sarah hesitated to open the curious little box for some reason. But that was ridiculous, because not a soul would know or care if she did. She had no family left at all.

Her sentimentality about unlocking this secret was even more ironic given that she curated the possessions of the dead for a living. Sarah was hardly unused to opening precious things left behind. In the end, she adopted the determination that she had assumed so often as a matter of necessity over the last tumultuous year and slid her nails under the tape. The key felt small and cold in her fingers when she inserted it in the lock. She pulled at the lid and stared at the contents. Or the content. Because there was only one thing in the box.

An envelope. And across this envelope, written clearly in the blue ink of a fountain pen, were both a name and an address that were perplexing in themselves—*Viscount Henry Duval, Île de la Cité, Paris.* Postmarked 1895.

Sarah took the letter over to the window that looked out over the genteel Boston street where she had grown up. Blossom petals floated from the stately trees that lined the grand street below. Nannies pushed expensive new strollers along the sidewalk, dodging the inevitable well-tailored office workers and the usual array of women who looked like they lunched. But none of this could draw Sarah in, not today. She turned back to the delicious little mystery in her hands instead.

Viscount Henry Duval had been veiled in intrigue for Sarah since she was a girl. The name was linked forever with Sarah's family, tied up with a tragedy that had captured her imagination when she was young.

The death of Sarah's great-great-aunt in the midst of a glamorous party in Paris during the Belle Époque had never been fully explained, as far as Sarah was concerned. Louisa Duval had, so the story went, jumped out of a window one night in Paris and died on the pavement below. Even though the mysterious young woman's death was declared a suicide, the circumstances had never been investigated.

The more Sarah had asked her father for details, the more she realized how little he knew. She hadn't had much time for curiosity in the last few months, having been confronted with a triple tragedy of her own: the deaths of both her parents, and her husband leaving for good. Now, as she worked through her parents' vacant apartment, the resurfacing of her ancestor's mystery tickled her mind. These older ghosts had a more comfortable distance than the painful, fresh ones right now.

There had always been an assumption that Louisa killed herself. But had this enigmatic young woman, from whom Sarah was descended, really taken her own life?

The more Sarah had thought about it, the more she wondered if there was a reason it had been kept quiet. What on earth was her father doing, hiding away a letter addressed to Louisa's husband in a decrepit green box?

But Sarah was late for a meeting and there was no time to linger over distant events. She had already missed some work over the past few months, and, while she was not directly involved in the new exhibition that was about to open at Boston's Museum of Fine Arts, where she worked, she had to go or she would wind up in trouble.

Sarah tucked the letter inside her handbag, took one last look at her parents' apartment—it would have to be sold—locked their heavy front door, and slipped down the front steps into the street.

It wasn't until that evening that she had the chance to pull the timeworn envelope out of her handbag. She had been accosted by emails and interruptions at work all afternoon, and while her thoughts had wanted to turn to Henry Duval's letter, she had forced herself to remain focused on her job.

Sarah poured herself a glass of wine in her galley kitchen and moved across to her living room, with its picture windows overlooking the Charles River. The days had started to lengthen, and she didn't need to turn on the lamps that she had bought after Steven had left during Boston's last cold, icy winter, but she switched the lights on anyway. She loved the warm glow they created.

Sarah still didn't know whether to sell her apartment, rent it out, or simply stay put. She had been too exhausted to face a move after Steven left. So she had replaced some of the furniture, had installed floor-to-ceiling bookshelves filled with books on things she loved—art, old jewelry, family heirlooms, and houses. And she had stayed where she was, for now.

Sarah sat down in her favorite pale blue armchair, took a sip of wine, and turned back to the letter. And opened it. And read.

Paris, 1895

My dear Henry,

I find myself unable to articulate my shock at the events that unfolded last night.

You must be appalled, mon cher. *And confused, I am in no doubt. What a tragedy, what a trauma—I simply cannot think how you are bearing up.*

And to have something as dreadful as this happen in Montmartre, our little homeland! Louisa's death throws a villainous shadow over our menagerie sociale. *The atmosphere is quite changed after one single night. I saw not a soul from the party when I rode in the Bois de Boulogne today. The park was empty of our little groups—and it suffered for it. It suffered with the stuffy bourgeoisie gliding like old ghosts on the paths—because we were not there, my dear.*

Later, I found myself extremely agitated at home in the apartment. I could not settle, and the idea of visitors! Can you imagine? No I think not!

Following this, I was in a mind to visit you. I even had on my kid gloves, but I feared that the sight of my carriage at your house on the Île St.-Louis would simply bring more gossip—and we cannot afford that, my dear friend, not at all. Which brings me to my next awful thought.

I know that you come to Paris to enjoy our wonderful "attributes": the cancan dancers, all our friends, and the razzle. Not to mention our wonderful theaters and dance halls. But my fear is that you need to think like one of us, my Henry. I want you to think like a true modern, I want you to move and move very fast. My darling, I sense that it is vital that you leave Paris, today.

Tragic as it is, tragic as must be your feelings about Louisa and about last night—no matter what she was, or what she was to you, she was your wife.

Go home to England. Bury yourself at Ashworth until it is over. You need to encircle yourself within your family. They will protect you. You must let the wheels of your parents' influence take over now. The authorities will want to question you if you stay here—you know everything, and that is too much.

Your father will be able to get rid of the press. And you will deal far better with the inevitable police investigations from the safety of your home. Your parents will shield you. They are not emotionally invested. They will know exactly what to say.

Just leave, or I will worry until it kills me.

When we meet next, we will talk as if we were never apart. It will be like it always is, but for now, à bientôt, my friend.

I will miss you, but I am always, always with you, you know that.

Au revoir,
Marthe de Florian

Sarah stared at the signature at the bottom of the page. No matter how used she was to researching other people's heirlooms, no matter how used she was to hearing about other people's pasts—this was her own family.

This was her past.

The fact that Viscount Henry Duval, Louisa's husband, seemed to be connected with one of the most famous Parisian courtesans who lived in the Belle Époque was one thing. The fact that the famous courtesan was telling Henry to leave Paris was quite another again.

Marthe's handwriting stared back at Sarah as if it were the most casual thing in the world. But Sarah knew how famous this woman had been. Sarah knew that Marthe de Florian's apartment had been rediscovered in Paris in 2010. Her granddaughter had fled Paris in June 1940, abandoning it on the eve of the Nazi occupation.

For seventy years, nobody had entered Marthe's grand home, no one had set foot inside. And nobody knew why the granddaughter had never returned. The discovery of Marthe's apartment had caused more than a buzz in the art world and had been a topic of interest among Sarah's colleagues.

The story had become even more fascinating. Marthe's apartment was not just a frozen replica from 1940, it was a time capsule from a generation before that. Sarah could only imagine how the curators who had discovered Marthe's gifts from her countless gentlemen "clients" must have felt walking into the veritable time warp when it was discovered. Imagine the jewels, paintings, furniture, objets d'art.

While getting her degree, Sarah had studied, albeit briefly, the life of Giovanni Boldini, the artist whose unsigned portrait of Marthe de Florian had been found in the apartment, causing such a stir in itself. It had sold at auction for over two million euros, no less.

But the thing that had touched Sarah, what had intrigued her most of all, was the discovery of a stash of letters to Marthe from her gentlemen admirers. They had been wrapped up in silk ribbons, all left intact.

And now, Sarah was holding such a thing right here, in her hands.

While she was tempted to sit and let some of the magic distill itself onto her, she knew that she had to investigate, and now.

Sarah went to her computer. First questions first.

When she read that the courtesan's apartment was now available for rent, Sarah simply stared at the screen in front of her and sat back in her seat.

But then, as she sat there, a thought began to kick in. It was mad, creative, the sort of plan that she would normally laugh off as ludicrous—but then, ideas that seemed mad at first were often valuable; how many artists had she studied over the years to learn that?

What if she were to go to Paris?

What if this was her chance to get close to her mysterious ancestor—to find out whether Louisa had ended her own life? If Sarah had no living relatives left, why shouldn't she find out about the past? After all, Louisa's father had lost nearly all of his old Boston wealth as a result of his terrible grief, and the family had been shunned by society because of the taint of suicide.

Sarah knew the feeling that gossip could bring. Rumors had led her to the sickening awareness that her ex-husband, Steven, had a girlfriend, an old flame of his whom Sarah had known nothing about. Once the horrible truth had come out, Sarah had avoided every place that she knew Steven frequented in Boston. In spite of this, she bumped into him and his girlfriend all too often—the woman always stared at Sarah as if she were something unpleasant that had crossed her path. Not the other way around.

But that was nothing compared to the death of a young woman at a party in Paris. Sarah looked at the letter sitting on the table in front of her. The idea that had started forming in her head was turning into a plan.

What if somewhere there were letters from Henry to Marthe that were as revealing as the one she had just found? If the courtesan had kept all her correspondence, this was not a long shot. What was more, the idea of getting away from Boston, from her own past, for a while was more than tempting; it seemed like a release. What if she could rent Marthe de Florian's apartment?

Summer in Paris was starting to sound like the perfect idea.

*

The following morning, Sarah steeled herself against any further doubts. Over breakfast in the museum's elegant café, she convinced her boss, Amanda, that she would like to use her sabbatical right now. Before she could think again, she would call the owner of Marthe's apartment—a Monsieur Loic Archer. What if Marthe had corresponded regularly with Henry? What then? There had to be more clues to Louisa's life and end in the apartment.

Once Sarah was in her office, she closed her door, swept a hand through her glossy black bob, and dialed France.

She explained, in her halting schoolgirl French, her reasons for wanting to rent the apartment. She said that she was hoping to make a reservation for the entire summer, but Loic Archer, the charming-sounding Frenchman who replied to her in English, speaking, curiously, without any French accent at all, sent all her hopes sinking like liquid down a smooth drain.

"I understand your interest in the apartment, Sarah, and to tell the truth, I'm intrigued by your ancestor's seeming connection with Marthe. But there is one problem. We have a clash. Laurent Chartier, the artist. I'm sure you've heard of him?"

Sarah nodded in silence down the line.

"Laurent," Loic Archer went on, "needs to be in Marthe's apartment for the entire summer—there is nothing I can do about it. He's one of my oldest friends. We grew up together in Provence. I'm sure you know how famous he is. He's been commissioned to paint a series of portraits for *Vogue* magazine in the style of Giovanni Boldini. You know, models, actresses, the sort of celebrities whom Boldini would have painted, were he alive now."

Sarah had heard of Laurent Chartier—he was a wunderkind, the next big French artist. He had held wildly successful exhibitions in Paris, London, and, more recently, New York. His style was ever changing. He adapted all the time. And that had made him extra famous, one to watch. His paintings sold for record prices because no one knew what mode of expression he would take on next.

"Laurent needs to be in the setting where Boldini painted while he works—the lighting, the props, Marthe's things. *Vogue* is fixated on the idea of using the famous courtesan's rediscovered apartment as a backdrop for the series of paintings. It makes sense that he stays there. I'm sorry. He paints all night when he's on a roll."

Loic was quiet for a moment. "This is a commission from the leading fashion magazine in the world in honor of one of our most famous portrait artists. The only option I can offer is that you share the apartment with Laurent. You would have your own bedroom, of course...otherwise, I'm happy to help you find somewhere else to stay in Paris."

Sarah stood up and paced around her office. While she adored her job, she hated to think how many hours she had spent stomping around this room during the past year. Typically, the stomping would be followed by a good dose of staring out the window at the street below, trying to contain her grief.

Sarah closed her eyes.

Loic Archer remained quiet.

Sarah moved back to her desk. She collected the folder of notes for her next appointment. A woman wanted to bequeath her mother's jewelry collection to the museum.

She ran a hand over her trouser suit. "Please, could you ask if I could share the apartment with Laurent?" She steeled herself and waited for Loic's response.

"I will."

"Thank you."

There was a silence. "There's a few things you should know about Laurent." Loic's voice dropped so low that it sounded as if he were about to reveal state secrets on an international scale.

Loic paused for a moment before he started to speak. "It might help—if you are going to live with him—if you understand what's going on. Laurent is a very refined individual. He has a strong aesthetic. He abhors anything obnoxious, tasteless, or crass. But at the moment..." Loic coughed.

Sarah stopped still for a moment, before moving toward the elevator.

"Nowadays, he's abandoned all that." Loic went on in a rush. "He seems to think he's some sort of Toulouse-Lautrec. He's hanging with models. His behavior is a bit...wild."

Sarah had also heard stories, gossip. Laurent hung around with the elite set and he had done something naughty at Miami Art Basel last year, but Sarah couldn't recall exactly what. She bit back her instinctive response and pressed the elevator button instead, gazing at the red numbers on the screen. She had made an art of focusing on what was right in front of her just to move forward every day after what had happened with Steven.

Was she a magnet for out-of-control men? And yet, why should she be intimidated or put off? What if this was a chance to get some behind-the-scenes experience with an artist? Usually she only dealt with people who owned the art. She realized that she was conjuring up excuses to leave Boston, but in the end, did it matter what this artist was like?

"I've read about him." She kept her voice deadpan.

"I'm sorry." Loic sounded resigned. "I guess some people might find it hard to...deal with Laurent right now. He's going through a rough patch. Something went wrong. But it's not my place to tell you. That's his story. It's just that, it might help you to understand that he is a good person. He is brilliant, you know—"

"Oh." Sarah felt a chuckle rising in her throat. "Well, that will help."

"He's incredibly talented."

Sarah stepped into the lift and felt her eyebrows rise to the roof.

"Anyway, by rights the apartment belongs to my wife, Cat. She's flat out with our first baby right now. Our little daughter is a month old. So I'm going to have to be the person you deal with, I'm afraid."

Sarah stepped out of the elevator and walked to the street. "Congratulations." She knew she sounded vague, but her mind was locked onto Paris and wild artists and, for some extraordinary reason, Toulouse-Lautrec. "Congratulations on the baby."

She shook her head, rounded the corner, unlocked her car door, slipped inside, and memorized the address of the house she was visiting.

"Laurent will be working hard all summer," Loic said. "Just tell him to be quiet when he comes back in the door late at night. If you have real problems, then I'll simply move you out. I can talk to him anytime too."

Sarah looked at her watch. It was time to go. She was never late. Never.

She took a few seconds to think, right there, right then. After what she had been through, what was an artist in a tailspin? He didn't have to affect her. No doubt Laurent would be all over his models and actresses anyway. He wouldn't even notice Sarah was in the apartment at all.

She collected her thoughts. "All right then. I'll still share with him. You know, I do appreciate this, thank you. I'm sure we will be fine."

"Thank you," he said.

They agreed that Loic would meet her at the apartment once she had arrived.

"I'll see you in Paris," she said. And hung up. And shook her head. She had let a mad idea run to fruition. So unlike her. What she was doing, she had no idea. But she had to get away, she knew that. She wanted to find out about Louisa. For some reason, she felt closer than ever to her ancestor. For some reason, Sarah felt as if Louisa were calling to her from the past.

Chapter Two

Sarah's boss, Amanda, insisted on hosting a farewell dinner for Sarah at her favorite tapas restaurant in town. It was one of Boston's hardest-to-get-into places, but Amanda had cultivated a friendship with one of the hip owners, and she liked to show off the fact that she could get a table at the drop of an emerald brooch.

Sarah knew the food would be as good as the tapas in Barcelona, or so everyone said. Long wooden tables ran down the center of the room. An artisan bar sat along the length of one exposed brick wall, and an oversize blackboard showcased the menu. Sarah hung her favorite leather jacket over the back of her chair, shook her coworkers' hands, and ran a hand through her black bob. She had taken great care with her makeup this evening—had spent some time on her dark brown eyes. This evening she wanted to look particularly professional. She suspected her workmates were stunned that she was going to Paris.

The first part of the evening passed well enough. Sarah found herself chatting her way through the entrées of smoked eggplant and wild mushrooms with summer herbs and plates of melt-in-your-mouth grilled corn, while her colleagues—graphic designers, along with art educators and marketing people, curators of paintings, and staff on research fellowships—kept up the sort of steady banter that Sarah always enjoyed on nights out.

But once the food was done, Brian Doolan, one of the museum's longest-standing curators, addressed Sarah, and the table fell quiet. "What we're going to miss is your efficiency." His eyes twinkled, and Sarah found herself raising her brow.

Sarah toyed with her dessert wine, watching the sticky liquid move around in the bottom of the glass. "My efficiency?" she said. "Wow. Thanks." She kept her tone light. She knew Brian. And she knew what he said was only a half joke.

"You have to hand it to yourself," Amanda chimed in from Sarah's other side. The older woman tossed her long blond hair and fixed Sarah with her green eyes. "It's what you do best. Don't know how we'll manage without you for the summer."

"Thanks." Sarah knew her voice sounded as flat as a sunken soufflé.

"You're so reliable." There was nothing nasty in Amanda's tone, but Sarah had heard these words too many times to count. Responsible, efficient, sensible. Rational. Sarah had to push away a sigh. Was that how Steven had seen her? Reliable? Not novel enough?

"You know," Brian said, "I always say, if we need someone dependable, then Sarah's our girl."

"Thanks." Sarah knew she was sounding like a record player with its needle stuck on one song.

"And you know what the best thing is?" Brian warmed to his theme. "You do things in an orderly fashion. Nothing is spontaneous with you. You work to a plan. Logical. We need people like that. I find you invaluable. Wish I had more of your qualities myself."

"So when you said you were going to Paris," Amanda laughed, "I nearly died on the spot. What, I thought, could Sarah possibly be wanting to do in the city of love? I mean, Paris is totally out of character for you. It's not the city I'd choose for you at all. London, yes, but never Paris."

"Are you planning a little liaison of your own? You know, revenge and all that on that vile ex-husband?" Brian leaned in closer to Sarah. "Do tell." He sounded wicked.

Sarah pulled away. She liked Brian, but right now she could smell stale wine and garlic on his breath.

"It's not that," she said.

"So you just want to go to Paris for the summer, because you can?" Brian was not giving up.

"Yup."

"Good for you." Amanda sounded cheerful.

"I don't believe you," Brian went on. "I've known you since you were twenty-three. Nine years is a long time, Sarah. You're too strategic to do this for no reason."

"I admit that I do enjoy a plan." Sarah shrugged. "But I don't have one this time."

Brian's eyes narrowed into a pair of tiny chinks. "I still don't believe you."

Sarah pulled her jacket on. She was not, she reminded herself, boring. She wore leather jackets. And she used to have a life. Until it exploded into a million tiny shards, and there was nothing she could do about it. Nothing at all.

"Well. You have a great time in Paris no matter why you're going." Brian had reverted to his usual affable self.

He leaned forward, kissed Sarah on the cheek. Chatter started up among the people at the table. Sarah smiled and patted her colleague on the arm. Hugged Amanda. Moved around the table and said good-bye to the rest of her workmates. As she walked out of the restaurant into the cool Boston air, she let her thoughts escape to Paris.

The next morning, Sarah took a last look around her apartment from the top of the spiral staircase to the living area below. She held a porcelain bowl that had belonged to Louisa's parents, Nathaniel and Charlotte West, which she was going to put away in her safe. She had collected the few precious items that her father had inherited from his parents, and now they were in her apartment. Nothing had been on display in her family; her father had always kept the few heirlooms that he did have protected, hidden away, and now Sarah felt compelled to do the same thing. It was almost as if she were following a script that she would never question. She took the porcelain bowl, which she had cleaned the evening before with her soft polishing cloth, and opened her safe up.

Nathaniel and Charlotte West, Louisa's parents, had inherited a tea-trading company from Charlotte's father, a successful business-man in old Boston's establishment. He had employed Nathaniel before he married Charlotte, and then once Charlotte's father had died, Nathaniel West had ended up running the business. The family had exported cloth, wood, and opium to China in exchange for tea. Sarah knew that Nathaniel had been based in Hong Kong, and then so had Louisa's brother after that.

Now she carried the Canton bowl to her safe, placing the precious piece with its hand-painted dragons and people taking tea right next to her pair of Chinese Foo dogs—gifts Nathaniel brought back for Charlotte from China.

As the late nineteenth century rolled on, Nathaniel had moved on to invest in railroads, seeking one lucrative opportunity after another. His fortune had been large back then. Other branches of the family included bankers and lawyers, with business and social ties to Harvard, the Boston Brahmins, and other blue bloods.

Sarah closed the safe and locked it with her key. The taxi to the airport would arrive shortly. She took one last look around the apartment. She was ready. It was time to go back to Paris.

Chapter Three

Hampshire, England, 1893

Willowdale was different from every other house that Louisa had visited in England. She felt removed, here, from the constant bustle that was London—the endless balls, the same dull young men at every party. The relentless pressure to make a fortunate marriage. It was summer, not winter, not officially the season, but it didn't seem to make any difference. Every mother and daughter was out for the same thing.

Willowdale was not far from London, but here Louisa felt a sense of the England she had imagined before she left Boston. Climbing roses adorned the old house's walls, framing the windows that overlooked the serene park.

A table was set for tea on the terrace. Everyone wore white, as if by some mutual agreement that it was the only color that would suit, Louisa thought. The young ladies' faces were shaded by parasols as the group sat, half-asleep in the afternoon sun. The two men sitting opposite her stretched their legs out in front of them, smoking cigarettes and staring out at the valley in the distance. Two villages sat in the valley below the house. Church spires peeped above the treetops, and rolling fields led down beyond the park.

Louisa could almost forget she had any troubles at all.

Almost.

But the truth was, Willowdale was going to afford her great happiness and deep sadness in equal parts. Happiness for her childhood friend, Meg, who had just married Willowdale's heir,

Guy Hamilton, and sadness, because this was where Louisa would bid farewell to someone more dear to her than anyone else in the world. This was where she had to say good-bye to Samuel.

Louisa regarded her brother with the air of an older sister who was a little proprietary, a little proud, and a little fearful at the same time. It was impossible to equate the grown man sitting near her with the childhood companion whom she had adored all her life. She was still becoming used to the idea that Samuel had grown up, even though she had been with him every step of the way, and they had gotten up to all manner of mischief together over the years.

Louisa's family had maintained the sort of cultivation, restraint, and dignity that was expected of those descended from the English colonists who arrived in the New World on the *Arbella* or the *Mayflower*. However, Louisa knew that she and her brother had enjoyed freedom that was uncommon to their class, largely due to their father's continued absence as a trade merchant in Hong Kong. Their mother had been so caught up in her own social aspirations that she had hardly noticed her children at all. Charlotte West's entire reason for living had always seemed to be to maintain an old aristocratic lifestyle in order to cement her social standing. Now, Louisa could see that her mother had dedicated herself to creating a replica of English life in America. Louisa grasped that she had not really understood either the motivations behind her mother's behavior, or the roots of social structure until she came to England.

Duty, restraint, discretion, these were ideals that Louisa's mother stuck to with a genteel smile. Charlotte West made an art form of cultivating the correct dress, manners, deportment, character traits, and personal virtues that were expected of her class. She devoted herself to the arts, to charity—hospitals and colleges—and to the good works of the Episcopal Church.

But Louisa had been blessed with a governess who had opened her mind to the fact that women should have better rights, rights equal to men's. Louisa had been so drawn to the idea that women deserved to determine their own destinies that she had read more on the topic over the last few years. Her governess shared with her Mrs. Pankhurst's pamphlets advocating universal women's suffrage through her Women's Franchise League. Louisa was inspired by the discovery that Mrs. Pankhurst had taken up an interest in women's rights at the age of fourteen, and she felt drawn to the woman's ideas.

She appreciated that Mrs. Pankhurst was a European woman living in the very society where Louisa found herself now, but Mrs. Pankhurst was leading the way for women in the New World too. The suffragettes proposed an alternative way to that of Louisa's mother. And that excited Louisa.

But Charlotte had found Louisa's pamphlets and had been furious at her new ideas. Charlotte had informed Louisa that being labeled a bluestocking would mean she'd never be seen as a suitable wife. Any form of activism among their class would simply not be tolerated, and Louisa would be dismissed from society faster than she could read one of her own silly pamphlets.

Charlotte sacked Louisa's governess and sent Louisa packing to England. Here she was kept under the watchful eyes of society and under a grueling social calendar to distract her, and to keep her from her unsuitable revolutionary ideas. Charlotte made it clear that Louisa would not be welcome back in Boston unless it was with an English husband, and that were Louisa to set foot near Mrs. Pankhurst in London, she would no longer be a member of the West family at all.

Samuel had been instructed to accompany Louisa on his way to Hong Kong, and here she was about to see him off. Her mother's plan had not worked so far—Louisa had not been distributed to a suitable husband, and she only wished that she could go to work in Hong Kong too.

She stood up. Samuel, ever intuitive, stood up too. Louisa held her parasol up against the sun, appreciating the coolness of the shade on her white cotton dress, with its high collar and full sleeves.

"I'm going for a walk," she said to the party on the terrace.

Guy Hamilton's sister, Alice, and her young friend smiled, waving Louisa on, while Louisa's dear friend Meg raised her hand in a nonchalant response. It had struck Louisa that Meg had become very content here—no doubt confident in the knowledge that she would spend hundreds of afternoons just like this one, with her new husband, Guy, who was famous for his good humor, his fine jawline, and his never having fallen in love until he met Meg.

Feigned delight at his engagement had fanned its way through debutante circles, while the innocent Meg remained oblivious to the fact that she was the object of both envy and hatred throughout half the English countryside. But Louisa sensed it, that tightness beneath the politeness of the other girls and their mothers, and she felt an odd need to protect Meg. She turned away from the terrace. Her mind was filled, as always, with too much. Which was what her mother always said.

"I'll join you." Samuel removed his white suit jacket, rolled up the sleeves of his shirt, and smoothed back his corn-colored hair. His face was lightly tanned. The English summer suited him, Louisa thought.

"You are agitated," he said, holding his arm out for her to take.

They stepped down from the terrace to the path that led through the rose garden. "No more than usual." She knew she sounded vague, but it was a lazy kind of day.

Samuel smiled and continued on to the park. "I hate the thought of being so far away from you. I don't want to miss out on any happiness of yours. You must keep me up to date when you make the most important decision in your life. You will need support. You know I'm always there for you."

Louisa turned her blue eyes to meet her brother's. Her wavy, golden hair was swept up on her head, but the clammy English summer played havoc with her curls, leaving tendrils running out of place, and she had become used to droplets of perspiration falling on her forehead.

"There's little chance of me getting married," she almost laughed.

"Do you want to talk about it?" Samuel spoke gently. He patted Louisa's hand where it rested in the crook of his elbow.

Louisa looped her hand away from Samuel's arm and tied the parasol up in a neat, straight line.

"Tell me." He stood still.

"Everything here is a game," Louisa said. They moved across the park and stopped in the shade of a great oak tree, one of the oldest in the county, according to the Hamilton family. "You know I don't want to play."

"Louisa. It's got to the point where neither of us has a choice. The forces are too great. Surely, even you can see that."

Louisa sensed frustration rising through her system and she could not stop it at all. "You have choices, Samuel."

"No I don't."

"You could marry, not marry, stay here, stay in Boston, go to Hong Kong. You are the center of your own life. And what's more, people take you seriously. People listen to you. They don't laugh when you speak. When you converse about a topic, as a man, you are seen as intelligent, not bossy; you are amusing, rather than mocked. But when I purport to have any opinions at all as a woman—"

"You are trying to fight against the tide again, Louisa."

Louisa dug the tip of her parasol into the soft English soil, then pulled it out again. "I'm right, though. You know that."

His voice dropped to a low bass. "You're upset about Meg, and I know it's hard for you, my leaving at the same time. Find someone who will make you happy and then be happy yourself. Don't complicate things any more. You know it won't work."

Louisa felt a terse smile cross her face. "For God's sake, Sam. Surely you, of all people, understand." The words bit themselves out.

Samuel took a step toward her, pulled the parasol out of its soft bed in the earth. "I think you haven't met anyone who interests you. I really do think that's all this is."

Louisa shook her head. "I've been stealing the papers once the men have read them after breakfast. If women have to obey the government's laws, then we should be part of the process of making those laws. We have to pay taxes just as men do, so we should have the same voting rights as men. How are we supposed to change anything if we cannot even have a say in who makes the decisions that bind us? And look at me. What if I wanted to do something more with my life? Most women probably do. But we simply don't have the chance. Can't you see, Samuel? We have to change things. I would hate to have a daughter who was brought up with the restrictions that I have had."

Samuel turned to her, took her hand in his own. "But if you get involved, it will brand you. You'll set yourself up for social and financial ruin, and I cannot stand by and watch. The forces against you are far stronger than you think. People will go to unthinkable lengths to protect the status quo. They will fight much harder than you think, Louisa. And women, I fear, will be your worst enemies."

Louisa heard her mother's insistent voice in her head—she shouldn't be complaining, or goodness knew, talking about herself! She turned away from the tree and began walking, fast, back to the house.

Samuel was right behind her. He pulled at her arm, turned her to face him. "It's our last evening. I don't want to remember you like this. I want you to promise me—"

"I can't promise you anything." Louisa whispered the words, but her heart had started to hammer and her hands were growing moister than her head. "Oh, drat!" she said, wiping away a hot tear from one eye.

"I know it's going to be hard, and different." Samuel leaned in closer, whispered right back at her. "But write to me. Let me know how you get on. Just do not settle for anything less than the best, which is what you deserve, and for heaven's sake, choose someone who will let you be yourself. You will be an influence on your children. You will instill your feelings and your intelligence into them. Louisa, you have so many gifts. You can share them. Find the right husband, start your family, and you can make it all work out. You know that."

But Louisa's words came out in a rush. "Gifts, Samuel? What use are they to any woman? Don't you see? We are simply viewed as packages. We don't do the choosing. We are the parcels, to be picked up—or not. Men choose us or discard us as they please, while all the older women look on like rival bidders at an auction house. Everyone is complicit. It's brutal." Louisa had to take several deep breaths. Fear and anger and even guilt, were she honest, and sadness and loss and homesickness, dare she admit to that, were all wrapped up in one whirling mess.

"You are worth more than anything in the world to me," Samuel said. "But I can't see that your dreams of freedom and independence are realistic in any way at all. You will need support if you want to take on anything. You will need a perceptive husband. Even your Mrs. Pankhurst has that."

"If there are going to be any husbands, they are going to have to be enlightened." Louisa almost laughed out the words. "Samuel, I wish I could come with you to Hong Kong, do what you are doing," she said through gritted teeth. "See the world. Gain experience. Contribute."

"I know." Samuel sounded distant now. "But we are stuck in the world as it is, Louisa. The changes you dream of are radical. And radical change requires a revolution. And revolution means violence. And as your brother, I do not want you involved. I don't know what will happen. I don't know what will come of Mrs. Pankhurst and her activities, but I do know that I care about you. And I want you to stay safe, and I want you to keep your dreams safe. Promise me that. Don't risk your reputation; don't ruin your chances of happiness over this. Just wait. It will work out. I believe that. I will write to you as often as I possibly can."

Louisa blew out a breath. "I want to be free to make my own decisions. I want to be free to run my own life. Like you are. That's all."

"None of us are free," Samuel said. He ran a hand over his head. "But I am in constant awe at your ability to hold down an argument."

Louisa shook her head. They had argued all their lives. But at least she knew she could trust Samuel with her thoughts. He would never betray her to anyone. She knew that he understood her, but he was not willing to upset the status quo. He thought one could hold views within the confines of society, and he viewed society as protective. And that was where they would always differ. The rub was that Louisa also understood that she lived in a world where an unmarried woman was considered of far less consequence than a married one. Were she not to marry, she would find it impossible to have a voice. She still had to think further about this matter, but the answer was not coming easily at all.

What was more, any marriage that she entered into would have to be considered suitable. What if she were to fall in love, heaven help her, with someone who did not fit her mother's idea of the perfect husband? She had spent sleepless nights dealing with the fact that she could not have a career, nor could she choose whom she might fall in love with.

So if she were to avoid an arranged marriage, if she were to join the fight for women's rights and hope to meet someone who might in fact interest her rather than simply be suitable for the circle in which she moved, she knew what she would be labeled—a blue-stocking, a renegade, a misfit. A young woman's reputation, once lost, was impossible to restore. Was she ready to throw everything that she had ever known away?

Louisa turned back toward the terrace. "Let's go and drink champagne for Meg and for Guy."

Samuel was right behind her. "She is happy with him, Louisa."

"I know." Louisa waved an arm at him, but she marched on ahead.

Sometimes she wondered where she fit into the world at all.

The next morning, Louisa changed into her riding habit straight after breakfast. Saying good-bye to Samuel had not been as bad as she had imagined. His buoyancy and excitement had shone through when she hugged him in the driveway shortly after dawn, no matter how tactfully he attempted to hide his feelings for her benefit. The last thing Louisa had wanted was to break his mood.

Now, she needed to be outside, to be free, preferably somewhere she could take a horse for a gallop. She strode through Willowdale's hallway, into the wing that housed Meg's bedroom. Meg had taken to having her breakfast brought up to her in bed since getting married. Louisa could hear the clink of a teacup settling on a porcelain saucer as she stood outside her friend's door and knocked.

It was a perfect summer's morning—still cool with the promise of heat later in the day. Louisa adored the early mornings. She couldn't abide the idea of staying in bed for too long. Today she had thrown her own windows open wide when she woke, breathing in the air scented with climbing roses.

Meg asked her to enter. The remains of her breakfast sat on a tray, along with a tiny posy of fresh petunias in a crystal vase.

"You are looking more and more at home here every time I see you." Louisa smiled, moving into the pretty room with its polished floorboards, pale rug, and marble fireplace.

"Oh, I confess, I'm in heaven." Meg stretched. Her long dark hair was still tousled and her cheeks were pink with good health.

"Are you coming for a ride?" Louisa went and stood by the window.

"Oh, goodness no. I'm supposed to be meeting with some of the neighbors. Then we're off to the church. Lady Hamilton has my morning all planned."

"Well, you'd best get going. Because the day will be half-over and you will have done nothing but indulge yourself in bed!"

"How delicious," Meg sighed.

"I have to get out," Louisa said, turning around all of a sudden. "It will be too gracious hot soon."

"Go and enjoy it," Meg said, but then her voice sank a little deeper. "How did Samuel's departure go?"

Louisa let out a long breath. "It was fine. He had to go."

Meg nodded, and for a moment, it was as if Louisa's old friend were back—the one who used to listen to Louisa's ideas, who shared some of them too. But Louisa had seen changes in Meg since their arrival in England, and once the other girl had fallen in love, she had stopped talking of such things at all.

Louisa had tossed in bed for most of the night. Her friend and her brother were both leaving her behind in different ways, but they were both happy. Louisa had finally decided that she would have to exercise some of the steel that her own mother had shown toward her. She would stick to her beliefs even harder. If she was going to be alone, why not be an explorer?

"I'm going out to the horses," she said.

"Enjoy!" Meg trilled, leaning back on her white cotton pillows, taking up a letter from her tray.

"And you," Louisa smiled.

Half an hour later, Louisa was sitting on a palomino mare in the courtyard outside the stone stables at the edge of the park. Something caught at the side of her eye. She turned the horse around on the spot, rather too fast, causing her to buck. She settled the mare quickly, but frowned.

"Morning." A young man stood under the arched gates that led to the stables. He was dressed in jodhpurs, long black boots, and a riding jacket. He looked up at Louisa and raised a brow.

"Good morning." Louisa hadn't seen him before—hadn't heard mention of more visitors arriving today. She frowned at him again. She wasn't in the mood for interruptions, nor was she in the mood for talking with vacuous young men, even if this one was tall and dark with brown hair that was, appealingly for some reason, in slight disarray on top of his head.

She took in his brown eyes, strong eyebrows, finely crafted cheekbones, and square chin. He looked amused, as if he held some secret. And this annoyed Louisa for some reason too.

She frowned down at him. She would have to be polite for a few moments, she supposed.

"Louisa West," he said. He sounded sardonic.

Her mare danced from side to side as if she were a pony in a circus. Louisa pulled gently on the reins and placed a little pressure into the stirrups to keep her charge still.

The young man strode closer and patted the horse on the neck.

"I'm Henry Duval," he said, holding up a gloved hand.

Louisa started at two things—his name and his informal manner. Even in Boston, the way he had appeared out of the blue would be considered improper. Did he think he could take liberties with an American? But then, what did she care for convention?

Louisa patted the mare to soothe her further and slowly reached her own gloved hand down to Henry. She let her hand rest in his, but only for a second, before pulling away. She wanted to get going.

But then, he had said his name was Henry Duval. She had heard of him. There had been chatter among the girls back in London. What were the particulars? She cursed herself now for not taking in the details of idle gossip. Too often, her thoughts were off somewhere else. She looked at him with more interest. At least, he did not at first appear dull, like every other young man she had met.

Henry Duval smiled, looking secretive again. "Would you like a riding companion, Louisa West?" he asked, still caressing the horse. "I never get up as early as this. So I think you should say yes."

Louisa regarded him. She had planned to take the path that led through the woods to the west of the property. Its entrance was directly beyond the stables, and once she had traversed her way through the forest, she was going to go for a gallop through the fields beyond, all of which still belonged to the Hamilton family. She had found this route on her first morning at Willowdale, when Guy had offered her free access to the stables.

Did she want Henry Duval with her, or not? If his conversation became a bore, then she could simply feign something—illness, hunger, thirst—and turn back to the house. On the other hand, if he was interesting, then perhaps he would prove a distraction from the ache she felt for Samuel. And Meg.

Henry had his head on one side. "I suppose I should tell you a bit more before I take you out riding for the morning."

Louisa watched him.

"I'm a friend of Guy's."

"I know that." Her mare took a circle, fast. She deplored that habit of deliberately playing dumb around young men. She had decided that it was fair neither to herself, nor to her companions. So she played things straight. And men could like it or not.

"Steady on," Henry said, catching the mare by the halter. "You know?" he raised an eyebrow.

"I'm fine with the horse," Louisa said. "You like horses?"

"They're not a passion for me."

Louisa stayed silent. At least he was not pretending to be something he was not. That was a point in his favor.

"I've just come back from Paris," he said suddenly, and he looked a little moody now.

"Paris?" Louisa felt something sharpen in her insides. She hadn't heard anything about him being in Paris. That was not it. But there was something the girls had been excited about—if only she could remember what.

Henry looked down at the ground and grinned. "You ever been to Paris?"

"I confess I have not." Her mount's patience was running out. If Henry wanted to talk about Paris, then that could be a real diversion from her relentless thoughts about Samuel and Hong Kong. She decided to take Henry up on his offer. "Why don't you saddle up and come with me, then? You can tell me about your travels if you like."

"Wait right there," he said, and strode off into the stables.

Louisa watched him go and couldn't help but shake her head. Had he created some scandal at a house party? Been involved in some sort of antic up in London? Was that it? But, gossip aside, the fact that he had been to Paris interested her. Travel was something she was endlessly passionate about. She admitted that she wanted to hear more about that. When he led out a handsome bay gelding and jumped on with an elegance that eluded many young men, Louisa was quite enjoying the sight of him. He was extraordinarily handsome, she thought, almost beautiful, and then checked herself. Why on earth was she thinking like that?

Once they reached the forest, shafts of sunlight flickered down through the trees, illuminating the foliage with delicate traceries. If Louisa had been the type to imagine, she would have said that this was a place for fairies or elves.

Unlike so many of the young men she had met in London, Henry did not seem eager to please her with trite conversation, nor did he barrage her with transparent questions about her father's business interests in the Far East.

It had been something of a distraction, she supposed, to be regarded as a foreign celebrity when she first arrived in London, but once Louisa had answered the same stock questions a dozen times, she had become more than bored with it all.

"How many times have you been to Paris?" she asked, urging her horse into a trot.

Henry kept up alongside her.

"Countless times. The crossing is easy from London so long as the weather is fine. I like it there."

They had come to the far edge of the forest. A wide expanse of green field stretched out before them. A few brown cattle stood about on the far side near the boundary fence, but they were far enough away to allow for a gallop.

"I'm off," Louisa said, her breath starting to quicken already. "You can come too, if you want."

"I'll keep up," Henry said, that satiric look returning again.

Louisa shook her head and took off.

She loved the feeling of freedom that riding in the open countryside afforded her. She had always sought out the most challenging horses to ride when she was young and her father had taken Louisa and Samuel to visit cousins with country retreats out of Boston.

Her horse seemed to understand her, so she urged the mare on, over a high jump that led to the next field. She rode on down its full slope, to the bottom of the hill, where she stopped at a pond and allowed the mare to have a drink.

Henry pulled up next to her.

"What is it about Paris?" she asked after a few moments.

"Paris is life," he said, patting his mount on the neck as it rounded in circles.

Louisa turned to face him.

"Montmartre is where it's all at. Paris is about being modern—it's about immersing yourself in the present moment, rather than the damned antiquities of the past."

Louisa started a little.

"Sorry," he said. "I don't expect you to understand."

"No, go on."

He let go of his horse's reins and leaned back in the saddle so that he was lying flat, his back against the horse, staring straight at the sky. "Cabarets that attract the literary crowd, theaters showing Molière and Jean Racine every night, dance halls, rough and seedy or deluxe and decadent, circuses—where the unimaginable becomes possible time and time again." He stayed where he was. "If I was born into a different life, I would have been an actor, Louisa. I hope I am not shocking you."

Louisa was silent for a moment. She looked down over the lower part of the valley. What Henry had said, she admitted to herself, had an element of shock. But if she were honest, he was making her excited.

Writers, poets, artists—was he talking about a free intellectual life in Paris? She turned to Henry, even more interested now. "I confess I'm intrigued," she said. "It sounds like the exact opposite of…here."

Henry sat up then, took up his reins. "That's exactly it. It's just what I mean. We should get back, you know." He sounded moody now. He paused for a moment, holding his horse's reins, but held off telling him to walk on. "I came to Willowdale because I was bored at home. I'd only been there two days." He looked at her as if challenging her to react.

"I imagine that it would not be difficult to become bored easily at home, given where you have just been," Louisa said, holding his gaze.

He nodded, as if she had given him the right answer. "I've invited Guy to my place, to Ashworth, for a few days, along with Meg. Before they go away. Would you like to come?" he asked, looking urgent, somehow.

Louisa pushed back the instinct to laugh again. She shrugged. "Ashworth?"

"As I say. It's my family's…place."

The horse's breathing had settled, and Louisa moved her forward at a slow walk. "Well, if Guy and Meg accept, then I cannot see any reason for me to stay here, nor can I see good cause to return to London on my own."

"I can't stand the thought of returning to London myself," he said, all of a sudden.

That made two of them. "I see. Well, then. I accept your kind invitation, pending everyone else's agreement, of course."

"Shall I firm things up with Guy?"

Louisa looked ahead. "Why not?" She had to work out what she was going to do without Meg, now she was married. Meg's governess was returning to Boston once Meg was established in her position. There was no reason for a governess to remain here. Louisa had no idea what she would do with herself in the long run.

"I'm going to race you back to the forest now." She urged her horse forward, pushing her legs into the mare's flank and leaning forward in her sidesaddle.

Henry was right alongside her. "Wait," he said. He reached over and took hold of her mare's halter for a moment.

The two horses were close, and Louisa resisted the impulse to pull hers away. Both animals were breathing hard as if keen to get moving, and she could smell the heady mix of leather and horse, but she was also aware, right then, of Henry.

"I've enjoyed meeting you. Thank you for letting me join you on your ride," he said. "I confess, I rose early this morning and came out here to find you. Because Guy had told me that you were not one of the...average debutantes."

Louisa pressed her lips together and held back a laugh. "Did he?" she asked. "And what exactly did he mean by that?"

"I don't know." Henry grinned. The horses started to jiggle around on the spot.

Louisa leaned forward and soothed her mare.

"But when I'm intrigued by something," he went on, still close.

Louisa sensed that she should not budge.

"I always follow it through," he finished. His voice was softer and frown lines had formed on his forehead.

"Well," she said. For some reason, she did not want to be on the back foot in the conversation. "You are certainly different from the other young men I have met. Your views are modern. And that, to me, is refreshing." She knew she had been bold, and she waited for his response.

But he chuckled and kicked his horse on. "I'll race you, Louisa," he said. "I'm glad I rose early this morning."

Louisa urged her own horse forward. Somehow the idea of going to Ashworth was more than appealing. Right now, it sounded like a lifesaver. Right now, it sounded like exactly what she wanted to do.

Chapter Four

Paris, 2015

Sarah felt wide awake once she was in the taxi in Paris, even after her sleepless flight. She couldn't help but be charmed by the city's grand old buildings and exquisite boutiques, not to mention the impeccably dressed people seated at sidewalk cafés on those charming wicker chairs.

A frisson of excitement ran through her as the taxi passed the Église de la Sainte-Trinité and turned on to Rue Blanche. This was the street where Marthe de Florian had lived. It was almost as if Sarah were receiving a jolt from the past. She couldn't help thinking that over one hundred years ago, Louisa, a young woman just like Sarah, fresh in Paris from Boston, had walked these very streets. And she couldn't help thinking that over one hundred years ago, Louisa had died close by.

A well-dressed man stood outside a building halfway up the street, where it narrowed beyond a couple of restaurants and an old theater. As the taxi slowed to a stop, it became clear that Marthe's apartment building was out of character with its surroundings—it did not follow Haussmann's strong, straight lines at all. The courtesan's building was sensual, flowing. Fancy ironwork adorned its curve-topped windows. A sweeping balcony on the top floor overlooked the street. It was built for the grand Belle Époque, and it wasn't hard to picture a courtesan living there.

Sarah paid the taxi driver, thanked him in what she hoped was passable French, and stepped out onto the sidewalk, still staring up at the building in front of her. She waited a few moments.

Loic looked exactly as Sarah had imagined him: tall, brown hair that curled slightly, warm eyes. He took her suitcase, insisting on carrying it up the short flight of steps to the front entrance.

"Are you sure you haven't changed your mind about Laurent?" Loic's unaccented English was something else. Sarah would have to remember to ask him about it sometime.

"Not at all. As long as your friend doesn't keep me awake tonight, we're all good," Sarah laughed.

Loic chuckled too as he turned his key in the solid front door to the building. The entrance foyer was airy and cool and tiled.

Loic led her to the other side of the lobby. "Oh, a very European elevator—one of my favorite kinds," Sarah said.

"I think we can both fit in." He hauled her suitcase into the tiny space. "How was your flight?"

"Fine. No, awful," she admitted with a smile.

The elevator came to a standstill and while Loic Archer seemed to be one of the nicest companions a girl could ask for when sharing a lift, Sarah was relieved to step out into the hallway on the top floor of the building. Her sense of anticipation, of actually being here, was heightened as she followed Loic across the floor, and her stomach started to flicker with nerves. She felt so close to Louisa right now that were her ancestor to appear in front of her, Sarah would have simply greeted the mysterious young woman with no surprise at all.

Loic held the door to the apartment open, and as Sarah stepped into what was clearly the salon, she gasped.

"We packed all of Marthe's things up, ready to sell everything, but then, well, Cat and I found we just couldn't part with any of it," Loic explained. "It was completely over the top when we found it. We left some of Marthe's pieces here, the Boldini painting went to auction, and we took the rest of Marthe's things down to Provence so that we could enjoy them, live with them surrounding us."

Sarah paused and looked at him. He simply lived with Marthe's treasures every day, as part of his life? She had to stop herself from shaking her head. It just wasn't what she would do—it was certainly not what her family ever did. You left the past where it belonged. Old pieces were for museums. You didn't live with them—you didn't integrate family history into your apartment, not at all. And with a baby around? Sarah waited for him to go on.

"This is Marthe's dining table, her sideboard." He led Sarah to the front of the room that looked over Rue Blanche. "We painted the walls, polished the floors."

Sarah looked down at the gleaming parquet. She would have to take care of it all. She would do so, as if it were her own.

"We replaced all the curtains, though. You should have seen them. They were hanging in strips!" He moved off to the left and opened a door into a long, narrow room. "The kitchen is here," he said, stopping in the doorway. "We are careful about who we rent the apartment out to, but we want it to be lived in, enjoyed. It was locked away for so long. Mostly, it gets rented out to friends. I'm confident that you'll treat Marthe's things with care. Go ahead and make yourself at home."

"Thank you," Sarah said. "You can be sure I'll treat Marthe's treasures with respect."

"The kitchen's all been renovated," Loic went on. "You should have everything you need."

Sarah nodded. A galley kitchen—just as she was used to at home. Atop the gleaming white kitchen counters were round canisters with all manner of cooking utensils. They stood at the ready for the kind of culinary adventures that must follow trips to the local markets. Sarah could already picture herself channeling Julia Child, roasting a capon.

"There are a couple of old maids' rooms upstairs beyond the kitchen," Loic said. "We've put a barrier on the old staircase because it's small and dangerous. Eventually, once we come up to Paris with our children, they can sleep up there, but for now, it's kind of set aside. Probably best not to go up the stairs."

"Of course." Sarah nodded.

Loic seemed to hesitate for a moment. "Right," he said. "Let me show you around the rest of the apartment."

The salon had been decorated by someone who had a good eye for placing old things in a modern context. The artwork, much of it from the early twentieth century, and original no less, had been chosen to complement the colors in the upholstery on the elegant Louis XV chairs.

Sarah was impressed.

Loic led her through an open double doorway into the next room. A large chaise longue sat in front of a set of curve-topped French doors, and a grand piano stood against one wall. An easel was set up in the middle of the space, and next to it was a palette with all manner of tubes and brushes.

The vast canvas was half-covered with a striking portrait of a young woman, her dress black and modern. The brushstrokes looked as if they had been flicked onto the canvas, flying around the woman's body and ricocheting away from her dress. Her blond hair hung loose around her shoulders, and she stared out of her portrait, confident. There was none of that half-secret look that so many of Boldini's subjects seemed to have. This was a modern woman, but the painting style was certainly reminiscent of the Belle Époque artist's style.

Sarah moved over to take a closer look.

"Are you familiar with Boldini's work?" Loic asked.

She nodded. "This is stunning," she breathed. "And I see a lot of art. I'm beginning to think that I'll forgive your friend's bad behavior if he can paint like this."

Loic laughed. "Good. I'll let you discuss art with him. Like I said, he's incredibly talented." Loic moved toward the next set of double doors, which led in turn to another room. "I'm afraid all the rooms lead off each other," he said. "It tends to be the way in these old apartments."

Sarah stopped in the middle of the next room—a bedroom. A vast four-poster bed sat against one wall, but its deep mattress was modern and it was covered in a tasteful blue-and-white patterned quilt. So, how was this supposed to work? She didn't want to sound prudish, but she wasn't keen on having Laurent walk through her room at night. She didn't want to complain to Loic, not on her very first day. But there was a limit…

"I put Laurent in here," Loic said. "Thought you'd prefer not to have him walking through your bedroom while you're asleep. Besides, I think he'll be back after you at night."

"Oh." Sarah was certain she sounded unconvinced. But when she cast about for thoughts, she couldn't come up with any alternative sleeping plans at all.

"He starts work before dawn, like I said, and he's often up all night. Has done that for years. I really don't know how he gets by," Loic said. He tilted his head to one side. "I hope you won't have to walk past him while he's asleep in the bed too often."

Sarah pressed her lips together. She also had the feeling that this room may have belonged to the courtesan once. That bed…

"The bed belonged to Marthe," Loic said. "And so did the chaise longue that you just saw in the sitting room. That was where she entertained most of her…guests."

Exhaustion from her long flight was starting to kick in, but Sarah's mind was spinning fast at the same time. She needed to sleep before she tackled any further discussions about the arrangements for her stay. And if her room was farther away from Laurent's and if he didn't sleep much, maybe it would all be fine. But still, she would reserve judgment, for the moment at the very least.

"You'd better get some rest. I'll show you to your room. You have your own dressing room and a bathroom. Laurent won't come in past this point."

Sarah nodded.

"There's another bathroom off the kitchen. Laurent is using that," Loic said, leading her through the next set of doors. These led into a smaller room, furnished with two single beds.

"This was Marthe's granddaughter's room—Isabelle's," Loic said.

"The one who fled." Sarah's words came out soft, and once again, she was hit with the sense of lingering ghosts, of other young women. She was not the only one who had sought solace here, perhaps.

The two beds were modern, covered all in white. White-painted shelves lined one wall, and these were filled with a collection of exquisite porcelain.

"All Marthe's," Loic said. "Gifts from her gentlemen friends."

The other walls were decorated with more paintings.

"Marthe had a keen interest in the arts," Loic said. "Most of the leading courtesans worked as actresses and dancers too—they were performers by rights, but only in the most exclusive of dance halls."

"The Folies Bergère?"

Loic nodded. "The top courtesans performed there," he said. "There were only a few who really made it."

"I hate to imagine what life was like for the rest of the women, or the ones who lived on the streets."

"I know."

Sarah had always wondered about Louisa. Family legend had it that Henry had been obsessed with Paris and the Belle Époque, but how had Louisa dealt with Montmartre's decadence, with the prostitutes and cabarets and wild artists and pimps? Not very well, perhaps.

Loic showed Sarah the bathroom, with its marble vanity and clean lines. Through this was a dressing room, filled with wardrobes and custom-made shelves.

"Oh, my goodness," Sarah breathed. A couple of the wardrobes stood slightly open. Inside, there were tantalizing glimpses of the most exquisite gowns Sarah had ever seen. Beaded silk scarves, parasols, and lace gloves were laid out on some of the shelves, which gleamed to perfection.

"Cat leaves a couple of wardrobes free for our guests," Loic said, opening some of them, wheeling Sarah's suitcase to a halt. "But she loves vintage fashion, so she couldn't part with most of Marthe's outfits."

Sarah was awestruck by the courtesan's shoes. She couldn't help but move closer and stare. They were all perfect examples of high fashion from the 1890s.

But as Sarah turned toward the back wall of the room, something struck her and she gasped. She had to move closer again. A dressing table, its mirror surrounded by delicate wood carvings, impressed even Sarah's trained eye. A set of cleaned and polished old perfume bottles sat atop the table, their silk hand pumps draped as if by an artist. Sarah turned to Loic.

"All Cat." He smiled, leaning against the door frame now.

Sarah smiled back at him and she couldn't help thinking how lucky this Cat was. Loic clearly adored her. And, perhaps, how lucky the apartment was to have ended up in Cat and Loic's hands.

"Laurent must have gone out for breakfast," Loic said. "Are you happy to settle into your rooms and meet him yourself?"

"Of course."

Loic shook her hand. "Just contact me," he said. "Won't you? If there's anything you need."

"Thank you."

"Your key is by your bed," Loic said.

"Actually, I meant to ask," Sarah said. "You have a baby daughter?"

A broad grin threw light all over Loic's handsome face. "A beautiful girl."

Sarah waited.

"Isabelle," he said, his voice soft. "She's dark, like my mother, but she has Cat's heavenly smile."

"Oh." Sarah couldn't help but smile herself. "How perfect."

"Long story," Loic said. "But yes, it's sort of perfect."

He turned then, and Sarah moved back toward the bathroom. A bath. A hot bath.

Then sleep.

Then, Paris.

Streetlights shone into Isabelle de Florian's old bedroom when Sarah woke that evening, sending flickering patterns onto the pale walls. She had been too tired to close the curtains before falling into one of the two perfect beds. Now she pulled her robe around her waist and padded over to the window, where she gazed down at the street outside. A few people were on the sidewalk; a scooter swung by, the noise of its buzzing engine reminding Sarah, suddenly, of other trips to Europe. Trips with Steven and, earlier, with her parents.

She forced thoughts of Steven out of her head as she had become used to doing for months, but she allowed herself to think about her parents for a moment. The fact that they had adored each other so much had been a blessing for Sarah. But she had never been able to forge such a close relationship with her own partner. She shook her head and turned back to the bedroom.

It was half past eight. Sarah moved into the dressing room and chose a simple black shift dress. Feeling fresh from her bath and her sleep, she dabbed on some perfume and applied light makeup. She would go out and find somewhere local for dinner. But now she stood at the closed doors to the bedroom that Laurent Chartier was using. She would have to knock before opening the door.

Sarah waited a few seconds, then tapped tentatively. Stood there. Nothing. Turned the handle. The room was empty, the bed made up. She couldn't hear any noises coming from the next room. So she moved toward the following set of doors.

After she opened them, Sarah stood stock-still. Laurent Chartier was working at his easel. He hadn't noticed her and was clearly so absorbed in his work that had Sarah danced the cancan in front of him, he probably wouldn't have looked up. She studied him for a few seconds. He was looking at the canvas, his dark eyes intent on one spot. His hair, which was silky and dark, was splattered with a few tiny spots of paint. His eyebrows were perfect. Sarah had no idea why she was noticing that, and he wore a white T-shirt, which was surprisingly paint-free, along with a pair of faded jeans.

Sarah took a step into the room.

"Bonsoir," he said, without looking up. "Sorry. I'm stuck," he went on in English with only the faintest hint of a French accent—he sounded like Loic. Was there something in the water in Provence? "I'm being rude." He frowned at his canvas.

"Bonsoir," Sarah said. She knew that it was always a good idea to say something in French when you were visiting Paris. Even a simple greeting was a fine start.

Laurent ran a hand over his chin. "Did you sleep well?"

"Yes!" Sarah almost laughed. "I was out of it for hours."

"Good. You'll want dinner."

"I do." Sarah moved toward his canvas. "Oh." The word came out involuntarily.

The painting had changed so much since the morning that Sarah had to do a double take. Somehow, he had captured even more of the sitter's personality. She looked even more thoughtful, but also more confident. More alive. And there was something in her expression that was whimsical now. Just a hint.

"This is exactly what Boldini did," Sarah said, taking another step closer. "You've captured it. Power and sensuality and poignancy all at the same time. And yet, she's a modern interpretation of Boldini's work. She's of our time, I can see that."

Laurent turned to her for a moment. He looked as if he were about to say something and then stopped, turned back to the painting, and folded his arms.

Sarah stood next to him. "What's the problem?"

"Her pose. Boldini emphasized the décolletage. But there's something about this model—"

"What's wrong?" She looked perfect.

"The décolletage thing isn't going to work with her."

Sarah felt her lips twitching into a smile. "So, don't paint her like that."

"But I have to be true to Boldini. Who threw light on his subjects' décolletage whenever he could."

"Not all of his portraits are...thrusty."

Laurent turned to her. His eyes twinkled. "Thrusty?"

Sarah felt a blush rise in her cheeks, but she went on. She was so struck by his work. "Think about his portrait of Adelaide Ristori, or *The Red Curtain*. To me, they are two of Boldini's most interesting works. No décolletage. I'd like to have known either of those women. He made them both look fascinating."

"Thrustiness," Laurent muttered. "You have me intrigued—although this is an intensely odd first conversation. And either you have a serious interest in art, or you're an expert on Boldini."

"I think you should be true to the model." Sarah couldn't stop staring at the painting. "True to her character. That's what matters; it's your work, not Boldini's."

Laurent looked more than amused now. "Okay, then, Sarah. I want you to tell me how you know all this. Loic didn't tell me much about you. And I didn't introduce myself. I'm Laurent." He held out a hand.

Sarah shook it. His fingers were slightly rough with dried paint. "Sarah West."

"Tell me about the art, Sarah West."

Sarah tapped her foot on the floor. "You know, I would, but I'm starving. I have to go out and eat. Can you tell me of a place that's good around here?"

He grinned then, his brown eyes warming too. "Go to Le Bon Georges. It's your first night in Paris and their menu is very French. It's a ten-minute walk down Rue la Bruyère, then take your first right and your next left. Have you organized a French SIM card for your phone?"

Sarah nodded. She had sorted that at home. Laurent showed her exactly where the restaurant was, using maps on her phone.

"I'll ring ahead for you and make a booking at nine. You'd better get going."

"Thanks." Sarah smiled at him. He seemed fine. And there was no obvious indication of any wild-boy lifestyle in his behavior right now. Nothing she could see that reminded her of Toulouse-Lautrec, for goodness' sakes. No bottles of absinthe decorating Marthe's mantelpiece, no lines of cocaine on the coffee table. His eyes weren't bloodshot and there were no actresses or models in sight. She moved toward the salon.

"Have you got your key?" he asked, tilting his head to one side.

"Yes." She was going to be sure she held on to that. She had to hold back a giggle. He sounded quite fatherly in his concerns about the phone and the key. Not what she expected. Not what she had been led to believe at all.

"Go and eat. I have more questions for you, though." He returned to his work.

Sarah felt a smile dance around her lips. Perhaps it was just Paris. But when she stepped out into the street, she felt lighter than she had in an age. It was as if a small part of the burden she had carried for the last twelve months like a deadweight on her back had lifted somewhat.

It had to be Paris.

Chapter Five

Hampshire, England, 1893

Henry insisted on taking Louisa to Ashworth in his spider phaeton. Louisa could not help but admire the carriage's elegant construction. There was no doubt that it showed off Henry's two light, spirited horses to spectacular effect. It was a terribly sporting little thing, but Louisa wondered whether it would make it the entire way to Ashworth.

"I drove it all the way here. It's really not as far as all that," Henry said, standing back and admiring the smart carriage. Its wheels were of polished wood, the front two only slightly inferior in size to those at the rear, and it had a great hood that could be pulled up in case of bad weather—not that there would be any need for that today.

Louisa hated to think what her mother's reaction would be to the idea of her driving across the English countryside in the company of a young man she had only met the day before, in his phaeton, no less.

Last night, Meg had revealed that Henry Duval was a viscount, heir to one of the largest estates in England and quite famous for having turned his nose up at all the eligible young women. According to gossip, his house parties could go on for weeks. To be invited to Ashworth was something indeed. Henry was the son of a duke and regarded as a colossal catch. Louisa had decided that she was not going to put herself in such a position that he could turn his nose up at her, at all.

"I like it," she said, turning back from the carriage to Meg and Guy. "And you tell me that Ashworth is still in Hampshire, so I suppose we'll make it in one piece."

"We'll be right behind you." Guy smiled, taking Meg's hand as she came down the front steps of the house.

Meg was looking particularly elegant this morning in a deep red dress trimmed with black lace. The outfit was finished with a fashionably high collar and puffed sleeves. But Louisa had chosen to wear one of her favorite simple white shirts and skirts for the journey—white was the only color she could stand in the heat.

Guy took Meg over to his chocolate- and gold-painted brougham, which was loaded up with everyone's luggage. The coachman and groom were already seated side by side, and a footman was on hand to help Meg into her superbly trimmed leather seat.

Once they had wound their way through several villages and passed the gates of a few enticing estates—Henry seemed to know the owners of them all and was happy to regale Louisa with juicy gossip about the inhabitants—he turned the phaeton off the road onto a raked gravel driveway. He drove for a while, until they reached an impressive archway that was set over a pair of elaborate black iron gates topped with gold spikes. To either side, a high pale stone wall stretched quite some way in either direction, and set into the wall, charmingly, there seemed to be a little gatehouse on each side.

Louisa's eyes roamed through the gates to the well-tended lawn that lay to each side of the driveway before it disappeared into a line of overhanging trees. The idea of traveling in the shade was appealing. Even though Louisa had her parasol, they had been jostling along in the sun for over two hours now.

The lodge keeper appeared and greeted Henry.

"Welcome to Ashworth, Louisa," Henry said. "A group of friends have come up from London—Parliament has closed and they are bored, so I sent word to them all to join us—junior ministers and so on. I must say, we have rather a lot of men." Henry moved the carriage on through the gate and toward the heavenly trees.

"No doubt they will attract a ton of young ladies then," Louisa said, not even trying to hide the sarcasm in her voice.

She stole a glance at Henry—a smile passed across his face.

Later, as the driveway tended up to a rise beyond the bank of trees, Louisa could not help but gasp. In front of her stood a palace—there was only one word for it—built entirely of honey-colored stone.

Louisa almost stood up in her seat, she was so entranced by the sight. A turret sat on each of the four corners of a vast, square-shaped building. Small spires and ornate decorations were inlaid into the elegant stone, visible even from the vantage point where they sat. A colossal square tower sat in the middle of the palace, overlooking the wide expanse of park that surrounded it. The contrast to Guy's elegant but small estate was marked, and while Louisa's family owned a house in Newport as well as one in Boston, she had not seen anything like Ashworth in her life.

Louisa found herself consumed with questions, some of which she suspected would cause Henry to laugh. How many people would it take to run a place like this? How many bedrooms did it have? And how on earth was she supposed to address his parents?

Henry pushed the horses into a trot. The road took them around the expansive park and through another copse of trees that edged the estate before wending its way to the left, straight toward the main entrance to Ashworth.

The house steward was waiting to greet them, along with Henry's valet, when they pulled up underneath the stately portico.

"I sent a telegram this morning to my parents. Asked them to get the servants to prepare for dancing over the weekend. And I have some other surprises planned. I do get bored easily, and I like to give the staff a bit of excitement," Henry said. He handed the reins to the footman who had appeared at his side and jumped down from the carriage.

Another footman appeared to hand Louisa down.

"Thank you," she said, smiling at the young man. He nodded, but remained poker-faced. Louisa caught Meg's eye and grinned as her friend made exactly the same mistake. The way the English handled their servants was more formal than back at home in Boston.

Henry proved himself to be one of the most exciting and charming hosts Louisa had ever had the fortune to know. The house party that had arrived for the summer's weekend turned into a moveable feast. Guests seemed to pop up and disappear during the course of the next two weeks. Every day there were different people for dinner, and Henry was tireless in his organization of dances, moonlit punts on the lakes dotting the estate, picnics, and drives to the follies that surrounded the park. Even pillow fights in the early mornings seemed to be de rigueur—Henry's parents turned a blind eye to any antics that went on in what were apparently more than fifty guest bedrooms. The duke and the duchess seemed to be utterly preoccupied with their own lives. Their appearances were occasional and their manner was formal. If Louisa's mother knew how lax the chaperoning was, Louisa suspected that she might be called back to Boston straightaway.

When Louisa found herself with any spare time, she would try to explore where she could. Henry had given her and Meg a tour of the staterooms—the vast library, lined with shelves of English oak; the music room, hung with priceless sixteenth-century Italian tapestries; the drawing room, decorated in pale silks by the fourth duchess of Ashworth; and the billiard room, its walls showing off the palace's collection of Flemish art.

Henry's stamina for fun was extraordinary. He slept until noon, appearing in his silk dressing gown on the main staircase that filled the central tower when he woke, swishing into the breakfast room, demanding tea laced with brandy and lashings of toast. The servants all obliged him, but Louisa had noticed a few wry looks pass between them behind his back.

When Louisa had returned from her early-morning walk through the park after nearly two weeks at Ashworth, she was surprised to find Henry up, fully dressed and holding court in the dining room, surrounded by several other guests.

"Louisa!" Henry called. "Just the person we need."

"How so?" Louisa asked, standing in the doorway. She was aware that the thick plait that she had asked the maid to put her hair into that morning was probably disheveled now. She raised a hand up to pat it back into place.

"You look beautiful as you are," a young man of the party called out, "especially charming as you stand there framed in the doorway."

Louisa raised a brow. She had become both sick of and used to empty compliments from countless men. Henry, on the other hand, still intrigued her. Several conversations with him had amused her, just as she had been surprised and diverted by him the first time they had met. But she was aware of whispered conversations, that things were being said behind her back. Other girls felt Henry gave her too much attention. She had been careful to keep out of any such talk.

When Meg had taken her aside one evening as they were about to go down to the library for drinks, Louisa had known exactly what her friend was going to say.

"There is talk that Henry is growing fond of you," Meg said in the ladies' sitting room before they met anyone else.

Louisa had folded her arms, held Meg's eyes. "I don't know what I think," she confessed.

"That is not very you."

"I know. But you see, Henry is modern, and that interests me, and yet look at his future. He will inherit one of the most important estates in this old country. His role, Meg, will be the antithesis of modernity."

Meg giggled. "Trust you to analyze it all. Louisa, how do you feel about him? That is all that matters. Could you love him? He is singling you out."

"I can't answer that question." At least with Meg, Louisa knew she could be honest. "The truth is I find him interesting, and fun, and unusual. He is charming and a talented, warm host. But is that enough? You know what my ambitions are. You know what I want. Is that ever going to be compatible with marriage?"

Meg ran her hand down Louisa's arm. "My dear friend, you will always have your ideas. You were born with opinions planted in your head. But you can keep them—they will evolve. You can work toward helping women, and have love, if you want it. Why not? And, as you say, if Henry is modern . . . Have you spoken with him about your feelings on women's roles?"

"We have hardly had the opportunity to have such a conversation," Louisa said. And she didn't add that she felt he would run away were she to raise the topic. But then, she should not be worried about a man running from her, just because she held opinions that were not the norm. Sometimes she found herself going in circles and becoming confused by her very own ideas. If only the two things were compatible—love and women's desire to contribute in a proper way to the running of the world.

"Why is it you need me, Henry?" she asked him now, keeping her tone light.

"Because I am having a ball."

"Oh, how delightful," Louisa said, hiding her disappointment. She had had enough of balls back in London.

"But I want to take you out today to talk about it. I want you to help me make plans. I suppose you have breakfasted already? I know that you do like your early-morning walks. I have made it my habit to become familiar with your routine."

Annoyingly, Louisa felt her cheeks redden. She was particularly aware of her status as an American. She hated the assumption that she was here in England only to find a husband, no matter how true it might appear to be.

"Louisa!" Henry was laughing at her now. "You are not hearing a word that I say."

"I apologize," Louisa said. "A ball will, of course, be delightful. Charming."

"I want you to give me the first dance," Henry said.

Louisa sensed a frisson pass between the ladies at the table.

"Of course," she said. "I would be honored, Henry. But now, I really must go upstairs and change." How easy it was to slip into formal politeness, but it worked, even if it meant nothing at all.

"Can you meet me in the salon at noon?"

"Certainly." Louisa nodded at him. "I will be ready."

She turned to go back out the door.

"Oh, and Louisa," Henry called after her, "my younger brother, Charlie, is returning home in time for the ball. He has been working at one of the other estates. But I'd like you to meet him. I think you'll like him, in fact."

The guests at the breakfast table took sips of their tea, and several of them cleared their throats in unison.

"Thank you, I would like to meet him very much." Louisa kept her tone even.

After her conversation with Meg, Louisa's thoughts had been in a whirl. Somehow, Meg had legitimized Louisa's trepidation. And she knew she had to consider carefully what she would do if Henry did propose. After all, girls she knew had received offers of marriage after only a few dances, a couple of morning visits in London, and, if they were lucky, a walk in Kensington Gardens. This was exactly what Louisa had always wanted to avoid, and exactly what she feared might happen with Henry.

But then, Louisa knew she would make her family more than happy were she to accept Henry. All social circles would be open to her. Henry could prove to be a fun companion, and his title and land might give Louisa freedom in some sense…but there would be social obligations. Even Meg was already caught up in her mother-in-law's ideas of what was right—endless charity events, volunteer work at the local parish, what one could say in society, whom she could talk to.

Again and again, Louisa came back to the same conclusion—marriage to Henry could mean being in a contented, gilded cage, doting on mini Henrys until she realized her moment for action and activism had passed.

What if she were to refuse him? The wheels of society turned like cogs in a machine. A decision to refuse Henry would haunt her forever—in Boston, in London, everywhere. The English aristocracy were the most powerful in the world, and their value as potential marriage partners was the highest in the world. The British Empire was on the rise, and the son of a duke was as close to royalty as one could get.

Louisa frowned and moved up the grand staircase.

She had thought about returning to America to seek work as a teacher. She had pondered joining Mrs. Pankhurst in London in her efforts to secure women's right to vote. Her mother would disown her if she did either of these things—cut her off—she knew that.

When she weighed this up with a marriage to Henry, there seemed to be no answer. No answer at all. But at lunchtime, she couldn't help but smile when Henry appeared on the vast staircase that led to the salon with a little dog in his arms.

"I thought you might enjoy her company for the afternoon," he said, holding the little spaniel out to Louisa. Henry was clever, she would give him that. She took the dog in her arms and caressed her long, soft ears. Suddenly, she was hit with a sense of homesickness, for Samuel, for her father. Not for her mother and her rigid sense of propriety, but for everything else. For her lost governess, for the old Meg.

"Cheer up," Henry said, taking her arm and leading her out to the driveway. "It's stunning weather."

Louisa found herself laughing. "You are correct about that."

"I want to show you my favorite folly. I don't take houseguests there as a rule. I like having a secret place where I can truly be myself, with no one watching," Henry said, leading her down the driveway and taking a turn to the right. He walked toward the stables, then turned left, away from them into a woodland walk, following a path that was narrow and shaded. Louisa placed the spaniel on the ground. A leash had been tied around her neck, and she trotted on next to them as if there was nothing to worry about at all.

"You have so many beautiful walks here," Louisa said. "It is hard to know where to start."

"You could spend a lifetime here exploring them," he said, his voice a little lower than usual. And then he chuckled, a sort of nonchalant aside. More like his usual self, Louisa thought as she kept pace beside him.

Soon the path took a turn to the right, going still deeper into the woods. "I hope you are not going to kidnap me and the dog," Louisa laughed.

"If only," he said.

Her thoughts were awhirl again. Perhaps she should ignore that niggling voice inside her that was telling her he was charming—was he too charming by far? Perhaps she should listen to the voice that was telling her that marrying Henry, should it be, indeed, an option, was probably her most sensible choice.

A real idea had begun to form in her head that morning while she walked, as ideas often did. What if she were to use her role here at Ashworth to promote women's rights? She agreed with Mrs. Pankhurst that the vote for women was the first step toward eventual equality. Wouldn't Emmeline Pankhurst be glad of a woman who would eventually have the rank and standing of a duchess to help with the cause? Louisa would have far more power as Viscountess Louisa Duval than she would as the unmarried Louisa West. Not to mention access to funds from her father once she married.

Possibilities had begun to open in her mind. Louisa was convinced that she had more chance of making progress here in Britain than she did at home in America. Were she to go home, her mother would put a stop to any activities that she tried to undertake. Were she to join the newly formed National American Woman Suffrage Association in America, she had no doubt that her mother would cut her off entirely from funds. But Louisa could see that this new group had been formed by bringing together women from largely middle-class backgrounds—the very participants in the charity organizations that Louisa would be expected to lead were she to marry Henry. And as his wife, not only would she have influence and power to galvanize women in these groups, but, dare she say it, she would have access to the money they needed.

They had come to a clearing in the forest. Scattered about, in the sudden sunshine, was a veritable collection of follies—tumbling-down replicas of Roman buildings, many of them draped in deep green ivy. Marble columns, some of them lying on their sides, some of them standing tall, caught the sun on their old, narrow bricks.

Louisa let the spaniel loose, but watched her as she trotted about.

A picnic table had been set up near an old upturned statue, complete with a white tablecloth strewn with wildflowers, as if some nymph had scattered them there. A plate of cucumber sandwiches was covered with a glass dome. There were silver pitchers of pink lemonade and two chairs were covered in pink brocade.

Louisa couldn't imagine a more romantic setting in her life. Had she entertained any doubts about Henry's intentions, they were dissipating fast now. Henry surveyed the scene, as if taking it in with his approval.

"Hungry?" he asked.

Louisa couldn't tear her eyes away from the charming surroundings. She wandered to one of the fallen statues and ran her hand over the warm old stone.

Henry stood near the table, leaning on the back of a chair. Next to it, a bottle of champagne chilled in a silver vessel on an elaborate stand. Louisa felt her breath quicken again, averted her eyes from it, and instead regarded Henry.

He poured her a glass of pink lemonade, holding it out for her.

"We had better not let the food turn bad in the heat." Louisa smiled, taking the glass that was decorated with the Ashworth coat of arms—several stag heads lined up in a row.

"I had it delivered five minutes ago," Henry said. He smiled then, a secretive, powerful smile, as if he enjoyed his ability to command others, the power it gave him. "Shall we sit down?"

Louisa hesitated a moment. She couldn't help but wonder if his invitation to sit at the table was indeed an invitation to join this power, or was he trying to use it over her?

Louisa moved to the table quickly, determined not to let him sense any confusion on her part. Her shoes sank into the soft green grass and she leaned forward, her hands wanting to play with something on the table. She settled for her fork.

Henry handed her the plate of sandwiches, and she thought how odd it was not to have servants around. It must be the only meal she had ever had at Ashworth where she was alone with a family member and no help.

"I think you would be very capable of running a place like this," Henry said suddenly.

A breeze picked up, sending the tablecloth into a small flurry. Louisa smoothed it out and focused on her plate of food. Cucumber sandwiches, egg sandwiches. Scones, cakes, and jellies. Did she want to become English, or not?

Apart from all the questions about what she wanted to do, how she was going to do it, and her feelings toward Henry, she had also experienced a strange sense of dislocation in England. For some reason, she seemed to have lost her sense of being American, and yet she felt foreign in Britain at the same time.

"I don't know that I would be terribly capable," she said, finally. "I rather think it would be a task that would take a special sort of person."

"A capable, strong sort of person, like you," Henry said. He leaned back in his seat. "Would you like some champagne?"

Louisa sensed her shoulders dropping from their tense state. So champagne at this point in the conversation, then. He was clearly not going to propose. "I'd love some," she said.

"About this ball," he went on. She sensed that he was trying to get her to relax. And yet she felt about as relaxed as a fox that was being pursued by the hunt.

"It sounds delightful, of course," she said.

"The salon, obviously. Sometimes we use the smaller ballroom or the theater on the odd occasion for smaller gatherings, but I want this to be big. I want it to be special. Louisa, is there anyone in particular whom you would like to invite?"

Louisa put down her champagne. Her throat seemed to have constricted. "I don't have anyone special in mind," she said. The conversation was awkward, stilted. She was having trouble finding words to say.

Henry lifted the lid from the food and was quiet for a few moments while they ate.

He folded his arms after a while and sat back in his seat. "I hope that you will get to make more friends among my acquaintances," he said. "I hope that you will get to know our neighbors. Have you walked around the village yet?"

Louisa shook her head. She gazed out at the landscape. The field bordered the forest on one side, and on the other led to a farther expanse, where cows grazed below wide cedar trees in the distance. She forced herself to focus on the man sitting opposite her.

And wondered, what would Samuel think of her sitting here like this?

Louisa nodded, but her insides churned. Suddenly, she put her napkin down on the table and stood up.

"I think I might go and have a rest," she said. The dog had fallen asleep by a statue.

Henry stood up too. "Of course, Louisa. As you wish," he said.

"Thank you," she said, her words coming out curter than she intended. "Thank you for bringing me here."

"My pleasure," he said. He walked around the table, and she stayed where she was, perfectly still. And she found she couldn't move, although she wanted to. She seemed stuck.

He stopped right in front of her. And he took her hand in his own, reaching it up to his lips and kissing it. Louisa started a little. He had never done that before. She had never seen him kiss another woman's hand since her arrival at Ashworth. Henry, while ever the attentive host, was all about putting on displays of entertainment rather than doting on individual guests.

Louisa nodded at him now, and she picked up the sleeping dog, and she made her way back to the path that led into the forest. She felt lost out here, for some reason. She wanted to go back to Ashworth, and she wanted, for some strange reason, to feel safe.

Chapter Six

Paris, 2015

Sarah was woken by the sound of rap. The beat belted about the bedroom, sweeping its way around Marthe's exquisite treasures as if it were taking over everything in the vicinity. If Sarah had started by feeling welcome and at home in the apartment, this noise was having the complete opposite effect on her now. She put her pillow on top of her head. Then she pulled it away again and looked at the clock. Seven in the morning. Darn Laurent! It was her first day in Paris. She was jet-lagged. She would have to confront him and fast.

She climbed out of bed and marched over to the door that connected to Laurent's room, aware that her black bob would be utterly tousled and her favorite polka-dotted silk pajamas were definitely only for her eyes. Problem was, she quite frankly didn't care. All she wanted was to go back to sleep.

Laurent was being ridiculous—this kind of music at this volume, especially at this time of day, was certainly inexcusable. What had Loic said Laurent disliked? Garish things, noise? Hardcore rap about bling and guns at the crack of dawn seemed to be up his alley nowadays. Sarah turned the handle and stuck her head around the door.

Nothing. No one in the bedroom. The grand four-poster was unmade. A couple of shirts were strewn across Marthe de Florian's magnificent old bed. Sarah moved farther into the room. The music was even louder in here; it throbbed through her entire system, causing her tired head to ache.

She turned the next door handle.

Laurent was not in the sitting room, although someone else was. Three someone elses, to be precise—three models, by the looks of it. Sarah felt her shoulders slump. One of the girls was clearly the subject of Laurent's latest portrait. Her green eyes were lined with black kohl. The other two girls were striking in their own ways. They all lolled about on Marthe de Florian's chaise longue.

Sarah could not help but gape.

But all three of them simply stared back as if they were appraising something unpleasant in the street.

Sarah wrapped her arms around her annoying, silly pajamas. She should have at least gotten dressed. But right now, all she cared about was turning down the music so she could go back to sleep, or, if not, at least think.

The portrait model beat her to it. The music retreated to a murmur with one flick of the girl's black-painted nails.

"You look angry," the girl said in stilted English. "Anger is not good for the complexion."

If Sarah were honest, right now, she was more focused on feeling like an alley cat having an encounter with a clutter of purebred Siamese than on any concerns with her skin.

"I just can't deal with that volume right now," she said. "I'm a bit jet-lagged."

"I am permanently jet-lagged," the portrait model retorted. "It means nothing."

Of course.

"No Parisian woman would wear that outfit," one of the others said, her accent heavy, French, sexy.

Perhaps they were triplets.

Sarah hated to think.

"Laurent told us there was an American in the apartment." The third one spoke English without much accent at all.

Sarah decided to take things into her own hands.

"I really should take a shower," she said, smiling. "I'm Sarah, by the way. Thanks for turning the music down." She turned back toward Laurent's bedroom, promising herself that she would never step out of her own room again without proper makeup and an outfit that was intended to kill.

"Sarah."

She closed her eyes and stopped, but did not turn around.

"Sleep well?"

The sound of Laurent's voice was accompanied by the delicious scent of freshly brewed coffee.

Sarah inhaled.

Heaven.

But she was going back to bed.

"Sarah, have you met Giselle, Suzette, and Adela?" Laurent sounded more than jovial now. The sound of his footsteps resonated through the room. "Sarah's the other guest in the apartment whom I told you about," he said.

Caffeine.

Sarah clutched at her wretched sleepwear.

"Would you like a coffee, Sarah?" Laurent sounded fine—relaxed and at ease. "You can have this one, if you like. The girls don't drink coffee, do you?"

There was a chorus of laughter.

Sarah sighed. She never got caught out like this. Never. She could either walk out of the room and look ridiculous, or turn around and take the coffee and look ridiculous again.

She was gasping for the coffee.

After a few moments, she turned around and walked over to Laurent. "Thank you," she said, with all the grace and dignity she could muster. "I would love some coffee."

She ignored the look of amusement on Laurent's face. He had gone from snicker-in-his-voice to outright I'm-trying-not-to-laugh-out-loud-at-you faster than a flick of his paintbrush on a canvas.

Sarah stood her ground in her pajamas and sipped the coffee. It was good. Seriously good.

"What are your plans for today, Sarah?" Laurent went on, deadpan.

"This is boring," the girl who was clearly the subject of the portrait announced. "We are going out for juices. You can drink that hideous stuff. Unless you need us, Laurent? We will take a twenty-minute break?"

Laurent caught Sarah's eye just then and raised a brow. "Fifteen-minute break," he said. "Then I'll do your preliminary sketches, Adela. And Giselle, we are nearly done."

Sarah wanted to protest. She needed a shower, makeup, and food. The last thing she wanted was a fifteen-minute conversation in her pajamas with a sultry French artist.

But Laurent looked like talking to her was exactly what he wanted to do.

Sarah sighed. The coffee was giving her the kick-start she so desperately needed, but if there was one thing she hated, it was being one step behind. She sipped away at the drink. She needed a plan to evacuate.

"Sarah, I've been wondering. What exactly brought you to Paris? And why are you so keen to stay in Marthe de Florian's apartment that you're willing to share with me?" Laurent sounded perfectly reasonable.

Sarah cursed herself for talking to him yesterday about Boldini. Why hadn't she kept quiet? She was in Paris on a mission—it didn't exactly need to be kept secret, but she was not in the mood to tell him the entire story of Louisa right now. And Laurent was very attractive—the absolute last thing she needed. She had sworn off men, after all. At least for a while longer.

But then, Laurent was an artist. He should know about the Belle Époque. What if she could ask him some questions? He seemed intent on telling her that he wanted answers, but what if she could swing things her way?

She sipped at the coffee. Another idea came into play. Now she was rolling, more like her usual self. Confidence and strategy, whether caffeine-induced or not, were always a good idea.

"The truth is," Sarah said, "I'm here on a personal mission."

Laurent smoothed out the white shirt that hung loose over his faded jeans. He slipped down onto Marthe de Florian's chaise longue and sat there, his eyes raking over her like an...artist... Sarah reminded herself. She stood a little taller, tugged at her own pajama top.

"I can't imagine many people wanting to share with me," he went on.

Sarah cleared her throat. What was she supposed to say to that? It hadn't been her choice. She had just wanted access to Marthe's letters.

She decided to plow on and not react to him. "My ancestor..." She looked at him to check his reaction.

But he didn't look bored. He was still watching her.

Sarah took in a long breath. "...Louisa West, was a debutante in the 1890s. A Bostonian who—"

"Came to Paris?" He tilted his head. "Unusual."

"England."

"Of course."

"Louisa married into English aristocracy. But we know that her husband, a Lord Henry Duval..." She looked at him.

"Go on."

"Well, Henry was something of a rake. He spent a lot of time in Paris, with the Montmartre set. Artists, actors...courtesans. Marthe, I think."

"So, are you interested in their lives, or—"

Sarah shook her head. She was still horribly aware of her appearance, but she sensed that Laurent didn't care about that a bit. He seemed to be listening. And for some reason, Sarah found herself wanting to talk.

"Legend has it that my great-great-aunt Louisa jumped out of a window to her death at a party in Montmartre. In 1895. But her death was hushed up by Henry's aristocratic family, so far as the story goes. They were keen to avoid scandal. No investigations, no questions. Nothing. Louisa's death was accepted as suicide—swept under the rug—and Henry's family simply moved on."

Laurent nodded.

Louisa took a deep breath. "But it turned out that my family wasn't able to deal with Louisa's death as easily as Henry's. Louisa's father lost everything he had built up—a successful trading company in Hong Kong, and interests in railways back home in the States. The rest of the family kept away, cousins deserted my branch of the family, and, well, I have no family left right now, and so it seems important to me to find out. It was never investigated. I think I should discover the truth." She stopped. Just short of saying that she had been desperate to get away from Boston as well.

"I'm interested," he said. "Tell me more."

When Sarah spoke again, she was acutely aware of the silence in the room. He had flicked the music off completely. "Last week, I found a letter from Marthe de Florian to Henry Duval among my late father's possessions. I don't know why my father kept it, and I don't know what it means. But it was hidden away."

"Go on," he said.

"It was written the morning after Louisa's death. Marthe was telling Henry to get out of Paris, to go back to England, because he knew too much. But what does that mean?"

"Why do you think your father never told you about the letter?"

Sarah shook her head. "That doesn't surprise me. My father never wanted to make waves. I'm certain that he would have wanted to leave the past in the past. He tended to accept things as they were. I expect he thought it was far too hard to open the family-collapse box of snakes. He might not have even thought about it. Some people don't take an interest in these things…" Her voice trailed off, but Laurent nodded as if he understood.

"That's true, they don't."

"I want to find out what happened to her now. Because there were personal repercussions for her, for her memory, let alone the impact on the family at the time. And I don't know if that was fair."

Laurent tilted his head to one side. "You want to find more correspondence between Henry and Marthe de Florian."

Sarah put her empty coffee cup up on the mantelpiece. "So far as the story goes, Henry spent more time in Montmartre than at the family estate in England. I know there weren't many top courtesans in Paris during the Belle Époque—Carolina Otero, Liane de Pougy, Marthe de Florian—it's not surprising that Marthe and Henry had been in touch, in some ways. It sounds as if Marthe knew what happened at the party, at the very least."

"Have you done any more research?"

"I've looked online at newspaper archives to see if I can find any references to Louisa's death. I've scanned 1895 and 1896. Even though my French is not very good, I can read the basics, and the only mention of my ancestor that I found was a brief statement: Louisa died at a party here in Paris. And the address where she died."

"Okay. That's good."

Sarah smiled. "I admit I was hoping that the party was here, right in this apartment. But it was in a building on the corner of Rue Lepic and Rue Robert Planquette."

"Rue Lepic is the extension of Rue Blanche." Laurent was frowning now.

"I know. I've google-mapped the building. It overlooks both streets. It's seven stories high, so if she was on the top floor it would have been awful. Her descent…"

"Yes." Laurent ran a hand over his chin. "Okay. You need to walk up there. Have a look at it."

"I was planning on doing that today. If I woke up. Which I did."

Laurent regarded his watch.

The front door opened. The entourage. Funnily enough, Sarah had forgotten about them, and when she heard the sounds of their singsongy voices ringing through the apartment, she frowned. She sensed that she had seen the real Laurent for the past few minutes. But that was silly. She had only just met him.

"Would you like me to come with you to look at the building later on this morning?" he asked, standing up, moving toward the door that the models would come through. "Why don't you go and have some breakfast, get yourself organized, and tell me when you want to set off."

"But aren't you working?"

"The models have a shoot with *Elle* magazine this afternoon. They have to be there at twelve to get ready. They are being picked up at eleven thirty."

The thought of having Laurent along was appealing. Sarah had not yet sorted out what she was going to do once she was standing in front of the place where Louisa had died.

"Thank you," she said.

Giselle appeared in the doorway. "We have had a fifteen-minute break, now," she muttered in her sultry French accent. "And you are still in your . . . negligee." She eyed Sarah with a particular brand of distaste.

Sarah looked down at the floor and fought the urge to giggle. "Negligee's not quite the right translation, Giselle." She shot a look under her eyelashes at Laurent. Something akin to a grin appeared on his face.

Sarah turned around and returned to her room. She had never had such a long conversation in her pajamas with a stranger—let alone a Frenchman—in her life.

After a bath scented with her very own Jo Malone and an indulgent breakfast of *pain au chocolat* and more coffee at a local café, where Sarah had managed to read a little of the newspaper in

French, she was back at the apartment, ready to go see the building where Louisa's life had ended so abruptly over a century earlier.

Laurent was wiping down his brushes when Sarah entered the room where he worked. All she could do was stand back and admire the portrait of Giselle that seemed very nearly complete now. The girl stared out of the painting, confident in who she was. It was all so very French.

"It's stunning," Sarah said.

"I don't know." Laurent put the last of his paintbrushes down. He seemed almost humble, looking at the painting with her. There was nothing of the show-off about him at all. "You get to a point where you just have to sign off. I've made some sketches of Adela and Suzette, taken some photographs. They are next."

"I can imagine that there comes a time where enough is enough." Sarah moved over to the window, leaned against the chaise longue for a moment.

There was such atmosphere in Marthe's apartment. When Sarah viewed the room from the window, she didn't see Loic and Cat's modern interpretation; she saw decadence, a crowded palette, a riot of expensive gifts and porcelain and shawls draped on ostriches and gilt wallpaper resplendent. She saw chandeliers and deep golden light. And a woman, lying on the chaise longue, all dressed in silk.

It was as if the place were pregnant with the past, as if everything that had happened here loomed somewhere unseen, just out of reach—like Louisa's story. Gone forever, but somehow not done yet.

"Are you ready?" Laurent pulled a jacket from where it hung over a chair near the canvas.

Sarah nodded. What she was going to do when she was standing in front of the place where Louisa had died was quite another question.

Laurent waited for Sarah to step first out of the apartment, before turning left along Rue Blanche and heading toward Montmartre.

Sarah had to admit that she enjoyed walking through old Paris with this handsome French artist in his chic black jacket and faded jeans. At the same time, she felt comfortable being quiet with him as they made their way toward that infamous old Parisian district of Montmartre.

She was so enjoying looking at the street. They passed several restaurants, their lunchtime menus set out on blackboards on the sidewalk. When the street opened up to the large square at its end—Place Blanche—the atmosphere altered so much that Sarah had to stand still and stare.

"The hub of the Belle Époque," Laurent said.

Sarah took in the iconic red windmill and the street entrance with its sign in faded old script: The Moulin Rouge. The square's fancy Parisian light posts and elegant buildings spoke of Haussmann's Paris, but the Moulin Rouge was something else. Nowadays, it looked seedy, a piece of Las Vegas dropped right into a square in Paris. The windmill no longer spun and it, like Marthe's apartment, was another silent reminder of the infamous Belle Époque.

"Would you like to go straight to the building?" Laurent asked after a few moments.

Sarah nodded. As they crossed the square and walked up Rue Lepic toward the apartment where Louisa had spent her final evening, the architecture changed again. The buildings here were simpler in style than those in other parts of Paris, and the street felt cluttered. Tiny shops took up every bit of space—from hot dog stands and French *tabacs* to lurid bars. The street was lined with cobblestones, and graffiti had been splashed onto some of the walls.

"It's like stepping into a different city," Sarah breathed. "What a contrast it must have been, coming here, for Henry, having grown up in England on some grand estate."

"I know," Laurent said. He walked straight ahead with purpose, but he stopped every now and then when Sarah did, seeming quite content to wait while she let her eyes roam.

"Imagine what it was like at the turn of the nineteenth century."

"Not the place for a well-brought-up girl from Boston," Laurent said.

"About that." Sarah turned to Laurent. "You see, this is where it gets a bit confusing. This is where I have trouble equating a suicidal Louisa with the girl who has been described through the generations. The information that has been passed down about Louisa may be scanty, but I do know a few things. My father told me that apparently Louisa wasn't keen on the idea of a conventional marriage. She was sympathetic to women's liberation and her mother had little time for her. I can't help wondering if that reputation caused her to be dismissed so easily after her death by society and by the family she had married into in England. Maybe Louisa's tragedy wasn't given the attention it deserved because she was unconventional, a bit of a problem. Clearly, neither family wanted scandal. I can see that. Does that make sense?" She shot a glance at Laurent. He was frowning.

"What was your father's attitude toward her?"

"He said it was very sad, but that she was regarded as something of a black sheep, and that there was nothing that could be done about it." Sarah marched on. Walking seemed to be getting her mind going. She was also feeling more alert—her jet lag had abated since this morning.

"I can't strike suicide out completely," she said. "I suppose she could have become depressed about her lot, felt trapped, and taken her life. And it seems that Marthe was trying to ensure Henry hushed things up too. There was a lot of protecting of everyone who was still alive—but what about Louisa? What about the way she has been portrayed? Did she become a scapegoat? Someone to blame for the family's misfortunes? It can happen. It's easy enough to get everything wrong. And I just don't know if that's entirely fair."

Laurent stopped for a moment. He leaned against a motorbike and something passed across his face. And Sarah remembered what Loic had told her about him. That something was troubling him so much that it had changed him completely. Sarah realized she was doing all the talking. She looked out at the shops around her—the cafés and restaurants of Montmartre, their shiny neon signs dull in the light of day.

"It's not good to cover things up. Let's go." Laurent brushed his hands down his jacket and moved on, his eyes focused straight ahead.

Sarah followed him in silence up the street. A few steps later he stopped. Neither of them spoke as they looked at the building on the corner of Rue Robert Planquette. It was a beautiful, typically Parisian building—its façade stood out among the other buildings on the street. The perfect setting for a party. The last place you would expect to see a death.

Each floor held floor-to-ceiling tall windows, with Parisian balconies decorated with low, wrought-iron railings that were intricately patterned and painted a smart black.

Sarah couldn't help visualizing the night of the party; light from the windows would have shone out onto the street. Her thoughts marched on, and she wondered which balcony had been the one... and stopped. Instead, she forced herself to focus on what the rest of the street must have looked like back then, with its secret dens and freethinking poets and artists, street hawkers, circus performers, prostitutes.

Laurent was staring at the building too. "Is there anything more you'd like to do while we are here?"

Sarah had thought about that. "The building would house a lot of apartments and I have no idea who owned the apartment that held the party. I very much doubt anyone living here today would have a clue about something that happened in the building over one hundred years ago. But I wanted to see it."

"The letters are a much safer bet."

"They are. I admit that I haven't gotten beyond this stage with my plans. Which is unlike me, because I'm such a planner—apparently."

Sarah shook her head. What was she saying? What did she mean? She had only just met Laurent, and here she was, telling him her family history and giving him a rundown of her personality as well.

Laurent sounded close. "Your determination to find out what happened for your family's sake, for Louisa's sake, is admirable. But I do think it's going to be very hard."

Sarah turned back toward Place Blanche. "I know." But she had to do something. She needed a focus, something that she cared about. She had lost everything that she held dear.

Laurent stopped at an intersection a short distance beyond Place Blanche. "Are you confident of finding your way back? I have to go to the magazine now. I need to touch base with the editor. And are you sorted for dinner tonight?"

"I can find my way back. And yes, I'll work things out for the evening. Thank you."

He smiled at her, turned, and disappeared down a street.

Chapter Seven

Ashworth, 1893

Louisa gasped when she came down the main oak staircase at Ashworth on the evening of the ball. The banisters had been decorated with twists of ivy and jasmine. The salon was resplendent with flowers from Ashworth's extensive hothouses and gardens, and a crowd of elegant people were already gathered in the vast room beneath the tower.

The duke and duchess, along with Henry and a man who was clearly Henry's younger brother, Charles, stood in line at the entrance to the salon, receiving guests.

Louisa stopped and regarded Charles. He looked very close in age to his older brother, and if she were honest, Charles was the more striking of the two. While he shared his brother's coloring—tawny eyes, dark eyebrows—Charles's features were finer than Henry's. He looked to have been cut from more delicate cloth.

Charles was chatting with a guest, his entire face lit up with warmth. Henry looked rather bored. She stopped herself from giggling and took another step down the stairs. The general opinion in society seemed to be that Charles's disposition was so different from his brother's that it was almost impossible they were of the same blood. Henry, of course, had the reputation of a rake. He was all about fun. And Charles, according to chat that Louisa had heard among the other ladies at the palace, was seen as the more serious of the pair.

Now, Louisa saw Henry spot her on the staircase. He excused himself and made his way over to where she stood. She watched while Charles looked up, fast as a whippet, his eyes taking her in. Even from this distance she could make out his frown. She held Charles's gaze for a moment, tilting her chin a little. She could guess his thoughts. An American, chasing his brother—after the title, like countless other women no doubt had been? The thought revolted her. Such a label was the last thing she wanted, but in some ways, she could understand the concerns Charles might have. A knot formed in her stomach.

"Louisa West," Henry said, stepping up to take her arm. "You look stunning. I could drop dead on the spot."

"Oh, thank you," Louisa laughed. Her new dress had been delivered from London just on time. It was pale pink silk—cut to show off her décolletage. Sheer, filmy gauze swept around the bodice and a black velvet belt was built into the waist. The skirt fell in swathes to the floor and finished with a train. She shot a glance back at Charles. He was still looking at her. For some odd reason, that pleased her. She turned back to Henry.

Henry was looking particularly dashing himself in his black formal suit and tie. His hair, which he often allowed to roam quite free, had been swept back, showing off his eyes to perfection.

He guided her around the dance floor, waltzing and chatting most amiably with his acquaintances as they turned about.

"Would you come with me for a moment?" Henry asked all of a sudden, after he had quite monopolized her for the dance.

He was smiling at her now, and if she were given to imaginings, she could have interpreted the way he was looking at her as indulgent—interested, keen. But there was none of that fluttering on her part—nothing building up in her system that her friends chattered on about when they talked about romantic encounters. She was able to think with absolute clarity. Louisa knew there were merits in that when it came to men. In some ways, she wanted to feel clearheaded around Henry, to be able to think. At least she was not feeling the annoyance that she usually experienced.

"Of course," she said, as he tucked her hand into his arm.

She walked with him through the salon, out into the wide entrance hall, and into the empty library. Sounds from the party drifted into the room.

If there was anywhere in the palace that conveyed a sense of timelessness and serenity, then the library, with its hundreds of well-dusted volumes, their dark navy and red leather bindings decorated with gold leaf, was the place. It was a room for tea in front of a roaring fire, an afternoon spent curled up reading. It was Louisa's favorite room in the palace.

Henry leaned against one of the velvet sofas in front of the fireplace. "I always think of this as rather a musty, old-fashioned room. All these old tomes. But it is the only place where I knew we could be alone." He ran a hand over his still-perfect hair and looked down at the floor.

"I see," Louisa said. She glanced at the beautiful old volumes, rows and rows of gold-leaf books, their spines holding treasures, she knew. Ladders were positioned around the room, up against the floor-to-ceiling shelves. How she would love to spend a day reading in here. Something stirred in her, something triggered again. That sense. It was as if someone had thrown a very small stone into a lake and it had pierced the soft sand at the bottom, and it told her, *He's not right.* Yet her rational self replied, *What other option do you have, Louisa?*

"You must know that I have come to regard you with some esteem," Henry said, his words coming out slowly, as if they were planned. Then he took her hand and knelt down in front of her. "I have corresponded with your father. I don't anticipate a problem, and therefore, I'm asking you to marry me. There's no point in delaying it."

Louisa looked down at the man in front of her.

Here it was.

She did care for Henry but she was certainly not in love. Was it better this way? She had heard countless women say it was. She looked down at the Turkish carpet, its patterns neat and structured. And thought about being a viscountess, then a duchess. Was this the way to gain control of her life?

Henry stood up, took her hand, raised it to his lips.

Louisa pushed away the strong instinct, almost violent this time, that this was all wrong.

She simply nodded, in the end. Forced herself to be calm about it. It was the best outcome, she thought. "If my parents consent, then, why not?" she said, her words coming out rather hoarse. All her thoughts tumbled about and the conclusion she had come to was that this was the right thing to do. It made sense. It made every sense in the world.

Henry dropped a light kiss on her forehead. She leaned up, allowing him to brush his lips onto hers. Then pulled away. That was quite enough.

She walked with him back out into the ball.

"Mama and Papa approve, by the way," he said.

"Oh, good." Louisa focused her eyes on the swirling scene in front of her, satin and taffeta ball gowns and handsome young men in formal attire. So, it was as easy as that. Her entire life decided in a second. In the swish of a conversation in a pink dress at a ball. She pressed her lips together and pushed down the feeling of trepidation that was mounting in her heart.

And came to a sudden halt on the edge of the dancers. Henry's brother appeared right between them. Louisa found herself reddening.

Henry spoke. "Charlie, I'd like you to meet Louisa. I'm going to get myself a drink."

Charlie folded his arms and didn't move an inch. "What an introduction! 'This is Charlie—I'm going to get a drink!' Hello, Louisa." Charlie held out a hand.

Louisa took it and looked up at him. He kissed her hand, but he was frowning, just as he had been when she first noticed him.

Vulnerability fell all over her suddenly. She did not know where to look. Henry had disappeared into the crowd.

"Louisa," Charlie said, "may I talk to you please?" His voice was far deeper than Henry's. Louisa chewed on her lip.

"Certainly," she said, and took in a breath.

Charlie took her arm and led her around the edge of the dancers. The sounds of laughter, the orchestra, all these things seemed to mingle in her head. The room felt quite hot all of a sudden.

"I want to ask you some questions. Let's go this way." He led her out of the room. They were standing in the hallway that led to the library.

And then he turned. "Come with me," he said.

He led her past the library and the sitting room, stopping at the entrance to the smoking room, waiting while Louisa entered first, then striding inside after her and closing the door. Louisa folded her arms and stood still. She forced herself to focus on the patterned rug and the hunting prints that decorated the walls.

"I brought you here because no one will disturb us," Charlie said. His tone was gentler now, in fact, his voice was quite soft.

Louisa nodded. She felt as nervous as if she were at an interview with a...duke.

"It's my father's domain. He doesn't tend to bring groups in here—there is another more formal billiards room for that."

Louisa nodded. Yes, that was right. Henry had shown her the formal billiards room. She focused on Charlie and frowned.

Charlie kept his voice low and soft as he spoke. "Henry will be telling our parents that you have accepted him as we speak. He nodded at me just then—so I understand what's happened tonight. I know you're engaged. It's a done deal, as far as Henry's concerned. All he needs now is confirmation from your parents, which I doubt will be a problem." He moved toward the fireplace, leaned against it, and ran a hand over his chin. "But Louisa, did Henry explain the implications of your acceptance?"

Louisa moved farther into the room herself. She moved, instinctively, perhaps, to a side table that held family photographs in silver frames. She ran her finger over the top of one of Henry standing on the lawn with a tennis racket. "I'm aware of the implications, of the responsibilities," she said. But she knew her voice sounded dull. And somehow, she couldn't help that.

"Do you know him?"

Louisa sensed a chuckle rising in her throat, but she pushed it back down again. Held it in check. "As far as anyone knows anyone when they are about to marry," she said.

"Do you love him?"

Louisa startled like a pony that had come across an aggressive dog. "You ask too many questions." She could not keep the annoyance out of her tone. Charlie, she sensed, was the sort of man who came right to the point. She squared her shoulders.

"I have more things I want to ask." He didn't seem embarrassed at his own forthright manner at all, and this bothered Louisa. Her nervousness was suddenly replaced with . . . something verging on anger.

And as it rose up in her, she did not even try to hold it back. "If you think, if you think for one moment that I am some aspiring American, then you have no idea who I am."

Charlie's voice was even more authoritative. He sounded more serious than before. "From what I've heard, I think an aspiring American, as you so delightfully put it, is the last thing you are. But you're confused."

Louisa felt heat flush in her cheeks. What was this? Where was Henry? But then, she reminded herself, she was perfectly capable of settling her own arguments. She reminded herself of the way she had always sparred with Samuel and braced herself some more.

"I noticed you this morning when you were walking around the park. You looked agitated. No one walks in circles unless they don't know what they're about." Charlie moved toward the fireplace and leaned against it in a most proprietary manner. "I'd hate to see you making a shocking mistake. And no matter what I think of Henry's actions with regard to you, I don't want to see him make the wrong decision either."

"We are perfectly happy. Thank you." Louisa lifted her chin. And knew she was lying. But she did not want, for some reason, to give an inch.

Charlie let out a laugh and regarded her with a smile on his lips. "Louisa, Henry isn't any ordinary heir. Henry has dreams and desires other than the role that was set out for him at birth. This might shock you, but he'd rather be an actor on the stage."

"I'm aware of that," Louisa said. "He told me. And furthermore, I sensed he was...different...the first time we met."

Charlie broke into a full-blown laugh now. "Did he tell you that he spends most of his time in Paris, frequenting the Moulin Rouge? I won't go into specifics, but—is that a life that appeals to you, Louisa? It's hardly the right milieu for a new husband and wife. I'd hate to think what it would do to you were you to accompany him on his...escapades. Because, quite frankly, if you are not interested in courtesans and the theater and dance halls, then you'll be spending most of your time at Ashworth by yourself. Don't underestimate his interests in Paris."

"Henry will have to be here to run the estate," Louisa pointed out. "He can hardly spend all his time in Paris. And if he finds it modern, and different from all this, then what is the harm in that? He might gain ideas on how to update things at Ashworth from his time in Paris." She was becoming quite agitated, but, she had to admit, stimulated and excited as well.

"I run all the estates. Henry doesn't do a thing." Charlie was not going to budge.

Louisa closed her eyes. Of course. Of course he did. Was Charlie, then, worried that her arrival would do him out of a job? That Henry might want to spend more time at Ashworth if he were married? That she might be a force for change within the family dynamic?

"I want you to understand what you are getting into, and I want you to promise me that you won't have any expectation that Henry will be here, that he will be a regular husband." His tone was darker again, more serious.

"Perhaps," Louisa said, her words coming out like bullets fired from a hunting rifle. "I never wanted a regular husband. Perhaps I was never interested in playing the role of a regular wife."

Charlie dropped his voice an octave. "I know that. I know you have your own inclinations. And I think that's a good thing."

As quick as a fox, Louisa glanced up at him.

He went on, and his voice was so soothing that she felt as if she were listening to a snake charmer casting a spell. "You must make sure that you don't get bored, in that case. You must make provisions for yourself to have an independent life once you marry Henry. Start making plans. Get yourself organized and make things clear from the word go."

"It's exactly what I want," she said, and it was as if she were in accordance with him now. It seemed that the conversation had shifted from a potential disaster into a duet that somehow worked. And she wasn't sure who had turned it. It bothered her that it just might have been Charlie.

"Very well then." Charlie pulled his hand down from where it had been leaning against the mantelpiece, adjusted his white sleeve.

"I have thought things through," she said, but she suspected she sounded more resolute than she felt.

Charlie moved toward the doorway.

A pang of disappointment hit Louisa. She wasn't sure why. But she wanted this seeming closeness that she felt to Charlie to linger longer than it had. He had one hand on the door.

"Meet me in the morning at the front entrance, at nine. I hear you are fond of riding. I am too. We'll go out together and I'll show you the estate. You should see it," he said.

Louisa felt a smile form on her lips, and something lightened in her entire system. "Do you always give unsolicited advice?" she asked.

He stayed silent, looking at her.

"Very well." She still kept her tone light, but he had unsettled her, again. "I'll meet you tomorrow. And thank you, it would be wonderful to learn something of the estate. I am interested, you know."

He held the door open. "I'll see you in the morning." He sounded firm. As if she were being dismissed.

"I do like to ride," Louisa said, moving toward him and through the door. Her shoulder brushed against his chest as she passed him, and she pulled away suddenly.

Charlie stayed where he was.

"You should have told Henry about your riding," Charlie muttered. "You could have gone out every morning. Would have saved you walking in circles. The horses won't let you do that."

Louisa stood still on the spot. Henry knew how much she loved to ride. He had never offered to lend her a horse.

Charlie nodded at her and followed her back out to the ball.

Chapter Eight

Paris, 2015

Once Laurent had gone, Sarah continued on down Rue Blanche, past a theater. Large billboards advertised the next performance. And then there was a school, the French flag hanging proudly outside its old stone façade. What a mix, what a blend of life every street in Paris was. Sarah continued walking toward the Seine and pulled out her phone. Her next stop had to be Loic. Her next stop had to be Marthe de Florian's letters.

But when she reached the end of Rue Blanche, where the street opened out into another square, altogether a far grander affair than Place Blanche, she stopped. Memories flooded back. She had been to this very place with Steven. Walked right here with him on a trip they had taken to Paris years ago.

Sarah turned left and walked along the sidewalk that surrounded the square. She stopped, unable to help herself, outside the chocolatier they had visited on that vacation, running into the sweet little shop after they had been on a tour of the Palais Garnier nearby. It had been raining.

But perhaps that afternoon had been an anomaly for Steven, who never did anything impulsive. He had pulled her into the chocolatier, bought her a cellophane bag of delectable truffles. Then, when they had left the shop, once the rain had stopped and he had charmed the assistant with his particular brand of self-confidence, he had taken her hand and led her into the center of the square, where there was a small park, with benches and a playground.

Sarah walked across the road, circling the park, not looking at it, her eyes straight ahead. Trying to push the memory out of her mind. She had thought Steven would never let her down.

She thought he would always be there.

As she went toward the river down another, narrower street, crowded with busses and cars and restaurants, more restaurants, she dialed Loic's number.

"Sarah," he said, "how are you settling in?"

"Fine, thank you, Loic." She smiled. Someone from her new life—there was, she had to remind herself, always a new life to be had.

She chatted with him about the apartment and moved past the Palais Garnier, past rows and rows of grand buildings now. Classic Haussmann territory. Then a hotel, marble steps, fancy black cars parked opposite a wide red carpet that was laid out on the sidewalk as if for celebrities.

If she kept going straight ahead, she would hit the Seine.

Loic asked about her plans, asked how her search was coming along.

He was going to make things easy for her. Sarah sent a sigh of thanks.

"I don't want to impose, but I mentioned Marthe's letters when we spoke on the phone."

Loic chuckled. "You are so very polite. I know you did. I've talked to Cat."

Sarah kept walking. She turned down Rue Cambon. It was quieter here. A man in a tuxedo walked past, looking as if he were going to a ball. She passed fashion shops, their sparkling windows decorated with alluring clothes, scarves, and high-heeled shoes. Rue Cambon ended at the Tuileries Garden. She walked straight through the first set of gates that she came to and traversed the paths. No one was allowed to walk on the perfect lawns, no matter how enticing they were in the heat.

"So you're thinking that your ancestor's husband could have been one of Marthe's clients?"

"It seems likely," she said. "They obviously had some sort of relationship, but I just don't know what. And I don't know what the implications of that could have been for my ancestor—for Louisa."

Sarah walked straight through the park, past the Orangerie. She had visited there with Steven too.

She focused again, left the park, crossed the Quay des Tuileries and walked right over to the stone wall that bounded the Seine, listening to Loic chatting about how he and Cat had found the letters. She leaned against the old wall under the shade of one of the trees that lined the river.

"Of course you can look at the letters," Loic said. There was real warmth in his voice. "When Cat and I read them, I had to translate them all. Hopefully you will be okay on your own. How's your French?"

"Interesting." She could probably manage to decipher the gist of it with a dictionary.

"Ask Laurent to help you if you get stuck," Loic said. "Just make sense of the flow of things. It's the best way to go when you're reading a foreign language."

"Loic, can you tell me something? I'm intrigued that you speak perfect English. Have you always lived in France?" She simply had to ask.

"English father, French mother," Loic explained. "My father insisted on speaking English to my sister and me at home."

"I see. I guess that has paid off for you in the end. I suppose you didn't come across a Henry Duval or a Louisa West when you were reading Marthe's letters with Cat?"

"When you see how many love letters Marthe collected, you'll realize how impossible it is for me to remember those sorts of details. It's hard to explain, but to remember one single name—"

"Yes. Of course." How many times had she searched people's estates herself with an eye out for that one elusive item? That one thing that might be of value to the museum. The piece that could be the star of a collection.

"The letters are in a safe in the dressing room. If I come to the apartment in a couple of hours, could I meet you there? Would that work?"

"Yes." Sarah found she felt more in control now. "Thank you."

"I'll see you around five."

Sarah thanked him. Hung up the phone. And she turned to walk along the Seine for a while. Alone, but hopeful.

There were worse ways to be.

Chapter Nine

Ashworth, 1893

Louisa did not sleep well after the ball. By the time she was able to go to bed, she only had a few hours to rest before she had agreed to meet Charles. She had lain awake—her mind awhirl with what her life was going to become. Then her thoughts would turn into a cycle of justification. Of course she had made the right choice. What else could she do?

She, Henry, Charles, and his parents had gathered in the library when all the guests had left. Charles had not stayed long. He stood by the fireplace, his arms crossed, while Henry told his parents that Louisa had accepted his offer. Straight after that, he had shaken Henry's hand, kissed Louisa on the cheek, reminding her quietly in her ear of their assignation at nine the following morning, and marched off to bed.

Henry's father came straight to the point.

"Henry has written to your father, Louisa," he said. "Helena and I are naturally delighted to accept you as a member of the family."

Louisa pushed aside the thought that this seemed like a formal address.

The duke coughed before going on. "Of course, matches between Americans and people from our country are becoming quite the norm. I will have no trouble explaining your ancestry and your position to our friends and family."

Louisa started a little at this, but the duke still pushed further. "I look forward to entertaining your father here at Ashworth in the future. His business interests in the Far East are strong enough to warrant this match."

Louisa had to stop herself from gasping at the duke's overt statement of the financial underpinnings that were always left unsaid in the New World. His candor had kept Louisa awake most of the night.

Now, she let her eyes roam over the park from where she stood at the palace's front door. She had arrived at the front entrance to the house right on time to meet Charles. A gardener tended the flower beds that sat against the edge of the palace—he looked at her, nodded, and then returned to his work. The lawns by the drive were dewy from their early-morning watering.

Charles came down the front steps a few moments later. He looked, at first glance, so like Henry had the first time she met him, with his dark riding jacket and pale jodhpurs, that she had to remind herself who he was.

She lifted the skirt of her own gray riding habit and moved up the front steps to greet him.

"Good morning. I think you and I are the only two awake," he said.

"I love the early mornings," Louisa said. "They are something that I confess I never want to miss."

"You were one of the only people up early yesterday morning. I noticed that," he said. His eyes seemed to roam over her face. "Is everything all right?" he asked, his tone dropping further.

Louisa started at this. He sounded as if he were asking an intimate question. As if he knew her. She had to shake her head. She sensed that he was reading her. But that was ridiculous. "Yes!" she said, her voice too bright. Lying. Then she pushed that unwelcome thought away.

She turned and moved down the steps.

"The stables are this way," he said, catching up and leading her away from the palace along the driveway.

Louisa focused on the sound of his boots crunching on the perfectly raked gravel.

"I think you'd like to learn something of the estate. You're going to want to get involved. And that's a good thing," he said.

Louisa smiled at this. And she wasn't surprised.

"I am interested. Very. And," she couldn't help adding, "thank you for understanding."

"Why?" His expression was serious.

Louisa stopped. "Because I fear that not many men would ask a woman such a thing."

"Why not?"

"You make it sound simple."

"Yes."

"I do want to get involved. I appreciate what you said to me last night," she said. "That's all." She felt a slight frisson pass through her.

"I know that." Charles moved toward the stables, and as he did so, he explained the details of the estate, including figures and facts that many men would have thought a woman wouldn't comprehend or appreciate. But Louisa was entranced to hear the specifics. Charles's sense of responsibility for the resources in his care seemed inspiring instead of oppressive. His face lit up as he answered her questions and asked her some. And he seemed more relaxed now. Once he started talking about his work, he seemed to forget to ask her probing questions.

Perhaps, she thought, he approved of her. And for some reason, this afforded her great relief.

They had come to the high wall that surrounded the stables. An archway, similar to, but on a far grander scale than that at Willowdale, marked the entrance to the stable courtyard.

"You are very fortunate," Louisa said, "to be able to have a definite role in life. A purpose that goes beyond, well, the menial, is something that women don't get to have."

Charles led her into the courtyard. Rows of smart horse boxes overlooked the large gravel space that was lined with wooden pots containing pink and white petunias. A groom cleaned out an empty stall while another young man held two horses ready for Louisa and Charles.

He stopped just out of earshot of the two young men and leaned down to her. "I want you to promise me that you will follow up on what we talked about last night. You need something to do. It's possible, but you'll have to push for it. Promise me you will give yourself a proper role too?"

Louisa couldn't help smiling. She couldn't help nodding right back.

"Good," he whispered. "Thank you, Dunlop." He strode over to one of the grooms. "Could you give Miss Louisa a hand up?"

Louisa mounted the large gray mare that he had ready for her. The prospect of a ride, and the sense of freedom that always came with it, gave her such pleasure that she almost forgot that she had hardly slept.

She allowed her horse to take a few steps around the courtyard. Her thoughts were running of their own accord. Henry had never spoken to her of day-to-day matters concerning the estate, and yet Charles had done so and they had only just met. She had always wanted to know about her own family's business interests, but when she had tried to discuss trading, or China, or anything to do with the firm's plans with her father, he had rebuffed her and turned the conversation to her latest dress. Now she felt animated, expectant. She had so many questions she wanted to ask, so much that she wanted to learn.

It was the idea of boredom that she couldn't stand. The idea of an idle life worried her. If she could help with the estate, work—she hoped—with Charles, and develop interest in starting up local women's franchise groups, then she could have a fulfilling life. She doubted Henry would object, not if his brother's attitude was anything to go by...

Perhaps things were starting to come together.

Maybe this was going to work, after all.

Charles pulled his horse to stand beside hers. "You look lost in thought." He grinned.

Louisa shook her head. "I'm just keen to see the real Ashworth, Charles. I've really only walked around the park, seen the follies."

He nodded. "I know you have," he said, urging his horse forward. "The first phase in this is to show you the closest farms to the estate. Today, there's also someone important I want you to meet. And Louisa, call me Charlie. Nobody calls me Charles."

Louisa smiled to herself. She kicked her horse on, enjoying the change into a trot as she followed Charlie out of the courtyard. They took the horses back along the driveway toward the palace for a time, the sound of the animals' footsteps resonating through the morning air.

"Canter?" Charlie asked, once they had passed the palace.

"Definitely." Louisa urged the gray mare into a gentle, rhythmic gait. They rode companionably for several more minutes, turning off the driveway and onto a wide, rough path that led away from the palace. Once they had reached the boundaries of the park, they skirted woodland on their left. The path turned left after a while, still edging the forest. Soon, a small chapel came into view. A graveyard sat next to it.

"The third duchess built this," Charlie said, slowing his horse to a walk. "It was created as a place of comfort for those who may be grieving. Anyone can come in here, if they want some respite. Services are still held here every so often. The graveyard beyond is where our ancestors are buried. I want you to get a sense of the whole of the estate. It's a working farm, essentially, but there's so much history here as well. And it's the people who have made the place what it is. Our ancestors might rest here, but there has been so much input from the villagers into the estate over the centuries too, and we make sure that we look after them as if they are part of the family."

Louisa felt a shiver at the sight of the family graves. She focused instead on the sweet little church. The chapel was built of light stone, and ivy hung over the front porch.

Charlie kept his horse at a slow pace as they passed the ancestral graveyard. It was well tended, and daisies grew among the stones. Louisa was unable to read any inscriptions, but the sight of several tiny headstones in one corner caused her to want to turn away.

Charlie seemed to sense her discomfort. He looked at her. "Enough of that," he said, softly. "I have something else to show you. I want you to meet someone I think you will adore."

Louisa tilted her head. She suspected that Charlie would never be far away from her new home, and for some reason she took comfort in that. She followed him along the path, past a small lake, and then into a garden planted with rhododendrons.

"Oh, how stunning," Louisa sighed. The sight of the flowers out here reminded her of her childhood, of visits with cousins at their country estate near Falmouth, Massachusetts. She had learned to ride there, had spent hours with Samuel and her cousins out exploring the countryside around that property.

Now they walked the horses through the garden and followed the path until it ended unexpectedly at a cottage that gave out to fields where sheep grazed. The small two-story house was bordered by a low stone wall. Flowers, typical of a cottage garden, waved in the breeze—hollyhocks, roses, windflowers, and Michaelmas daisies.

Charlie was on the ground and had hold of both horses before Louisa was able to tear her eyes away from the delectable sight in front of her.

"The estate employed a vicar here once," he said. "But now the house belongs to our old governess, Jess. Although, you'll see, she's not old at all. I want you to meet her. She was a wonderful teacher until we both went away to school. If there is one person who had a great influence on our lives, it's Jess."

Louisa dismounted. Once Charlie had tethered the horses, she followed him through the low front gate, through the impossibly pretty garden, to the pale blue front door, waiting while he knocked and stood on the doorstep, his arms folded.

"Jess's mother, Kate, was the family governess for years," Charlie said. "But Kate died when Henry and I were young. Jess was only twenty, but she took over her mother's role. We had a fearsome nanny, so having a wonderful governess was a saving grace. My parents gave her this cottage after she finished her duties with us. She spends her time teaching at the local school and she tends the chapel. Once you and Henry... well. Once there is another generation at Ashworth, she will be helping with your children, as long as you are happy. You must make sure that you have a say in those things, you know. Don't let wheels roll without your approval."

"Oh, how serious!" Louisa laughed. But again, she sensed she had an ally. And that, she knew, was not something to take lightly.

A twinkle of amusement passed through Charlie's eyes. "Come on."

Half an hour later, Louisa felt settled in Jess's sweet little home.

"I will always love Ashworth," Jess said, while pouring out tea and giving them warm scones with raspberry jam. "I am sure that Charles will help you with everything you want to know."

Louisa pushed away the thought that Jess had not mentioned Henry. She focused on the woman—her soft brown hair was in a loose bun and tendrils fell around her face. Had she ever married? She seemed quite content with her life as it was...

"Louisa?" Charlie was chuckling at her.

"Sorry, I am prone to going off into random thoughts," Louisa laughed. She had lost the drift of the conversation, but the sense of rapport and contentment between Charlie and Jess was clear. They chatted for a while longer. Jess congratulated Louisa on her engagement, and Charlie shared that he wanted Louisa to find herself a proper role on the estate.

"I think that is an admirable thing." Jess's brown eyes were warm. "I commend any woman who wants to make a contribution to the world beyond the domestic sphere."

Louisa held the woman's gaze for a second, sensed Charlie's approval and warmth toward Jess, and felt, somehow, that she was among kindred spirits here, in this little cottage. She couldn't help but contrast this with the cold comments her future father-in-law had made the previous night. But still, she supposed he was only playing the role he had been brought up to play.

She only hoped Henry would take a more modern approach. By all rights, it seemed that he would do so. She doubted his father frequented Paris, or questioned the role he was born to play in any way at all. So she reminded herself of that for now.

When it was time to leave, Charlie leaned down and hugged his old governess. "I'm going to show Louisa some of the tenant farms," he told her. "And, on the way, we'll ride through the village."

"Excellent, Charlie."

Clearly, Jess held him in high esteem.

And as they left the cottage, Louisa couldn't help wondering what sort of student each of the boys had made. She pushed the picture of Henry as a young boy out of her head for some reason.

"Let's go," Charlie said.

"Jess is lovely." Louisa smiled. She followed Charlie back down the path to the horses.

"She is," Charlie replied. They walked the horses through the field beyond Jess's cottage toward Ashworth village, which was set in the valley. Charlie kicked his horse into a canter, and Louisa followed him. There was a square, one side of which was bordered by a low stone wall that led to the churchyard and the village cemetery. Other than that, the square was bordered by a rectory and several well-tended cottages. Everything looked prosperous here. It was clear that the family did take care of their villagers, and the person who was responsible for that was also clearly Charlie.

Charlie stopped at a row of cottages. Old trees lined the road in front of them, providing cool shade for the horses for a few moments. "These houses are for workers on the estate. We also have the farms that surround the area. I'll show you those, if you like. Then we'd better get you back to Ashworth. Henry will be up soon."

Louisa sensed Charlie watching her. She urged her horse on.

As they rode past several tenant farms, Charlie chatting easily with the farmers who were out in their fields, Louisa felt more at home at Ashworth than she ever had before.

He took her back to the palace along a different road than the one they had taken on the way out. It was overhung with trees, and a small stream ran along one side of it. They walked their horses back, which suited Louisa. She didn't want to rush the return journey by cantering or galloping.

Louisa leaned forward and patted her horse as they rounded the driveway and made their way back to the stables. As always, she had bonded with the animal.

Charlie pulled his mount to a halt. "Louisa, I'm going to go back out to work now. Are you happy to see yourself back into the house?"

"Of course," she said. She looked across at him. Her horse took a few steps toward the stable. "Someone's tired," she said.

Charlie patted his own horse. "I know. I'll feed Ruby once we're at the farm I'm going to. She can rest while I meet with the farmer."

Louisa nodded. "Thank you," she said.

"A pleasure. Just let me know if you want to go out again, or if you need anything else. I'm always here."

She smiled at him.

He caught her eye for a moment, but then he turned his horse and cantered off toward the forest.

*

Three days later, Louisa sat at her dressing table in her bedroom at Ashworth. Her thick golden hair had been dressed in the most fashionable style—soft curls fell around her face while the rest of her hair was gathered high on the back of her head. Her dress had a golden bodice that was scooped across her décolletage. The silk skirt fell from a tight waist and was hemmed with layers of gold and silver.

It was the perfect dress in which to be engaged.

A telegram had been sent to Louisa's father in Hong Kong, and he had wired back his approval. But another piece of correspondence had arrived at almost exactly the same time as Louisa's father's, and it was the second letter that, were she to be honest, had afforded her far more interest than her father's expected response.

Louisa gazed at the two envelopes. They sat near her silver brushes and her bottles of perfume. The second letter was from Mrs. Emmeline Pankhurst. Louisa had continued to read about the Women's Franchise League and had written to Mrs. Pankhurst directly, having come to the conclusion that if she were marrying the heir to a dukedom, then her mother could hardly banish her for writing to Mrs. Pankhurst.

Louisa's interest in Mrs. Pankhurst had deepened even further once she had received a letter back so promptly. She had also become increasingly drawn to the fact that the woman had combined marriage and motherhood with her passionate advocacy for women to be the center of their own worlds.

Louisa surveyed her reflection in the glass. Mrs. Pankhurst's husband was a barrister who supported her involvement in women's rights. There seemed no reason that a woman could not furnish her heart at the same time as her mind.

Mrs. Pankhurst's house in Russell Square was the center of this movement. Louisa agreed with the League's view that the vote for women was the first fundamental step toward an equal world. And she planned to visit London as soon as she possibly could.

She wanted to talk with Mrs. Pankhurst, to establish what could be done to help.

Louisa took one last look at her reflection and made her way out of her bedroom and down to the library, where the family and their dinner guests were assembled for drinks.

The duchess, Helena, whose legendary beauty was complemented by her gown of pale blue silk, stood near the fireplace alongside her husband, the Duke of Ashworth, who smiled when he saw Louisa enter the room, his dark eyes lighting up at the sight of her no doubt suitable and elegant appearance. Louisa pushed away the unkind thought that he was only interested in her appearance, and probably her ability to bear a child. He had never smiled at her until now, never.

The room was filled with nearly forty guests—close friends and neighbors and people with whom the family felt it was important to share the official announcement of Henry's engagement.

When Henry came to stand by Louisa's side, and his father made the announcement, it was as if wheels had been set in motion. Louisa knew that were she a different type of girl, she could simply let everything happen from here on out and not do a thing, save be at the center of everyone's attention and be delightful. She suspected that this was what everyone expected her to do. She was going to do the opposite, and she was determined to stay on her own path.

Charlie came and stood with her once the champagne toast was done. Henry moved across to stand with his father, who patted him on the back as if he were the prodigal son.

"Are you sure?" Charlie asked, all of a sudden, his voice so close that if she had moved one inch she would have made contact with his cheek.

She jumped a little at this, but he held her gaze and his brown eyes looked serious, just as they had the first time she had met him.

"What an odd question," she murmured back.

"It's not odd." Charlie sounded as if he were the only person in the room.

Louisa lifted her chin. When she spoke, she felt as if her words were coming out automatically. "I love Henry and I am looking forward to a perfectly thrilling future." She frowned and gathered her skirts. The second part of her sentence was true. She had thought everything out. She must not let Charlie get under her skin. He seemed to have the ability to read her like a poem. Louisa frowned again.

"I see," Charlie said.

"I'm pleased," Louisa spoke through gritted teeth.

But she glanced up at Charlie, and he was looking utterly intent.

The sound of Henry's laughter rang through the room. He had moved away from his father and was entertaining a group of friends, who looked perplexed at his antics, but Louisa nodded at Charlie and went to stand by her fiancé.

She liked Henry.

Love would grow out of it.

Wouldn't it?

Chapter Ten

Paris, 2015

Sarah spent the afternoon wandering along the Seine, wanting to soak up every bit of Paris that she could, but half-distracted by predictions of what she would find when she read Marthe's letters. She stopped for coffee in a café that overlooked Notre Dame, gazing at its famous flying buttresses before asking for her bill in half-English half-French and then wandering back to the apartment.

Loic and Laurent were in Marthe's sitting room, frowning at Laurent's painting of Giselle.

"Sarah," Loic said. Neither of the men turned around. Laurent held a large sheet of bubble wrap, while Loic ran a hand across his chin. Both men were clearly concentrating hard on some problem. Sarah wasn't sure whether to interrupt them to ask if she could help.

So she stood there for a moment, a smile forming on her face at the sight of these two handsome Frenchmen in a courtesan's apartment, both dressed in faded designer jeans. Sarah was sure they were designer jeans—no Frenchman would be seen in anything less. The long sleeves of their shirts were rolled halfway up their forearms to almost exactly the same spot. How did the French do this so well? How did they always know what looked good, what worked?

At least, Sarah thought, she was not in her pajamas. She was intrigued by what was going on, so she decided to probe a little. "You both look very focused," she said.

"Sarah." Laurent spoke this time.

"I believe that's my name," Sarah chuckled. She saw amusement pass across both men's faces.

"We want to know if you can drive a truck." Loic looked perfectly serious.

Sarah had to hold back her snicker. "I had a boyfriend who drove a truck when I was eighteen," she said, her lips twitching.

But Laurent and Loic were looking at each other as if they were cooking up a plan.

"Have you got a driver's license that you can use here in France?" Loic said, turning to face her.

Why did she feel as if she were about to enter into an escapade? She wasn't used to men who did Bonnie and Clyde.

"Yes…" The word dripped with suspicion, but both men looked more earnest than two boys planning a fishing trip.

"Okay. Sarah." Laurent started unrolling the bubble wrap. "Loic's truck is parked down the street. Could you drive it up to the entrance of the building, while Loic and I load the painting of Giselle in the back? You shouldn't be picked up by the police if you're lucky. Just talk to them in French, keep them chatting while we bring down the painting, if that happens."

"Really?" Sarah couldn't help but roll her eyes.

"Yup." Laurent began wrapping the painting in earnest now. "Try to stay put. Don't let them move you on. Be French."

"It looks like rain," Loic said, catching Sarah's eye. "We just need to load this up. I'll take it to Condé Nast—it's not far, should only take me about half an hour, and then I'll be back. We can sort out Marthe's letters then."

"Right." Sarah nodded. "So where are the keys to this truck?"

Loic handed her an elegant leather key ring. Sarah took it. She had no idea why she was doing this. She was always reluctant to drive her friends' cars back home. Steven had been so risk-averse that Sarah often found herself calculating the likelihood of disaster in her head whenever anyone asked her to do something out of the ordinary. But now, she dismissed the concerns that were forming out of habit. Somehow, she wanted to drive a truck in Paris. *Why not?* a little voice in her mind said.

"Thanks, Sarah." Laurent grinned. "We'll see you in front in about ten minutes."

"The truck is green," Loic said. "It's more of a van, really. When you get out of the apartment, turn right and walk down Rue Blanche. It's parked outside the old school. It's pretty straightforward—you should be fine."

"I will be fine!" Sarah trilled, utterly unlike her. But she pushed the old cautions away and trotted out of the apartment, taking the stairs rather than the elevator, and feeling quite light.

In some ways, Loic and Laurent's confidence in her was also reassuring. Neither of them had lectured her about what she should and shouldn't do. As she reached the front door, pushing it open and stepping out into the pretty street, Sarah felt something lift. She hadn't always been cautious. Somehow her partner's concerns had infiltrated themselves into her way of living . . . She frowned and made her way up the street. She must not let that happen again.

The truck was exactly where Loic had said it was. And it was easy enough to work out. Sarah pulled out into the traffic and chugged up the narrow street, enjoying the sense of being on the road in Paris, behind the wheel. She pulled up outside Marthe's building, and Loic and Laurent loaded the painting in the back. Then Laurent held the door open for her, and Loic climbed in after she stepped out.

"Thanks, Sarah." Laurent smiled. Loic drove off, and they turned back toward the building. Laurent stopped for a moment. "Would you like to go for a coffee while we wait for Loic to come back?"

Sarah looked up at him. "Sure," she said.

He led her down the street, stopping at a café. "Shall we go inside?" he asked. "I'd love to give you the classic Paris experience of chairs outside on the sidewalk, but I think Loic's right. I think we're going to get some rain."

Sarah looked at the cozy interior. Wicker chairs were lined up against a long bench by the window. Several people sat inside, reading the newspaper, chatting, looking out at the street. She had no doubt some were probably looking at Laurent. He was so effortlessly cool that even in Paris, he looked chic.

"Inside sounds like a good idea," she said.

He held the door open for her and chose a table for two in the corner. The coffee, when it came, was delectably good. It woke Sarah up further. She had questions that she wanted to ask. But Laurent, it seemed, had exactly the same plan.

"Okay," he said, putting his coffee cup down on the table and leaning forward. "Tell me how you know so much about art."

Sarah raised a brow.

"Not many people know about Boldini," he went on. "Let alone do they have knowledge about his specific works. Did you research him before you came to Paris, given his connections with the apartment, or is it something else? Because I suspect the latter. And I admit, you've got me intrigued."

Sarah sat back in her seat. She sipped at her coffee. "You see, the way I was brought up, it was inevitable that I was going to develop an interest in art."

"Tell me," Laurent said. "I'm interested."

Sarah sighed. Steven had never been interested in culture. It was funny, the more she thought about her relationship with him from a distance—from the perspective of Paris—the more she wondered whether it had been inevitable that it wouldn't work out.

"Are you okay?" Laurent asked, leaning forward, reaching a hand out to touch her arm.

Sarah jolted a little at the feel of his hand brushing her bare arm, but she shook this away. He was French. European. Men kissed people on the cheek all the time. Personal space wasn't the same as in Boston. She must stay focused, not allow her thoughts to drift to the past in a constant swirl of memories. But then, she was, in a way, half in the past, half reaching tentative tendrils out to make a new life, not sure whether she was ready to let go, knowing that she must. She took in a breath. "Well," she said, "with my mother, it was inevitable that I was going to have a good knowledge of art."

"Go on," Laurent said. He sounded close now, and Sarah, suddenly, simply wanted to talk.

"My mother was a lecturer in art history," she said. "So, she's the culprit for my interest. Instead of taking me to the beach for vacations, we went to New York. She took me to every exhibition that she could. I think, while she was indulging her own passion, she definitely was instilling a love for culture in me too. I'm sure, had I told her that I didn't want to be taken to such things, she would have stopped."

"But you loved art as much as she did?"

His use of the word love also made Sarah smile. Again, it seemed so French, so natural. She felt that the French were not uncomfortable talking about such things—passion, love, art. They surrounded themselves with beauty every day. Paris was replete with elegance and romance. "I did. I do. I admit that I didn't have to grow to love it. But I think I wanted to do something different than what my mother did. Her knowledge of the subject was prolific. There was no way I was going to try to compete."

"So what career did you take up?"

"Fine arts. My main interest is in jewelry, but my job is to visit people who want to donate family heirlooms to Boston's Museum of Fine Arts. I look through their collections and sort out what the museum will accept, and what it won't. I also help curate some exhibitions. I have a special fascination for the nineteenth century. So when Marthe's apartment was available to rent, it was a double hit for me, I have to say. I wanted somehow to connect with family; I had this real need, since my parents both died at the same time as...well, never mind. But I was also fascinated, from a professional point of view as well as indulging my—"

"Passion." Laurent was firm. A slight French accent had slipped into his otherwise immaculate English.

Sarah sensed something in him that she had not picked up before. Something, somehow, had shifted. She found herself biting on her bottom lip. "Yes, I suppose it is a passion."

"And this quest to find out about Louisa is also a passion for you. She is your ancestor, of your blood. You have to find out."

"Yes," Sarah said. "I suppose I do." And she couldn't help thinking what an honest, direct conversation this was. Laurent seemed to be talking in such a direct manner that she felt as if she were in a tiny bubble with him right now. She felt drawn to him. Was it Paris? Was it just France?

She was well aware that European men were charming. She was well aware that she was possibly in a vulnerable state. But she was attracted to the way that he seemed interested in her—in her as a person, in her interests, in her past.

"Tell me about your father," he said.

"He adored my mother," she said. "And she adored him right back. He was a cellist."

"What a combination," Laurent said. His eyes had crinkled up at the corners, in genuine warmth. "You were lucky. And you have a fascinating career, and one that you love."

"Yes, yes I do," she said. And her voice dropped a little. "And so, it seems, do you."

Laurent tapped his fingers on the table. His skin was olive toned, and his hands were beautiful. Artist's hands, Sarah thought suddenly, then felt her heart dance. She really should not be thinking like that about a man she hardly knew. And yet, Laurent had been kind to her this morning. She was intrigued, she had to admit.

And she wanted to know more about him. She wondered if he would be open to talk. She wouldn't push whatever secret he had, what was upsetting him, not that, not now—although, she admitted to herself, she did want to know about that. But she would start, like he had, with his childhood.

By the time they were strolling back to the apartment, she had learned something of his life. His father owned an art gallery in Aix-en-Provence, and Laurent was the eldest of three children. He had been to school with Loic, and they had been friends since they were eight. Laurent had always loved drawing, had spent hours on his own, away from his rambunctious, busy, social family, who lived in a *mas*, or farmhouse, near Aix. As a boy, he would go off and find a quiet tree in the garden, climb it, open a book and his painting materials, and draw in the warm climate for hours until his parents called him in for dinner.

His mother had her boutique in Aix, so both his parents were busy, and his younger sisters both worked in the fashion industry. One had moved to Carmel-by-the-Sea, and the other lived in Reims, where she was newly married to an advertising executive. His parents were still very much wrapped up in their careers, but he saw them when he went down to Provence, usually staying with Loic and Cat.

Loic was waiting in the salon when they wandered inside. Sarah was quite lost in Laurent's imaginative and dreamy childhood—she couldn't help but picture his glamorous sisters, and his mother, the owner of a smart boutique. She wondered if any of them had been much support for Laurent in what he was currently going through, whatever it was.

Loic stood up from where he had been waiting on one of Marthe de Florian's restored Louis XV chairs. "Sarah—do you want me to help you with the letters now?"

Sarah nodded. Laurent's eyes caught hers and they twinkled at her. She followed Loic through her bedroom to the dressing room and forced herself to focus on Marthe's letters.

Loic opened a drawer, one of the many drawers that had held shoes once, Sarah guessed. Inside it, there was a safe. This was back to her comfort zone. Sarah did this all the time. It was her job. But she couldn't help feeling, in some ways, that she was intruding here, searching for the truth about Louisa's past. She couldn't help wondering what Marthe and Louisa would make of her, delving a hundred years later into this tragedy in Paris, wanting to know what had really happened that night in Montmartre. But she wanted to find out, and that was it. She must push her doubts about feeling nosy aside. Sarah would assume her familiar, professional role of researcher.

"We haven't worked out where Marthe's letters are going to be stored yet. So, they're still here."

Sarah's resolve took another nosedive as Loic placed bundles of crisp, yellowing paper on the dressing table. Each pile was tied with a different-colored silk ribbon, many of them faded, fraying at their old edges. Gently, he moved Marthe de Florian's silver-backed brushes aside, lining them up on the polished wood to make room for the papers.

Sarah dealt with objects—works of art, jewelry, old porcelain things. Not words. Not feelings.

"Sarah," Loic said. "There's nothing else in the safe. I'm going to leave you the key, so would you make sure the letters are locked away when you're not here? I know it's a funny thing to ask, given that they sat here undisturbed for over seventy years. But I would hate to lose any of them now. I think they could be quite important. They are history—albeit a secret one."

Sarah held back from saying outright that she hoped they would be important to her. "Of course," she said instead.

Loic leaned across, rested a hand on her shoulder. "Good luck."

Sarah gathered up the little collection and took it into her bedroom. Into the bedroom that she knew had belonged to Isabelle de Florian, to Marthe's granddaughter, who had left the apartment for good when she was in her early twenties, never to return. And no one, not a soul, knew why she had done it.

She could understand parts of the letters—names, dates, and the gist. She had her phone on next to her and looked up words whenever she needed to. She became entranced with Marthe de Florian's secret history. The men who wrote to her chronicled a Paris of velvets and satin and corsets so clearly that Sarah began to form pictures in her head, of the old Paris, the Paris of the Belle Époque, the Paris that had existed right in these streets, all that time ago. But she also found herself wondering about Marthe. The letters never spoke of the real courtesan hidden beneath the façade. Instead, there were carriage rides in the Bois de Boulogne, men offering her trips to the races, assignations in quiet Parisian cafés, soirees in grand people's homes, lavish dinners in famous restaurants and bars—Maxim's, Lapérouse, Café Riche Plume. Countless powerful men wanted secret, private afternoons with the famous courtesan.

Marthe clearly chose her own lovers—it was they who had to woo her—and she was not short of offers: carriages, gifts, publicity in high-fashion magazines in return for an hour or two spent in this very apartment. There were calling cards from the press—dates set for Marthe to receive magazine editors here on Rue Blanche. Invitations to charity events, the promise of season tickets to the opera from her many admirers, pleas to join men at Longchamp Racecourse, personal cards from gentlemen all over Europe. Some of the letters held flowers that Marthe had kept, touchingly, pressed between the old papers.

One admirer compared Marthe favorably to Liane de Pougy—a rival courtesan who Sarah learned in the letter had recently entertained the Prince of Wales. Marthe was presented with diamonds, pearls, sapphires, gold, rubies, and emeralds in exchange for her favors. One gentleman offered her a jewelry collection to outshine that of Carolina Otero, who was famous for entering Maxim's wearing her entire collection of tiaras, bracelets, necklaces, and earrings at once in a blaze of wealth that was only enhanced by her evening gown with its plunging neckline. Liane de Pougy had arrived in Otero's wake wearing a simple white evening gown, with her lady's maid behind her carrying a velvet cushion on which sat a jewelry box weighted with jewels. Another gentleman promised Marthe his mother's tiara in payment for dinner at Maxim's, where he swore they would not be caught out if they were discreet.

Sarah kept on reading even when she saw the light disappear from underneath Laurent's door. She could not stop. She was simply going to have to devour the letters in one gluttonous feast.

There was a declaration of love from Georges Clemenceau, and another from Paul Deschanel, whom she looked up. He was the eleventh president of France.

By two o'clock in the morning, Sarah had laid the last letter aside.

There was not one reference to Louisa West or Henry Duval.

Not a thing.

If she hadn't found the letter in her father's locked box, Sarah would never have thought there was any link between Henry and Marthe whatsoever. But there was a connection. She just had to find it. And somehow, the fact that she had not discovered anything yet spurred her on even harder, because she suspected now that everything between Henry and Marthe had to be hidden.

In the early hours, Sarah fell asleep, her head resting on the desk. The next morning, she woke in exactly the same spot to the sound of knocking on her door. She stood up, ran a hand over her hair.

"Sarah, are you okay?" Laurent's voice resonated into the room.

Sarah took a glance around the bedroom. Marthe's letters were arranged on the floor in neat, orderly rows. Sarah had tied up the bundles in turn, careful not to separate them from where they had been kept. They appeared to make some sort of chronological sense and she did not want to upset the order of things.

"I'm fine, thank you."

"Can I talk to you for a moment?"

"Now?" she asked, her nose crinkling up at the very idea of her appearance. The idea of a daily audience with him in her pajamas was not appealing at all. Not that she had even changed into sleepwear last night. She ran a hand down her tousled, day-old dress.

"I have to go out to meet with the magazine right away. Can we please have a chat?"

Sarah cleared her throat. Laurent was her roommate. He didn't care what she looked like. She moved toward the door. Then stopped.

"Just one moment," she called, scuttling off to her bathroom.

"Okay—but I'm running late. It's late. I want to check how it went with Marthe's letters. I went out last night and arrived home too late to disturb you."

Sarah ran to the basin and took a look at her face. Old mascara rendered her already big eyes huge. Her bob was a mess—she brushed that. Other than that, she swished some breath freshener around in her mouth, brushed loose powder over her face, squirted on some perfume, performed a quick flick with lip gloss, and cleaned up the panda eyes.

"I hope you found something?" Laurent was calling through the door.

Sarah faced herself in the mirror. She looked fine. She would take a shower immediately after this, though.

"Sarah?"

"Yes." She zipped back to the bedroom door, slowing down as she neared it.

She opened the door. Sensed her eyebrows raising in what she hoped was not an impertinent stare.

Laurent leaned against the door frame, one arm resting high above Sarah's head. She didn't move, although she was a little too close, she knew. He stayed put. His eyes looked pained somehow, and she felt her head tilt to one side in response. He cleared his throat.

"So, anything of interest?"

Sarah shook her head. "No…"

"Okay. You look exhausted." He leaned forward. "Look, why don't you take a break from it, for today, and then work out what the next step forward is? I'm happy to help if I can. I have to rush off. Have a good day, and don't worry. I think you should push on with it."

Sarah ran a hand down her dress. "Yes," she said. "I'll work something out. And thank you, I'd love to have a chat about it."

"No problem." He grinned, his handsome face lighting up with genuine warmth. "I'll see you this evening. I should be back about eight."

Sarah watched him leave. For some reason, the thought that he would be back in the apartment tonight was reassuring. She would like to take him up on his offer. She would like to talk to him about what she should plan to do next.

Laurent was not in the apartment that evening. Sarah fought with irritation at her expectation that he would stick to his word and irritation that she was, in fact, disappointed that he hadn't come home. After all, she had enjoyed a gorgeous day in Paris—visiting the Musée d'Orsay, wandering across to the Eiffel Tower. She had ridden right to the top. She would be perfectly fine on her own for the evening.

There was no reason Laurent had to tell her if his plans had changed since this morning. He had just been being polite, letting her know what was happening, that was all it was.

At eight o'clock, Sarah looked around the apartment. Normally, she would have reveled in the opportunity to spend an evening surrounded by Marthe de Florian's beautiful things. But it was warm outside. And she was in Paris. Twilight was starting to settle in, and that lent an even more romantic feel to the air—that half-dimmed light that was filled with a sense of quiet—before the magical dark-velvet evening ahead. Sarah moved to the window in Marthe's sitting room and threw open the set of double French doors that led out to the wide balcony over the street. Sarah stood out there for a moment, reveling in the warm Paris air. The restaurants in the street were starting to open, and people, dressed for dinner, strolled up and down, looking for places to eat.

She lingered, enjoying the view from the balcony, and the sense of possibility that an evening in Paris could bring. Then she went to her bedroom, put on a little black dress and a pair of strappy patent-leather sandals, sprayed her favorite Jo Malone, and walked into it, to be enveloped by the enticing mist. She changed her earrings. Even though Steven had bought them, she still liked them and had decided to keep them. It was no good letting go of every last piece from her history. Diamonds, Sarah had decided, could be an exception when throwing things from a troubled past away.

Once she was out in the street, she looked up and down. Suddenly feeling vulnerable, alone in Paris, she decided to head toward Le Bon Georges, the restaurant that Laurent had chosen for her on her first evening in the city. After all, some of the restaurants around Montmartre looked as if they were fully geared for tourists, and she didn't want to get caught in a trap. She had made an effort and if she was going to eat alone, she was going to eat somewhere lovely.

The waiters, in typical charming French style, remembered her. Of course they did. She was led, with great courtesy and aplomb, to the exact table she had occupied the first time she came. A complimentary glass of champagne appeared a few seconds later, and after a few sips, she sat back to read the menu.

Two hours later, having enjoyed a melt-in-the-mouth meal of legume tart, roast shoulder of lamb, and crème caramel, Sarah decided it was time to wander back to the apartment. She strolled back slowly, admiring the pretty lamp-lit streets, until she reached Marthe's stunning old building. She stopped at the entrance. Lights shone from every room in the apartment. So. Laurent was back.

Glad that she was wearing one of her favorite dresses for once, Sarah took the elevator up to the top floor.

She slipped her key in the lock. The kitchen was lit up, but no one was inside. Sarah poured herself a glass of water. Jet lag was starting to kick in again. The wine she enjoyed with dinner had made her sleepy, and now all she wanted to do was rest. After she said goodnight to Laurent. She was going to have to talk to him—to someone—in order to come up with a plan about Louisa. Laurent, or Loic—they were both so helpful. But for now, yawning was taking over and the thought of her comfortable bed was delicious. Loic and Cat had spared no expense in furnishing the apartment, and Sarah couldn't wait to snuggle into the gorgeous surroundings.

She moved through Marthe's sitting room. The beginnings of the next portrait that Laurent was working on sat on his easel. It was strange, looking at his work when he wasn't there. There was something eerie about the just-started piece. The confident face of one of the models whom Sarah had met stared out of the picture at her. She was no doubt famous here, Sarah thought, worthy, most probably, of a front cover on *Vogue*, if the magazine was sending her off to be painted by the likes of Laurent. Sarah moved on toward Laurent's bedroom. And stopped with her hand resting on the handle. The handle would not turn. The handle was most definitely locked.

Unmistakable sounds did not drift out of the room—they resounded. Sarah closed her eyes and stood there. It was as if she were paralyzed. What was she supposed to do? Knock? Interrupt Laurent during what was clearly a very unsubtle tryst? A huge sense of disappointment rushed through her system, which was ridiculous, so she pushed it away. Sarah decided that the only thing to do was to wait until they had...finished. She must be practical. Logic told her that he would realize that she would need to go to her own room sooner rather than later.

Sarah moved back into the sitting room, still frowning at her own sense of disappointment. And questioning herself. Had she wanted to see Laurent while she was wearing something strappy and almost French?

The evening had become cooler and her little black dress afforded her no warmth. It was a dress for hot summer evenings, for dancing on well-lit terraces with crowds of people, for strolling through Paris with a man who would lend you his jacket. Would that ever happen to her again?

She had often found herself thinking the same thoughts. Would she ever fall in love again? She had thought she loved Steven. She was sure she had, once. It was just that trying to equate the new Steven, the new cold, cheating husband whom he had turned out to be, with the man she had married, the man with whom she had thought she would spend the rest of her life, was not only a difficult task, it was something that still caused her stomach to turn.

Now she closed the curtains, pulled the window closed, drew the wooden shutters, and clipped them together, with what she hoped was a bit of a resonant thud. But this didn't make the room any warmer.

She stood on the spot, hideously awkward, hearing talk now, a confident woman's voice. Fast French. Nothing she could understand. Then a response, much quieter than the female tones. Sarah bit her lip. He sounded intimate, close. It was the sound of a lover's voice. Again, she had to stop herself from wondering what was going to happen in her life.

She moved to Marthe's chaise longue. She could fall asleep on her feet, given a chance. She had to sit down.

She perched on the edge of Marthe's infamous piece of furniture, pushed away thoughts of Marthe's antics right here on this chaise longue, and heard the voices, again, through the bedroom door. His, soft, gentle. Caring. She closed her eyes. And tears started to build up, slipping through her eyelashes, falling silently onto her cheeks.

She didn't know why the thought of him with someone else mattered. After all, he had most likely only been kind to her today out of a sense of responsibility because she was, in effect, Loic's guest. But, somehow, she had thought of him as a different person than who he clearly was.

Loic had warned her.

What had she been thinking?

The sounds from the bedroom started up again and Sarah slipped her shoes off, lying back on the chaise longue. She had enjoyed his company, that was all. And the thing was, it was the first time in months she had really enjoyed the presence of any man. She had holed herself up in Boston, not going out, except to the odd film with her girlfriends, shocked from the loss not only of her husband, but of both her parents, reeling from the reality of finding herself, suddenly, all alone.

She rested a hand on her forehead. Her thoughts started to become more blurred. There was no way to know what was going to happen tomorrow, let alone in the more distant future. She just had to stop worrying about that. Closing her eyes, she sensed that delicious drifting, away from everything—off into sleep.

Chapter Eleven

Paris, 1894

Louisa's wedding was a sea of white dresses, white bouquets, white kid gloves, white silk stockings, and white satin slippers. Henry presented her with a set of diamonds and pearls the night before the ceremony—a necklace, a bracelet, a tiara, and earrings. Louisa wore a sixpence for luck in one of her shoes. Everything was perfect, a painting with every brushstroke in place. Only one thing was missing. None of Louisa's family were there from Boston.

As she passed through Ashworth village in the Duval ceremonial carriage, she waved at the locals who had lined up for a glimpse before she walked up the aisle. The village church that she had passed the first day she had gone riding with Charlie had been turned into a blooming version of itself. Flowers and palms cascaded on pedestals under every stained-glass window, and the pews dripped with roses.

After the wedding breakfast at Ashworth, she and Henry took the carriage, along with six white horses for luck, to the train station for the trip to Dover and the continuing journey on to France. Henry had organized the honeymoon. And Louisa could not contain her excitement at going to Paris.

The only poignancy was that she had to say farewell to Meg as she embarked on a grand tour of Europe with Guy. The fact that she would not see her close friend for several months while she traveled with Guy was a mixed blessing—though Louisa was happy for Meg, she couldn't help but sense that she was waving good-bye to the last vestige of her life in America. And she felt that now she was facing her new life, completely alone.

After the wedding breakfast, Charlie came and stood by Louisa's side. He leaned down, kissed her on the cheek, shook Henry's hand, and then told his parents he was going back to work. Louisa had watched him stride away and had ignored another strange pang as he disappeared.

Now it was her first night in Paris. And she was alone in the vast Duval residence.

Henry had, almost immediately upon their arrival, gone out.

Louisa had to admit that she was entranced by the Duvals' Paris house. It was on Île Saint-Louis, overlooking the Seine. A grand gateway on Rue Saint-Louis en l'Île led to a square courtyard surrounded by two-story buildings. The top floor of one wing contained a gallery, on either side of which were various formal salons, while below was a home filled with treasures. There were paintings and porcelain, along with flowers, family photographs, and small, intimate pieces that would all bear witness to old friendships and infatuations that had affected generations of the Duval family.

Henry had insisted that Louisa rest after the long journey from Ashworth. She had accepted this. She was tired, but now as she sat in the dining room having dinner by herself, she wished she had gone out, wished he had come back to dine with her. She had thought he was only going out for the duration of the afternoon. What was more, she had to stop herself from dwelling on the fact that he had not invited her to accompany him at all.

Two footmen stood in attendance in the otherwise silent, empty dining room. The long mahogany table was decorated with an elaborate silver candelabra that had been lit for Louisa's sole benefit. Tiny candle flames shone out through the open windows that overlooked the Seine, sending flickering light onto the trees outside, their leaves almost touching the old window panes.

The sounds of people strolling and laughing outside drifted up through the darkness into the room while Louisa stared at her entrée.

She had lost her appetite.

The maid had taken great care with Louisa's appearance, not seeming to consider that she was dining alone. Louisa took a sip from her wineglass. She had barely picked at her food—salmon and pheasant and venison were all laid on as if she were going to eat for twenty, but all she had been doing was sitting in a carriage, then resting in her gold-leaf bed. Her appetite was nonexistent. She yearned to go out for a walk.

After what she decided was a decent amount of time to sit there at the table, Louisa placed her gold cutlery back down on her porcelain plate. The clink of it resonated in the silence. One of the footmen startled at the sound, then took her food away. The other footman was behind her faster than she could move to stand up.

She sighed and moved toward the magnificent entry hall, with its black-and-white tiles and elaborate wood-paneled walls. How she had admired it all when she had first walked through the front door. How she had complimented Henry. Now, she felt as if she had behaved like a fool. Like a young American ingenue.

Green palms in brass pots were dotted about the vast space, and gilt-edged chairs sat about, waiting for something to happen. Louisa's shoes clattered as if mocking her for being the only one there.

She moved into the family's private salon, struggling with thoughts about whether Henry could have let her know she would be dining alone. Part of her still hoped that he simply wanted her to rest. The other half of her was irritated that this was her first night in Paris. The least he could have done was be at home. In the salon, yet another candelabra lent the room a ghostly, shimmering air. As Louisa sat down in one of the red velvet chairs, she gazed at the portraits on the walls.

Ancestors.

Lines of people.

She was going to be one of them too.

She drew her arms around herself. Henry had hardly uttered a word to her throughout the entire journey to Paris. When Louisa had tried to chatter about things that she thought might interest him, he had replied in monosyllables and pulled out a book.

A servant appeared in the salon holding a silver tray. He moved over to where she sat. "A letter, Madame. From Hong Kong."

"Oh!" Louisa gasped, delight blending with an ache for Samuel—and for something else that she could not define.

She took the letter and the brass opener from the tray, slitting the thick cream envelope with a satisfying rip, her fingers delving, searching for the folded paper inside.

Samuel sent congratulations, asked her to promise him that she would always ensure Henry was up to the mark once they were married.

Louisa laid the letter aside and closed her eyes. Samuel wrote for the remainder of the letter about his life as a China trade merchant—he was being mentored in the tea business by a local trader. He told her of the Cantonese table of hand-carved rosewood that he was sending back to their mother, along with a Chinese lantern decorated with peacocks, which were the symbol of good, healthy living in that country.

She stood up, took a look around the room that was stuffed with such treasures, wondered, in the end, what they all meant, if anything, and turned toward the doorway.

She would retire.

She and Henry had separate rooms, as they would in Ashworth. So far, he had only kissed her once. While this had bothered her somewhat, and she had found it most odd, she could hardly initiate things with Henry. She put her hand on the warm wooden banister and made her way up to bed.

Louisa woke the next morning as her maid pulled open the shutters, throwing warm, bright light into the room. Her room was decorated in pale blues and gold brocade—a largesse of gilt-edged opulence. Clocks and vases adorned with gold filigree sat atop the white marble mantelpiece, and the parquet floors were laden with soft, pale rugs.

She sat up, ate her breakfast, lay in the bath while the maid washed her back, held out her arms like a young child while she was dressed, had her hair done, and was sprayed with perfume.

Now what?

She wandered out of her room and down the grand staircase to the first floor. And stood in the entrance hall.

Henry would not be up for hours.

She wondered what on earth she had done.

That evening, Louisa tried a different tack. Henry was pacing about in the salon. She had thought about what to say to him all day.

"Are you planning on going out this evening?" she asked. A question seemed a good place to start.

Henry stopped near the window, adjusting his shirtsleeves. He was dressed formally and his hair was slicked back as it had been the night of the ball.

One of the footmen had brought a nightingale in a cage into the salon that afternoon, for Louisa's amusement, so she had been told. The solitary bird had sung for hours. His whistles and clear calls had resonated through the family apartments. Now, he hovered on his perch, his brown eyes still, watching. He had given up his flurry of sad notes.

"Yes. I am going out." Henry faced the window. He leaned both hands against the sill. "Do you know anyone in Paris?"

Louisa allowed the tight smile that was forming on her lips to reach fruition. "You know the answer to that question," she said.

Henry's voice was low, controlled. He didn't turn to face her. "I could contact some friends of Mama's if you like. That might amuse you while you are here."

Louisa took in a breath. She had to reach through to him. Somehow, someway. "Do you remember the first conversation we ever had?"

Louisa stared at the ramrod straight line of his hair that was cut in a perfect parallel with the unswerving top of his white shirt.

"Remember what you told me about Paris?" she asked. "I want to see what it is that fascinates you so much. Please, show me."

"You do not want to come to Montmartre. I can't possibly take you there."

"Why not?" She stared, resolute, at Henry's back. "Perhaps I want to take an interest in what you do. You told me that Montmartre was . . . life. Henry, goodness knows I want to see that. I want to see modern. You know I'm not entirely . . . traditional." She would have to tread with soft footsteps. Be clear about what she meant. She had not broached her views on women's rights with Henry. She had planned to save that conversation for when they were surrounded with modern life here in Paris. The idea had made sense to her. She assumed he would be up-to-the-minute in his outlook here. Now, she chose her words with care. All she wanted tonight was not to be left in this vast mansion all on her own again. "I did not come here to stagnate, Henry."

"Montmartre would be unthinkable." He cut her off.

But Louisa fought irritation, and anger. "So. What am I expected to do, Henry? You sleep all morning. You spend the afternoons riding out with your friends. Your evenings at dance halls!"

"I expected that you would have things to do. I'm so sorry. It's just what I do here. I thought you would enjoy other aspects of Paris. Like my mother does. Like respectable women do."

Louisa took in a breath. "I am not suggesting that we live in each other's pockets. But, I should like to come with you." She struggled with the desire to speak out. "I am not like other women. I assumed that was why you married me. I have, Henry, my own ideas and thoughts. And I do not wish to be left here alone. Surely, you understand that."

She saw Henry's knuckles tighten and blanch white as he leaned on the sill. "What is it you want, Louisa?"

For the ten thousandth time, Louisa fought the sickening idea that he had simply made a marriage of convenience with a wealthy American. She thought he saw her as different. She thought he saw her as unique. She simply had to get through to him. She had done so before; she was sure of it. Or had she? She pushed that question right out of her head. "I want us to have a partnership that works. I want us both to be free to live our lives, but I want there to be things that we share, together," she said, barely maintaining control.

He stood motionless, still staring at the trees outside. Louisa glanced at the nightingale. It was staring straight ahead too, as if at nothing.

"Henry."

Still he did not turn around.

Louisa closed her eyes. "Henry," she said. "I am coming out with you tonight. I want to see it. I want to see these artists and writers that you talked about."

He turned then, to face her.

She felt ill at his expression. It was cold, yes, but there was something else lurking as well. And if she were really pressed, she would say that he looked as if he despised her.

Louisa stood up suddenly and flurried across to the open door. She was not going to give in, not now. She must not be left, a doormat, to be walked on when Henry felt he would, and stepped over when Henry thought he would ignore her. She remembered what Charlie had said—she must have a role in the family. She must not let herself be neglected. She stopped in the doorway.

"I will get my cape," she said.

Henry muttered something, but it was too hard to catch.

Ten minutes later, Louisa climbed into his carriage.

Henry stared out the window at the narrow street. "I can't believe you are doing this." Darkness did not begin to describe his tone. He was a thundercloud. Louisa reached out and placed a hand in his, only to abruptly pull it back when he moved away from her.

"Irish and American Bar," Henry told the driver, his voice tight.

"Sounds interesting," Louisa said.

"Interesting's the word." Sarcasm exuded from his voice.

There was a silence.

Louisa opened her mouth and closed it again. The carriage rolled forward with a small jolt.

Henry let out a sigh. He turned to her then, his face tortured. "Look, Louisa, what goes on in the places that I go to is not going to work for you. It's not what you are looking for, believe me."

"I want to be a part of your life," she said.

Henry stared out of the carriage window to the street.

Several minutes later, the carriage rolled to a stop on the grand Rue Royale, outside what looked like a public house. Louisa craned her head to peer at the long wooden bar inside the window. Men, dressed in the typical garb of the working class, were seated at it. Several of them turned at the sight of the grand Duval carriage.

Henry had his hand on the door. The footman had jumped down and was about to open it for them. "I've changed my mind," he said to the young man, suddenly. "Take us to Le Chat Noir."

The clientele at the Irish and American Bar stared at them through the murky glass panes.

"I can't take you in there," Henry muttered. "I just cannot do it."

Louisa chewed on her lip.

Twilight lingered over Paris as the coach traveled on. The glittering lights from the restaurants, theaters, and clubs flashed through the windows. The farther they moved away from the Seine, the narrower the streets became, the smaller the buildings. They were no longer grand, but crowded, their old bricks painted with simple whitewash. It couldn't be more of a contrast to Haussmann's grand boulevards—the Paris of Louisa's imagination. She stared at the seedy cafés and nightclubs, at the women on the streets, clearly disreputable, lingering in lurid shop windows and at the entrances to unmarked buildings. These were Paris's *maisons closes*, she supposed—houses for prostitutes, infamous the world over. Louisa gawped at the women's faces painted in garish, tacky colors. And a big part of her couldn't help but feel sympathy for them.

There had to be better ways for women.

Surely, Henry mixed with writers, with poets and artists; that was what he had said. But what did he think about the streets? She was shocked at what was going on out here. "Louisa." His voice came from beside her, but she couldn't tear herself away from the scene outside. "You have to understand. *All* the classes mix in Montmartre. Entertainers, courtesans, dandies, artists, writers—everyone is here. It is the ability to shock that is the key to success in Paris. It's the opposite from everything at home. Montmartre isn't about holding one's ancestors in esteem. You come here, you see all walks of life in one small community. And that's what concerns me. *You* seeing it."

Louisa drew her cape around her body, but she didn't turn away.

Henry was leaning close now, looking out the window with her. "These streets are the new stage. In Montmartre, shop assistants, milliners, and *les cocottes* are thrown into contact with the old elite. Everyone wants to pose. The lines of identity between the classes have blurred in Paris."

"I suppose it is good that you don't find this threatening." She turned to look at him, and his expression was unreadable in the gathering darkness.

"To the contrary, as I told you, I feel far more at home here than I do at Ashworth. It is freedom for me, coming here. Freedom from the endless cycle of the same sorts of people, of the expectation that I must be one of them. We all need to work out who we are. But at the same time, we are all labeled from birth."

Rue Victor Massé was so narrow that the carriage had to slow down in order not to clip the crowds on the sidewalks. Noise swelled from the buildings that crammed each side of the road, and an even more extraordinary array of people wormed their way up the impossibly narrow footpaths. Louisa took in the women's mocking faces, their hair dressed as if in cheapened copies of what was fashionable. Gaudy, filthy feathers sat atop their heads, while their ill-fitting clothes either pressed tightly into their bursting busts or hung on emaciated, unfed frames.

The footman, his eyes diverted from everything, including Louisa, held the carriage door open for her to step outside. As soon as she did so, she was assailed with the squalid stench of cheap perfume blended with human sweat and the rank, turgid odor that emanated from every restaurant in the unbearably warm street. She lifted the hem of her dress instinctively, tried not to look too superior, too interested, or too shocked at the sight of number twelve in front of her.

Le Chat Noir was three stories high, with a row of dormer windows running across its top floor. It was not a large building—there was no room for such a thing here—but largesse pulsed out of it as if it swelled with its own singular life force. The solid sound of brass band music belted into the street. Raucous conversation and laughter escaped into any space that was left in the air.

"Welcome to the Cabaret Artistique, madame," a woman shouted in English at Louisa, flashing a row of hard black stumps that made do for teeth; her hair was a gaudy mess of clown-like fervor.

Louisa fought turmoil. She felt confusion and empathy for these poor, desperate creatures, but she could not evict her own revulsion and fascination at the entire scene.

A man dressed as a Swiss Guard waved them through the entrance to Le Chat Noir. Louisa stopped inside. A vast ironwork sculpture of a black cat loomed over the entrance hall, its head portrayed in front of a silhouette of the sun. Beyond this, at the entrance to the cabaret theater, she stared at a canvas of another imperious cat on its hind legs, holding a red flag.

Henry moved ahead.

Louisa followed him.

The theater beyond the entrance hall was decorated like a gaudy medieval palace—heavy oak tables were stuffed with guests who drank from pewter mugs, while suits of armor lined the walls, along with tapestries and more stained-glass designs.

And then Louisa stopped. Several people pushed past her, shoving her aside while she simply stared. Henry had moved into the center of the room. He stood right between two tables, kissing a woman full on the lips, his own mouth lingering on hers. The woman was beautiful. Her thick, luxurious, henna-dyed hair framed a stunning face. Her large, clear brown eyes rendered her ethereal. For a moment, Louisa wondered if this might be a lady. Relief fought with confusion, but only for a moment.

The woman's manner of dress, while exquisite, showed far too much creamy décolletage for any lady of taste. And yet she held herself like a dancer—the tilt of her chin was distinguished, her look haughty. Her eyes caught Louisa's and she frowned, turning back to Henry, whispering something into his ear that obviously amused him. He laughed, his features lighting up in a way that Louisa had never seen before, and leaned down again, replying to her comment, placing a hand on her elegant, straight back.

Louisa stood alone. She sensed people, other guests, staring at her. She knew their laughter was indiscriminate, but she felt with acuteness that it was directed at her.

The extraordinary woman handed Henry her own drink, filled with some concoction that was half-green and half-purple. Absinthe? Louisa couldn't move from the spot. She watched, fascinated, yet horrified, while Henry, the man she had married, her husband, tipped his head back and soaked up the lot in one long draft. Then he handed the glass back to his beautiful accomplice, and she raised it to her own lips, taking in the last few drops of his drink, running her tongue over where his lips had been to lap up any drops he might have left, her eyes locked on Louisa's the entire time.

A dancer appeared on the stage. Henry's companion linked her arm with his, and they stood there, their backs to Louisa, intertwined, watching whatever performance this was. After a few moments, the music stopped. The sounds of conversation, bawdy laughter, and jeers shot through the room unaccompanied by any loud music, and then the musicians picked up their instruments again.

Now, a seductive, lone trumpet performed a slow fanfare while a new female performer, who was dressed in nothing but a couple of slivers of silver gauze covering her breasts and the lower half of her body, writhed about on the stage, waving oversize white feathers. The sensuous music swelled into a fast, intense rhythm, and the woman kept up with her body. She kicked up her heels and twirled in never-ending circles while the entire band joined in. Everyone in the room seemed hypnotized by her dance.

Louisa, feeling dizzy with heat and noise and faint at Henry's brazen antics, took a step back, moved toward the entrance again, and passed the Swiss Guard, who shouted, "You didn't like La Goulue, Madame?" and laughed at her in a torrid, raucous way. She made her way out into the fetid night air, where her arms were stroked and her skirts were pulled at as she bustled her way up the street.

And stopped.

What was she going to do?

And then, thank goodness. Henry's carriage was parked halfway up the street. Solid, its navy blue presence was like some sort of relief from the gods—whatever gods presided over a place like this.

Louisa pushed her way through the prostitutes and past the pimps, and when she arrived at the carriage, she looked up at the footman and the driver, who were smoking on their seat.

Her eyes, she knew, told them everything. She didn't need to speak French. The footman jumped down, crushed his cigarette butt into the pavement with his highly polished shoe, took Louisa's elbow, and helped her back into the carriage.

Once in there, back among the velvet cushions and the plush gold decorations, locked away with all of Henry's gilt, she closed her eyes as the door shut on the noise and the debauchery outside. And the carriage, blessedly, started moving forward after some shouted negotiations between the driver and those who were parked in front of him in the crowded, filthy street.

As they turned, slowly, out of the narrow streets that were Montmartre, back to the chic boulevards of Paris, Louisa rested her hand over her face and did not look out the window.

Because, now, with the clear dread of certainty, she knew that she had not only made a terrible, impetuous mistake, but had also probably ruined any chance of happiness in her marriage. And that was it. She had done it without any help. She had made the decision. She had chosen to marry Henry. She had been swept up with the romance of Ashworth, with the idea that she could somehow combine love with her own goals, and she had ignored that voice in her head that had warned her. She had not listened to her own instincts at all.

She had no one to blame but herself.

Striped patterns of clear sunlight ran across the floor of Louisa's bedroom the following morning. She had tossed most of the night, her mind awhirl with what she should do next. She had stood limp while the maid undressed her the evening before, removing her tight corset, setting her jewels on the dressing table with delicate precision. Louisa had turned her head away from their sparkles. She had tried to convince herself that Henry's distance since their marriage did not matter. But now she knew the opposite was true.

He was, of course, a rake. She knew that now. Not a man for marriage. The signs had been there—his sleeping all morning, his endless rounds of entertainment at home. His constant need to be entertained. He was like a child craving constant attention. He would have been perfect for a life on the stage. He could not possibly be an actor. Instead, he surrounded himself with the only theatricality he could find. And he had found a natural place for himself here in Paris.

But none of this helped her relentless thoughts. Henry was the last person she should have married. What had she been thinking? Had she been so determined to find a life for herself that she had accepted what was clearly not in her best interests just because it was on offer?

What on earth was she going to do?

Henry had told her who he was the first time they had met, and she had not listened. She had grabbed onto his life raft before she had thought twice. She had been vulnerable, bereft at losing Samuel to the Orient, Meg to marriage. She had read far more into Henry than it seemed that there was to read. She had thought too much of him. Overassessed him. She had wanted to believe he was more than he was. She had wanted to believe he could be who she needed him to be.

And for Henry's part, she understood that now too. She was the perfect foil, and she was there. Available. He didn't care who or what she was. She was an American heiress, that was all that mattered. Marrying Louisa pleased his parents. He was one step closer to providing an heir.

The maid appeared with breakfast on a silver tray. A newspaper was folded next to the plate. Louisa reached for the paper. She could not stomach food.

The news consisted of only four pages. Louisa sighed. Presumably, it was all that the staff thought she, as a woman, could digest. Of course, it was all in French, but Louisa spoke and read French anyway. Not for the first time, she wondered why her mother had bothered to have her educated at all.

She took in the front page. There was a picture of people strolling along what looked like a wide, tree-lined boulevard. A horse was to their left. A gentleman in a top hat sat astride it. But what was extraordinary was that there was an elephant in the center of the photograph. A group of people sat atop the great creature, and a man, dressed in white trousers, a black coat, and a black, peaked cap, walked alongside the animal, leading it along the pavement.

The wide pathway, for that was what it must be, was otherwise filled with pedestrians. Ladies held their parasols up against the sun, and the pavement was dotted with shadows from the trees. Even with the elephant, the scene looked blessedly normal after the abominations of last night.

Louisa forced herself to eat her breakfast, read the rest of the journal, and put the paper aside.

But then she returned to the picture. It was taken in the Bois de Boulogne. She knew that was the fashionable place to walk. Louisa needed somewhere to think. She needed a survival plan. The caption on the picture said that the Bois de Boulogne possessed beauty and a charm that made it the perfect place to promenade, whether on foot or on horseback, by bicycle or carriage.

Louisa rang for the maid.

The same footman who had attended her last night seemed astounded that Louisa did not wish to ride around the Bois de Boulogne in her carriage. Once they arrived in the park, it took her some time to convince him to wait for her while she walked about on her own.

The wide road for carriages gave off to several smaller, meandering paths. Louisa put up her silk parasol against the relentless sun and took one of these, passing children with their nannies having picnics on the lawns, a vast pond full of ducks and other waterfowl, and a café, where people sat on iron chairs and sipped coffee. But all the while, Louisa's thoughts churned on without getting her anywhere at all.

She stopped at another pond. White swans hassled a woman who threw them chunks of white bread. Louisa watched this for a while, until the unmistakable clatter of carriage wheels rolled to a stop right behind her on the wide road that circled the lake.

"Bonjour," a voice called out.

Louisa turned. She doubted the person in the carriage was addressing her.

And found herself face-to-face with the bizarre woman whom Henry had been with in Le Chat Noir last night. Her hair was swept back, and her long neck was decorated with the most fantastic array of jewels for a morning tour around the park. The woman wore a dress of pale green silk. Her gloved hand rested on the windowsill of her smart carriage, her long fingers dangling over its edge. She appeared to have no embarrassment when approaching Louisa, staring at her in the same way she had the evening before when she had been whispering with Henry.

Something kicked in and Louisa decided that she would show no discomposure herself. "Bonjour," she replied, meeting the woman's gaze directly.

She was extraordinarily beautiful, only a few years older than Louisa.

But this woman would never be invited to Ashworth, Louisa thought suddenly. And then she tilted her chin. This thought somehow gave her a sense of superiority over the outrageous yet exceptional creature. But, at the same time, the idea of her own preeminence unsettled Louisa. She was judging a woman based on her morality. Furthermore, she had been so sickened by the depravity and the state of things last night that she had run away.

Wasn't this the sort of hypocrisy that she had railed against for years? The dichotomy that divided women into two separate camps:

respectable and not? The very thing that made it seem even more justifiable for her to contact Emmeline Pankhurst?

Louisa sighed and waited for her companion to speak.

"You were not comfortable at Le Chat Noir last evening?" The woman, whatever she was, spoke English with hardly any French accent at all. Elocution lessons, Louisa thought, then chastised herself again. Was her own idea of good taste merely a method of asserting superiority of rank over others?

"I don't think we have been formally introduced," Louisa said. "I am Louisa Duval."

"I am Marthe de Florian," the woman said. She held out a hand.

Just then, a man leaned forward in the carriage next to Marthe and peered at Louisa. She had not noticed him in there before. He was well built, tall. His face was pockmarked and although his jacket looked well cut, his appearance was rough.

Marthe firmly pushed the man back into his spot. Who was he? A bodyguard? "Madame Duval, I am pleased to meet you, because I adore Henry," Marthe announced.

Louisa almost laughed. But then, realization hit her, and she felt her forehead crease into a frown. She had seen posters on her way to the park. They were dotted about everywhere: La Goulue—the dancer who had shocked her so last night—Carolina Otero, Liane de Pougy. Even from the posters one could tell that these women were fashion leaders, women in the smart set, dancers, actresses, and...prostitutes. So. This Marthe de Florian looked as if she, too, was in their league. One of the handful who had made it to the top of the world of the night. Louisa shuddered whenever she thought of the rest of them, the poor, starved, dolled-up creatures that she had seen in the streets.

"Well," the courtesan said, "I must keep moving. I have a list of engagements as long as my glove."

Louisa stood stock-still while the carriage rolled away.

The woman had done the exact same thing that she had done last night. She had won the round. She had finished the conversation first and taken the upper hand.

Louisa frowned and turned back along the direct route that would lead her to her own carriage. She had no plans as to how to deal with Henry. And she had absolutely no idea how to handle Marthe de Florian.

Chapter Twelve

Paris, 2015

Sarah didn't wake until light crept through the slats in the shutters. Consciousness stirred her slowly out of the deep, deep sleep that she must have enjoyed all night. But it didn't take her more than one second to remember what had happened, how she had ended up in the sitting room while she should have been in her warm bed. It didn't take her more than one second for irritation and annoyance to kick in. She sat up and stretched, ran her hand through her tousled hair, and then realized she was not alone.

Laurent was working away right next to her at his easel.

Sarah peered at him, still half-asleep, and he looked down at her. And put down his paintbrush.

"Morning," he said. "Bonjour," he added, softly.

If Sarah had felt vulnerable when she had made her entrée in her pajamas on her first morning in Paris, now she felt like a naked model caught in floodlights on a catwalk with an audience staring at her morning-mussed-up hair.

But Laurent simply reached down to the table beside him and handed her one of two cups of coffee that were sitting there.

"I will take that, thank you," Sarah said, her voice coming out far more husky than she had planned. "But as soon as I'm done with it, and I can think straight, we need to talk."

Laurent moved closer. She breathed in the smell of his gorgeous aftershave. She had always had a thing about men's aftershave, and now she wanted to close her eyes and inhale it along with the freshly brewed coffee. Instead she shook herself and sipped at the jolting, delicious warm drink. She had to get her thoughts under control. She had to say something stern to Laurent. She couldn't let what happened last night occur again.

But Laurent started to speak first. "Sarah," he said, "I am so sorry about last night. I really had no idea."

No idea? She put her coffee back down, and then picked it up. She was determined to sort this out, but she needed to be able to think. The caffeine was good.

But then she found herself grimacing at the thought that occurred to her. Wasn't that what Steven had said? That he had no idea—no idea about the impact of his betrayal on her? Was that the stock excuse for this kind of behavior?

She sipped at the coffee. Laurent still stood there. He looked genuinely concerned. Sarah reminded herself that Laurent was not Steven. She needed to sort out some fair house rules, that's all. Even though, for some reason, if she were honest, she would admit to a pang of disappointment that he had lived down to Loic's description.

She took one last sip of her coffee, and drew in a breath. "Laurent—"

"Sarah." He came a step closer.

Sarah sat up straight. "I have to have access to my room. I didn't want to disturb you and your... thing last night, but I'm going to have to..." Her voice was sleep filled, morning-time sexy. She cleared her throat, folded her arms. She simply had to stay firm.

Something twitched in Laurent's cheek. He crouched down next to her now, and when he spoke, his voice was soft, penitent. "I am so sorry. I would never ever do what you thought was happening here last night, ever." He ran a hand across his chin, which was tickled with stubble, and went on. "I gave my key to a friend when we were out. He left his jacket here before we went out for the evening, and he wanted to come back here to get it. He left the club earlier than I did and I gave him a key.

"I'm sorry, Sarah, I feel so badly for trusting this friend who didn't deserve it, for not realizing that it could have been awkward for you if some random man had walked in on you, and for being out so late that it simply didn't occur to me what could go wrong. And, I'm sorry for ditching you last night for dinner.

"By the time I came home—and I admit it was late—you were asleep, and I was locked out of my room too. So I've been working."

Sarah frowned. Images of him working here next to her while she was fast asleep rushed into her head. She was startled that she felt comforted at the thought of his quiet companionship and protectiveness. But embarrassment crept in. Had she talked in her sleep? The thought of a handsome Frenchman beside her all night, painting while she slept, stirred some feelings she would rather not acknowledge. She was not, she thought firmly, going down that path.

She folded her arms and frowned. "So, hang on."

Something twinkled in Laurent's eyes now. His hand rested right near her knee.

"You're telling me that your friend was locked in your bedroom, and you were locked out too?"

Laurent nodded, and the amused expression on his face morphed into something more serious. "It was not fair to you. I shouldn't have lent him the key. I don't know what I'm doing..." He stood up, moved back to his easel, picked up his brush, then put it back down.

He stood there, his hands in the pockets of his jeans. And suddenly, Sarah wanted to listen. Why was he spending time with people like that? People who she suspected were absolutely not right for him. She sensed that he was not a European playboy, and she wanted to understand what was wrong to make him surround himself with that type. He moved then, over toward the window.

"I'd better get on with my work," he said.

Questions ran on in Sarah's mind. But she gathered her shoes and stood up. Whatever the answers were, it was clear that he was not going to talk now.

"I guess we should wake them…" she began.

Laurent shook his head. "I roused them a couple of hours ago. Made them keep quiet so they didn't wake you. They've gone. You can go through to your rooms and get ready for the day." He sounded tired, resigned. "What are your plans, Sarah?"

She stood there, her eyes wanting to search his face for answers. He was talented. He seemed an incredibly thoughtful, sensitive person. He was absolutely gorgeous. He had everything in the world going for him. So what on earth was wrong? Why was he spending time with people who clearly took liberties with him like this? She looked directly at him. "I don't know. I really haven't thought about today. I'll sort something out."

"I want to make it up to you."

"You don't have to do that."

"Yes I do. I want to," he said. His lips curved into a smile, but his eyes remained serious.

Sarah kept her tone light. "Are you going to clean the apartment from top to bottom? Decorate it with flowers? Massage all the kinks out of my neck that I got sleeping out here?" Whoops—too far! She bit at her bottom lip.

"Nope." The expression on his face softened.

Sarah felt some of the tension in her shoulders easing too.

"Come out with me tonight," he said. "I promise it won't be crazy, and I'll introduce you to my friends—dear friends I think you'll like. It would be good for you to start meeting people in Paris."

Sarah folded her arms.

He waited.

She pressed her lips together.

"It won't be out of control, I promise," he said, his voice soft.

Sarah looked up at him. And for some irrational reason, she did not want him to think she was boring. She might like a bit of organization. She might like a plan. She might prefer sleeping in a bed to sleeping on Marthe de Florian's scandalous chaise longue. But she was definitely not dull.

"Tell me what time to be ready," she said, aware that she was gritting her teeth.

"Nine," Laurent said. He was still close. She sensed him laughing again. "See you then?"

"See you then," Sarah said. "I'm going to go out for breakfast."

He stood up. "Good. Enjoy your day."

"Thank you." She smiled. "Excuse me…" She had to move past him to get to the bedroom door.

"Sorry," he said, quieter as he stepped aside. "Looking forward to seeing you tonight."

He moved away from the door. She went into her room, closed the door behind her, and leaned against it on the other side.

Two things were perfectly clear. Laurent was devastatingly attractive, and the thoughts that were coming into her head were quite the opposite of the ones she had had about any man for months.

After brunch at a *boulangerie* near the Palais-Royal, Sarah wandered around the boulevards on the Right Bank. It was strange, not having a plan as to what to do next. Being adrift certainly wasn't how she had gotten through the last year. But somehow, walking around Paris made plans seem rather too efficient for the first time in ages. Instead of thinking about Louisa or the future, or her work or the apartment, Sarah simply enjoyed the city.

She found herself lured by makeup in Galeries Lafayette for the evening ahead. Sarah debated the reasons for her browsing while coveting the pretty, shimmering glosses and eye shadows in the famous department store; she wondered if she was becoming too anxious about an evening spent with Laurent's glamorous Parisian friends. What if they found her dull?

She bought the makeup.

Once outside Galeries Lafayette, she stopped on Boulevard Haussmann. One of the store's window displays caught her eye. A mannequin wearing a Chanel dress lounged on a designer sofa. A set of delicate porcelain teacups sat on a coffee table in front of the model, and behind her, there was a painting. One of Laurent's prints—a rainy Paris street. Against a lamppost shrouded in mist, a woman leaned, staring out of the canvas as if she couldn't care less. "So what?" the woman seemed to ask anyone who cared to look.

People had skirted around Sarah while she stared. No one seemed bothered whether she stood still, moved ahead, or went backward; all these Parisians were busy following their own paths. So what, then?

Did it matter if she didn't have a plan? Did it matter if she didn't know where she was going from here in her life? Couldn't she just live, taking things one day at a time, enjoying each moment as if it were precious, the way she had been doing today? What was stopping her from doing that, apart from herself?

With a sudden rush, she realized how tense she had always been when she was with Steven. His insistence on being on time, his insistence on impressing certain people, his insistence on Sarah's perfection had all become a part of her.

But then her mother had died after a desperate, valiant fight with cancer, and her father had died of grief only months after. Sarah had not been able to give her husband the time he seemed to require; tragedy didn't fit well with perfection. Steven had left her.

Sarah folded her arms and frowned. There were two ways of looking at this.

She could be devastated at Steven's betrayal, at what she realized now was weakness. Or, instead of regarding herself as alone and abandoned, she could see herself as free. She could see that anything could happen. The possibilities were endless. Her life was not over just because she had lost so much. The old life was, but somehow, a new life would begin.

She looked some more at the woman in Laurent's painting. She could be at a crossroads too. Standing there, in the rain.

Back at the apartment, Sarah unlocked Loic's safe and took out Marthe de Florian's letters, handling the delicate, ribbon-wrapped bundles with care. These little remnants held memories that had long passed. They told of people's secret feelings, of men and women who would never return to this world again. Finally, Sarah checked that Loic had not missed any papers in some hidden corner at the back of the safe.

He hadn't.

So after one last look, one last run of her fingers over Marthe's precious love letters, Sarah locked the safe again. The afternoon was drawing in. Shadows fell across the floorboards in Isabelle de Florian's old bedroom.

Once Sarah was done, she walked over to the kitchen window, where she looked out at the street and dialed Loic's number. He didn't pick up. So she left a brief message, thanking him for allowing her to read Marthe's letters, telling him that she had not found what she sought.

Sarah moved back through the dressing room to her bedroom. She was going to have a nap. She was tired, tired after this year, this long, long year, and she had to take care of herself. It had seemed as if the agony of it all would never end at times … but now it had.

And here she was in Paris. Amanda had said it was the most romantic city in the world. Amanda had said that it didn't suit Sarah. But what if it did? What if she were, quite simply, prepared to embrace its beauty, prepared to embrace every possibility she could?

Later, she woke to the sound of the front door closing.

"Bonsoir, Sarah," Laurent called through the apartment.

"Hi!" Sarah leapt out of bed.

What time was it? But then, she looked at her watch. She still had an hour or so before they were going out. An hour to get ready.

Goodness, that was enough. She stepped toward the bathroom, throwing her clothes onto the floor and leaving them there. There was warm water to savor as it ran over her bare shoulders, luxurious suds to shampoo through her hair. Then she applied makeup just as she knew how to do, how she used to—before there had been Steven and his insistence on rushing and pressuring her. She used to love spending ages getting her dark eyes right, using the new colors to highlight her cheekbones, blow-drying her hair and brushing it until it shone. She would treat herself; she would take her time.

She put on a gold dress that she had brought with her, just in case, its spaghetti straps showing off her slim, brown arms. One last look in the dressing room mirror.

She was ready.

She walked toward her bedroom door.

And was hit with shyness. Was her dress too much? Would Laurent get the wrong idea? Would he think she had gone too far? Then full-scale panic. Loic had said Laurent hated certain things—garish clothes, was it? Horrid aesthetics? Would he hate this dress too?

But then she caught herself. She had to stop thinking that way.

She could hear Laurent moving about in his room. Heard the sound of him opening and closing wardrobes. He was probably still getting dressed.

Sarah wandered over to her bedroom window. It was dusk. People walked by, and the signs of the theater across the road flashed neon in the stillness.

Laurent's room was quiet now. She would give him a few more minutes. A long bookshelf lined the space underneath the window in her bedroom. Sarah leaned down to have a look. It was filled with old books—Hemingway, Fitzgerald. She picked out a copy of *Tender Is the Night* and leafed through it. She hadn't read it for years. She wondered whom it had belonged to—the granddaughter, Isabelle, or perhaps Marthe, in her later years?

Sarah wandered back to her bed, her fingers gently opening the book's cover, turning back the first page with the reverence that she always reserved for old things.

And something slipped out of the book.

An envelope.

On the back, in neat italics, was the name of the sender. Lord Henry Duval, Ashworth, England, 1895.

"Sarah?" Laurent's voice was whisper-soft through the door.

"Coming," she said, her own voice barely sounding at all. She looked at the envelope in her hand, her insides darting about like a kite in the wind. "I'm on my way." She put the envelope back between the thin pages of the novel, back into its spot in the bookshelf.

She went through Laurent's room to the sitting room.

"You look gorgeous," Laurent said. A smile played on his lips. He was dressed in a dark jacket and trousers. His shirt was open at the collar.

Sarah didn't tell him he looked like heaven, but she thought as much.

"I've chosen one of my favorite places in Paris. Some of my oldest friends are coming. Loic and Cat, along with two artist friends. I thought you'd like to meet them."

Sarah couldn't help but smile. Any tension about the evening that she may have felt slipped right away.

Laurent stood aside for her to leave the apartment first, then waited for her to choose the elevator or the stairs. She chose the stairs. Somehow, the idea of being confined in the tiny elevator with him seemed a bit too awkward right now.

The warm summer night lent a festive atmosphere to the street. Lights shone up and down Rue Blanche, reminders of the Belle Époque. The old theater sat, still resplendent, surrounded by restaurants advertising post-theater suppers. People milled about and chatted.

Laurent stopped at a black Alfa Romeo that was parked a little way down the street. "Hop in."

Sarah ran her eyes over the sleek car. She felt her lips curve into a thought-so smile, but she didn't say anything to Laurent while he held the passenger door open for her. The interior was all soft cream leather. The car still smelled new.

"What an enigma you are," Sarah muttered, almost to herself. She bit her lip once the words had come out.

"What on earth do you mean by that?" Laurent asked.

"Nothing." Sarah shook her head. She looked out at the streets as he drove. They were heading toward the Seine. Laurent was quiet as they pulled onto the tree-lined Avenue Montaigne. Sarah let her eyes feast on the gorgeous boutiques on either side of the wide boulevard—Prada, Valentino, Ralph Lauren.

Laurent found a spot and pulled over.

And turned to face her.

"No, tell me what you mean," he said. His voice sounded tender.

But Sarah put her hand on her door. She hadn't meant to say anything. Suddenly, she was hit with a basket of nerves. "Sorry," she said, feeling her cheeks redden. She didn't want to cross a line here.

She climbed out onto the street.

Laurent was right beside her. "You're going to have to tell me."

But Sarah shook her head.

He led her down the street, stopping at a wide glass door. Sarah cast about for somewhere to look. She shouldn't have said that. He was being kind. What he did in his spare time was no concern of hers. "I'm sorry," she said again. "I seem to have developed the ability to come out with things I don't mean lately. It must be Paris."

"You don't have to apologize. Anything can happen in Paris."

Laurent held open the door to the entry foyer. A pale sofa and a couple of blue Louis XV chairs were grouped in front of an elegant bar, its deep wood polished to a sheen. Table lamps sat along its top. Black-and-white photographs of famous artists lined the walls.

"This is beautiful," Sarah breathed.

"It's the sort of place I like to come to with my close friends," Laurent said. "My real friends," he added.

He moved inside, where Loic, another two men, and a beautiful blond woman—Cat, Sarah thought—sat. They all stopped chatting when Laurent and Sarah arrived. The men stood up and shook Laurent's hand.

"Sarah, you know Loic, and this is Jacques and Marc," Laurent said. "And here is Cat."

Sarah shook the men's hands and leaned down to take Cat's outstretched hand. The other woman smiled up at her with such genuine warmth that Sarah found herself smiling right back into Cat's eyes.

Five minutes later, Sarah felt at home with everyone, from the tall and lean Jacques, with his shock of black hair and round, tortoiseshell glasses, to Marc, even though at first, she had noticed him appraising her with gray eyes that sat below his gingery hair. But then, she reasoned, Laurent had said that the other two men were artists. Marc was probably just studying her. After a few moments, he smiled at her. Sarah relaxed.

"Have you settled into the apartment, Sarah?" Cat asked.

The men had started a riotous conversation about a football match.

"I love the apartment," Sarah said. "I can't imagine what it must have been like, finding it untouched."

"Loic and I literally walked into a time warp together," Cat said. "Although it took us a while to get the door open, you know. No one had entered the place since 1940, and the dust was something else. Everything inside it was so precious—Marthe de Florian clearly hadn't thrown out a thing since about 1890."

Sarah chewed on her lip. She really should tell Loic that she had found the letter from Henry. But raising Louisa's death and then answering personal questions about her family in front of these people she had just met was not appealing. The last thing Sarah wanted to do was let all her skeletons loose here.

And a part of her wanted the chance to read Henry's letter to Marthe alone, before she told anyone else. After all, she usually read documents, or examined pieces of jewelry, forming her own opinions before getting back to the owners.

Cat seemed happy to chat about her baby and her life in Provence, which sounded bucolic, along with her burgeoning photography studio in Aix. After half an hour or so, a waiter came to tell them that their table was ready. As Sarah stood up, her thoughts reverted back to Henry's letter.

What if there was more correspondence from him hidden in those books? And why had Marthe kept Henry's letter separate from everyone else's? After all, every letter that Sarah had found was from a man. What was so special about Henry's mail?

Once Sarah was at the table, she found herself seated between Laurent and Cat. The other tables were full but the restaurant wasn't noisy. The soft lighting, smooth carpets, and rich, warm wooden tables lent an atmosphere of quiet.

When their first course arrived—Sarah had ordered a warm goat's cheese salad—silence lingered between her and Laurent for a few moments while they ate. Cat had joined in a conversation about wine-making with Loic and the others.

Sarah put down her fork, and so did Laurent at the same time.

"Laurent—"

"Sarah—"

They both laughed.

"You go ahead," Laurent said. He had put on a pair of glasses to read the menu and hadn't taken them off yet. They made him even more attractive, Sarah thought, framing his classic features to perfection.

"I didn't mean to make a funny comment earlier," she started. "Don't mind me."

He put his wineglass down and waited.

She rapped her fingers on the table. Everyone else was laughing and having fun, exactly as they ought to be doing, and here she was, feeling awkward, like a teenager on her first date. Which this wasn't. Not at all.

She needed to pull this together.

"Okay," she said. "It was only that, well..."

He still waited. Clearly, he wasn't going to make this any easier for her.

Sarah grabbed at her wineglass. This was ridiculous. Moronic. Couldn't she just think of another topic? Anything?

Laurent coughed.

"You all right, Laurent?" Cat turned around, her pretty eyes crinkling with a smile.

"Yes, fine, thanks." And turned back to Sarah.

"I want to know what you meant, though," he said, his voice laced with something else. He sounded close.

"I don't know what I meant," Sarah said. She tried to laugh. Took another gulp of her wine.

And then Laurent reached out, placed his hand over hers on the wineglass, and put it back down on the table.

"I want you to tell me," he said, sounding as if they were in complete privacy now.

She frowned again and sat back in her seat. "I didn't mean anything," she said.

But he rested his elbow on the table, facing her, and waited.

"Shouldn't you talk to the other guests?" She was flailing around like a duck trapped in a storm.

Laurent caught her eye and shook his head. "Nope," he said. "I'm more intrigued by you."

Sarah felt her cheeks heat up. She stared at the white tablecloth. "You mean you are intrigued by what I said."

"No. I'm intrigued by you."

Suddenly, the other conversation stopped. Sarah was still staring down at the table. She was aware of the curve of Laurent's arm where it rested nearby, creating a circle around them. She was aware of his closeness.

This was mad.

She lifted her head and addressed everyone else in a loud voice. "I'm going to have to go somewhere cool tomorrow," she announced. "I saw it's going to be horribly hot."

"It is." Loic grinned.

But Sarah felt her face flushing again. Had they all noticed that she and Laurent were...what, exactly?

"Go to the Orangerie," Cat said. She, at least, didn't sound as if she were making fun of her. "It's my favorite place in Paris."

Thank goodness for Cat.

"Sit among Monet's water lilies and you'll soon forget about the heat," Cat went on.

Loic threw his arm across the back of her chair. "Your favorite place, Cat?" he asked.

She leaned in toward him. "Second favorite," she laughed. "Some other places have a bit more of a personal connection."

"I should hope so," Loic said.

"Laurent could take you to the top floor of the Pompidou Center." Marc's serious expression was back.

Everyone went quiet.

"He has a whole section of that floor devoted to his work."

Laurent twirled his wineglass in circles. "Thank you, Marc. I'm sure Sarah wanted to know that."

"Really?" Sarah asked. "How intriguing."

A smile played around Laurent's lips.

The main course arrived. Jacques started chatting about a film he had seen.

Sarah started her mushroom risotto.

Laurent stayed quiet next to her for a moment.

Sarah put her fork down.

"Okay," she said.

"Yes."

"If you want to know—"

"Yes."

"And this is none of my business, by the way, but I'm—"

"Going back to Boston, so it doesn't matter if you mess things up with me, because you might never see me again after the summer..." he prompted.

"Exactly." Sarah nodded. Utterly emphatic. But then she thought about going back to Boston and had to push aside the downward feeling in her stomach.

"So tell me," Laurent said.

"Okay. Here's the thing. Well, after the other day, and something I read...like I said, it's none of my business what you do...but I hope everything's okay with you." Sarah folded her arms. "It's none of my business."

"Why would you think something was wrong?" he asked, but his voice was you-have-hit-on-a-nerve dead serious.

Sarah reached for the pepper grinder and twisted pepper all over her meal.

"Sarah, you're going to choke," he said.

Sarah started taking small mouthfuls of her food, but it was becoming difficult to get it down. Laurent would think she was an idiot.

She ate with the concentration of a surgeon who was saving a life.

"It's not nosy," Laurent said suddenly, out of the blue. "It's no huge secret. I'll tell you, if you like."

Sarah placed her fork down on the table. She could not eat at all now. This was crazy.

"Laurent," Loic said. Everyone else appeared to have finished their main course. "We're going to have a drink in the bar. And you can't monopolize Sarah anymore. We want to get to know her too."

"Yes, we do." Cat smiled.

Loic leaned over and kissed Cat on the cheek.

"Sarah, you're going to have to come and sit with me, away from Laurent." Cat moved her chair to make room.

"He's trouble. I'd keep away if I were you, Sarah," Jacques piped up. His hair seemed to be sticking up even farther now.

Laurent grunted and pushed back his chair. "I'll buy the first round," he growled.

"Let's stay here, for a moment," Cat said, when the men had gone to the bar. "We can follow them soon enough. Please, tell me all about Boston. Much as I love living in France, I do miss the States. I get back there every so often, but not enough, and it's going to be even harder now, with the baby."

When the party broke up, and Sarah had swapped phone numbers with Cat, and Jacques had told her to get in touch if she wanted to hang with a proper artist—an unsuccessful one, he said, unlike Laurent—Sarah found herself back out on the Rue Montaigne with Laurent.

"Are you okay to drive?" she asked.

Laurent tilted his head from side to side. "You know what," he said, "the car's going to be just fine here overnight. As long as I'm back here early in the morning, when the parking restrictions start up again, no one's going to tow it away."

Sarah looked up and down the enchanting street. The top floors of the buildings all looked like apartments, sitting atop the most exclusive and fashionable stores in the world.

"You have to walk along the Seine at night while you're in Paris," Laurent said.

Sarah looked at the pavement. Things had been so hard since Steven had left. She had been through every emotion under the sun until she had ended up wrung out, feeling nothing at all anymore. And at the same time she had been through the process of grieving for her parents—she had only started to reach a sense of closure when she had been able to pack up their apartment.

It was her father's death that had been such a deadly blow. While Sarah had known that her mother was ill for some time, she had relied on her father still being around, assuming that she and he would care for each other in the ways that they always had. The depth of his suffering at the loss of her mother had shocked Sarah more than she cared to admit. He had suffered a heart attack soon after Sarah's mother's death, leaving Sarah reeling. Lost. And the fact that she had been embroiled in a divorce right at the time they were both clearly sick and needing her had left her feeling terrible guilt—the very worst part of grief had hit her hard.

For some time she hadn't known if she ever wanted to risk a relationship again. But lately, she had been thinking that there was no harm in talking to other men; there was nothing wrong with making friends. Devastatingly attractive as Laurent was, there was nothing wrong with chatting with him while she was in Paris. Even if he were hardly ideal friendship material.

"It's only a walk." His voice broke into her thoughts.

"I'd love that." Sarah kept her voice firm.

"Good," he said.

They wandered along the quiet street. Lights shone onto the pavement from the shop windows. Sarah stopped to admire them and Laurent seemed happy to look at the pieces on display with her. He shared her appreciation of fine things, but in a different way. His eye was clearly drawn to color and shape, while she looked at intricacy and craftsmanship. She was enjoying his company. When they came to the Place de l'Alma, which was on the edge of the Seine, Sarah gasped.

The Eiffel Tower was directly opposite them, lit up, sitting there—iconic, unchanging, classic.

"Paris is all about pure grace," Sarah said. She couldn't help but sigh.

"It is," Laurent said. "Everywhere you turn, that's what you see. I'll always love Paris."

Sarah smiled.

She walked with Laurent across the street toward the river after they had gazed at the Eiffel Tower for a while. Laurent clearly had the soul of an artist. No one who lacked sensitivity could begin to paint like he did. And yet, Loic had seemed to be warning her off. She frowned at her thoughts. Why was she thinking in that way? There was no call for her to do so. She must not get ahead of herself.

Laurent turned left, following the path that ran along the edge of the Seine. Soon, they passed underneath a line of trees, their leaves trimmed into the neat, boxlike shapes that the French so loved. They passed couples, their arms linked. Walking through Paris at midnight seemed the most natural thing to do.

But Sarah's thoughts were niggling at her. Laurent had stopped making conversation. While this had felt comfortable the first time she had walked through Paris with him, now Sarah found herself wanting to find out more. But how should she start?

"I've talked my head off about me," she said.

They had reached the Pont de la Concorde. To their left the Egyptian column pointed to the night sky in the center of the elegant yet tragic square.

Laurent strolled along next to her. He had his hands in his pockets now.

Sarah tried something else. "It's great that you have a career that you love so much."

She sensed him relaxing a bit. "If I'm not painting, I'm not very good company, I'm afraid." He turned onto the bridge, leaning against the stone balustrade for a moment. "I'm probably not the easiest person to live with. Sorry you're stuck with me."

"You're not difficult to live with." Sarah gazed down at the dark water. The river was still, silent, a deep millpond.

"And you're very polite." Laurent moved off the bridge, walking farther up the Seine.

Darkness cloaked the Tuileries Garden on their left.

"No I'm not," she laughed. This was becoming awkward. But Sarah sensed that it was better to stay quiet. She had the feeling that Laurent might be going to talk to her, and the last thing she wanted to do was discourage him.

Laurent was quiet again. Was he waiting for her to ask questions? And then she stopped and stared.

"Oh, wow," she said. The Louvre was right in front of them, its ornate decorations lit up by spotlights in the dark.

"I'm working there after this project's done." Laurent dropped this as casually as ever. "I've got an artist in residency program lined up."

"Of course you have." Maybe it was because it was late, maybe it was Paris, but for some overwhelming reason, she did not want to get to the end of this night and not know a bit more about the man standing next to her.

"Laurent," she said. "I'm going to come clean about what I said in the car. I can't help but ask you a question. It's just that, well … you seemed so at home with your friends tonight, but … sorry. I don't know. I'm being a nosy roommate."

She stopped on the spot. Waited. Had she gone too far?

Something tightened in his cheek. "I'd been living with Eva for over eight years," he said, his voice low. "I'd known her since we were teenagers."

Sarah leaned in close so as not to miss what he said.

"I thought—assumed—that we'd spend the rest of our lives together. When I was working in New York, I decided I was going to ask her to marry me. But while I was in New York, she met someone else. And she moved out with that someone else, and they went to Switzerland, and they got married while I was away."

Sarah stayed quiet. She wanted to reach out a hand to him, but sensed this was not the thing to do. He didn't want sympathy. He only wanted to talk. She could understand that.

"You see, the thing is, as well as leaving, Eva took everything out of the apartment that we had bought together. Including all my paintings—the ones I had wanted to keep—all my early work, every last piece of the furniture that we had bought together, my music, even my photo albums; she cleared it out. I still don't know where it is. I was so devastated about Eva that I haven't followed up. I don't know if I will. The things she took were only things, and I had to question their worth in the end, but...the thing was, I came back to an empty space. There was nothing left—not her, not my work. It was as if everything I held precious had been obliterated in one sudden swoop."

"It doesn't make any sense at the time," Sarah said. But she wanted him to go on.

Laurent shook his head. "I didn't understand why. I had no idea what I'd done wrong. I kept questioning that. The only answer I have is that she wasn't comfortable with my career. I think she was worried about being with an artist..." He looked down at the ground, made a face, and looked back up at Sarah. "I just—it was the loss of trust, of everything I'd planned, and of her. Of who I thought she was."

Sarah knew.

"Eva and her husband are living in London now, and apparently, well. Eva's having a baby." His voice trailed off. "And I know I can't keep on hanging with models and going out all night. It's not me. It never was. You know, going out with old friends tonight has helped. I hope that makes sense."

"It makes sense." Sarah smiled. For some reason, a sense of warmth had come into her system. She loved that Laurent had talked to her. She felt pleased—of some use, finally, to someone else, perhaps for the first time in the last year.

Laurent was looking down at her. His expression was difficult to fathom. It was as if he were thinking about whether he should say something more.

"Okay," he said, his voice softer. "Now you tell me. Why did you really come to Paris? The family history is compelling, but why right now? There must be a reason for that."

Sarah folded her arms around her waist. "I had to leave Boston," she said. Her words came out with too much force.

"I sensed that."

Sarah turned to the river. She wished she had a stick or a stone that she could hurl into its depths. "Cheating husband," she said. "My mother was dying at the time, and…I don't know. I was overwhelmed. Then my father died a couple of months after my mother. He had a heart attack. He didn't want to go on without her. I felt guilty, as if I hadn't been there enough for him. As if I'd been too focused on my silly divorce. It was just…like you say. Everything gone. Like that. And then you are faced with the future…Coming to Paris was like a lifeline. Finding out the truth about Louisa is a connection with family—if I couldn't make any sense of the present, then perhaps I could learn from the past…" Her voice trailed off.

Laurent took a step closer to her. Sarah focused hard on the river. A barge appeared—its slow pace laborious to watch. For some reason, it irritated Sarah. For some reason, she wanted to speed it up.

"But you know, being here, being away, has helped. I've been able to look at everything from a distance. And I'm coming to see that, perhaps, what I thought was right wasn't so great after all."

"That's good," he said, and he reached out, placing a hand on her cheek for a moment. "But I'm sorry."

Sarah turned, looked up at his face. "You know what is strange? I thought I had everything all lined up. I would be married to Steven for the rest of my life. We would have a family. My parents would be there for our children. You know—I thought things would be regular. Normal."

"Sarah." Laurent sounded intimately close. "I'm not sure I should say this, but if Steven wasn't going to be there for you at a time like that, then he was hopeless. Sorry to be blunt."

Before Sarah could catch them, the words came out in a whisper: "Anything could happen now."

Laurent caught her eye. "Yes. It could." And suddenly, he leaned down and kissed her on the cheek.

It was very French, Sarah thought, as he lingered close for a moment before moving back, just a friendly kiss.

But something inside her tweaked. And she still could not stop the grin from spreading across her face. "It's so strange," she said.

"What?"

"You. You are in exactly the same position as me."

He tilted his head to one side. "I know."

"But you've taken your freedom and your career is completely stellar, it's just that your lifestyle is a bit..."

He leaned out then, pulled her into a clumsy hug. "Don't go there," he muttered into her ear. And then, as quickly as he had pulled her toward him, he took a step right back. "We should go home," he said, his tone completely different. "I have to work tomorrow, and you, you have to decide what to do next with your investigations. You really need to think about that."

He moved toward the street and, after a few moments, waved down a taxi.

Sarah struggled with her thoughts—happiness, for some reason, even though nothing at all was secure, and sadness, because she quite simply didn't want the evening with Laurent to ever, ever end.

Chapter Thirteen

Paris, 1894

Louisa alighted from the carriage outside the Duvals' Paris house in Île Saint-Louis, her mind still concentrating on her encounter with Marthe de Florian. The footman helped her down onto the cobblestones. Henry wouldn't be up yet but she was impatient to talk to him about the woman, even though she suspected any such conversation between them would only end badly. The simple fact was, Louisa felt that she had a right to know. She had a right to know about this woman. What was her relationship with Henry? Did they have a past? Louisa had become even more sure that Marthe had to be a courtesan, a demimondaine—otherwise known as a high-class prostitute—who seemed quite content to hold court over Louisa.

Of course, she knew that these women only turned to prostitution out of desperation, and her conscience persisted with questions surrounding her own beliefs about women's equal rights. She did not want to judge Marthe de Florian, but when confronted with her so close to home…the situation in which she found herself was confusing. If she were honest, it seemed as if her beliefs were being tested right here in Paris.

And yet, what she struggled with was this. The thought of Henry, of her husband, being with one of these women made Louisa feel ill. Were they—she hated to think about it—lovers? Half of her knew she would be naïve to think that they were not. But the other half of her still hoped. She still wanted to believe that Henry would not betray her now, to believe that even if he had a former relationship with the courtesan, he would stop it out of respect for his marriage.

She stopped in the middle of the cool marble entrance hall at the Duval house. And told herself she was definitely being unsophisticated. Everything she had seen since her arrival in Paris had pointed to the fact that Henry was not going to change his way of life, not for her, not for the future of his family, not for any reason at all. Waves of disgust seeped through her, along with indignation at the brazen manner in which the courtesan had approached her at the Bois de Boulogne. Suddenly, the hall in which she stood seemed even colder than usual.

Marthe de Florian didn't seem to care in the least that Louisa was Henry's wife. It didn't seem to factor at all. It was as if the courtesan was above the rules of normal society. It was as if she had thumbed her nose at every rule that had been dreamed up, while being a terrible product of the restrictions on women in society, and at the same time being utterly owned by men. Louisa frowned, took off her hat, and went into the salon. The nightingale shifted on its perch. Louisa stroked the bars of its gold-leaf cage.

She sank down on one of the delicate sofas and closed her eyes for a moment in the silence. Louisa hated to think how one stopped the cycle—wealthy men handing over jewels, apartments, carriages, dresses; women having no shame, selling their bodies for material gain, enjoying the perks of high society life in return, being seen where it mattered, at Longchamp, at the opera, at the theater. Where did it end?

The answers were education, universal franchise, and freedom of opportunity for women. Coming to Paris and seeing so many desperate women in the streets had only made Louisa's convictions stronger.

"Louisa." Henry appeared, dressed, which was unusual this early in the day. He wore a coat. He was clearly about to go out.

"Good morning," Louisa said, stultified by the paradox of her own situation. Who was she dependent on? What was her role in all of this? She ran a hand across her forehead. But her mind simply would not stop.

Henry leaned against the mantelpiece. He looked at the clock, checked it with his fob watch. *Sorry to interrupt your plans for the day,* she wanted to say, but instead, she held her breath.

Henry pulled a miniature portrait out of his pocket. He was admiring it, smiling in some secret way.

Louisa sat up. She had to talk to him. So she stood up, moved over to where he stood. And gasped as she looked over his shoulder. Henry held a perfect miniature of Marthe de Florian in the palm of his hand. Marthe's hair was swept back but strands of it fell across her cheeks, and one of her arms was thrown up behind her head in a most suggestive fashion.

He placed it on the mantelpiece, under the gold-edged mirror.

"For God's sake, Henry," Louisa whispered. "What will everyone think?"

"I don't see the problem." He adjusted the miniature slightly, so that it was dead in the center of the space.

Did he think the courtesan only had eyes for him? Was he so innocent as to think that a woman like Marthe de Florian loved him?

Louisa laughed then, a hollow, empty sound. He thought he was sophisticated, and yet, he was blindingly naïve. She walked back to the window. Stared at the leaves outside that were sun-dappled and moving gently, as if nothing was wrong at all.

Suddenly she saw Henry for what he was. A charlatan. A fool. Someone who was simply trying to avoid the reality of his life by being in Paris. Someone who thought a courtesan, a coquette, cared about him.

Louisa stared out at the street. Her mind had become clear. In one instant, she had ceased being intimidated by Henry. In one instant, she realized that there was simply nothing she could do that would change him. In one instant, she made up her mind. There was only one thing to do. There was only one thing that was remotely palatable right now, and urgency propelled her to speak.

"I am returning to England," she said. "I am going back to Ashworth. There is nothing, Henry, for me here."

Henry was quiet for a few moments. "You'll need to stay here a few days. Then you can go. You'll have to remain in Paris with me until it's seemly that you leave."

The practicality of his statement came as a blow to her. But she nodded and closed her eyes. Then opened them again. Of course. That was all it had always been for him. Practical. His marrying her. The puppy, the lunch by the follies. She had been stupid. She had fallen for it all. But he hadn't meant it. Suddenly, Louisa felt something loosen.

If Henry was doing what he wanted to do, then why couldn't she?

She turned to him, but he drew out his cigarette case and lit up. "I really didn't want you to show up in Montmartre last night. You know that."

The stink of smoke filtered through the room, reminding Louisa of the ghastly night before. The club. The heat. *Sorry to have besmirched your plans*, she wanted to retort. But she held it in, knowing that it would only start an argument. And now, the only way forward was to be formal right back to him. Practical. They had an arrangement, almost a business one at that. Louisa thought about it. Perhaps there was a reassurance in this. Plenty of marriages survived on those terms. It wasn't what she had wanted. But perhaps there were advantages in the relative freedom that such an arrangement offered—the release from any expectation that she would have a relationship with Henry that was anything more than superficial. If he could look at her as a means to an end, then why couldn't she, as a woman, do exactly the same thing back?

Louisa tilted her chin. "Very well, then, Henry," she said. "I will stay for a few days to make things look good. But only on one condition."

Henry looked up at her, his expression very much as if he was only mildly interested in what she said.

Louisa resisted the urge to bat at his cigarette smoke. "I want you to tell me about Marthe de Florian."

If Henry was surprised that Louisa knew the courtesan's name, he didn't give anything away. Regarding her blankly through the haze, he said, "She's a friend."

"Really."

"Why not?"

"Henry."

"I've known Marthe a long time. There are things that you don't understand, and I don't blame you for that, but—"

"I'm not brokenhearted."

Henry muttered something.

Louisa went on. "Quite frankly, I'm more interested in women's rights. Marthe seems a clever person. But how did she end up as a—"

"Demimondaine?" Henry stubbed out his cigarette. Sat down in a chair and crossed his long, elegant legs. Aristocratic legs, Louisa thought. In some ways, he came across as a spoilt child, in others, he was sophisticated. She understood his yearning to act on the stage. She understood how restricted he felt back in England. What he failed to grasp was that he had drastically underestimated her.

"Like so many of them, Marthe was a poor seamstress in the garment district," Henry said. "She had two sons to two men by the time she was twenty. Like all women without support, she is only trying to survive."

Louisa nodded. Exactly. Because Marthe de Florian had no other choice. What else could she do? Become a governess? A maid? Never see her children? "Henry, I want to do something to change that. To change things for women like Marthe. Can you understand that?"

Henry's mouth formed into a cynical smile. She could see he was taking in what she had said, but he was quiet for a while. Finally, when he spoke, his tone was cold. "I have already heard of your...interests. Your involvement with radical women—with bluestockings—will not be tolerated by my family. You are not unintelligent. Surely you understood the role you were taking on when you married me, Louisa.

"As long as you toe the line, you can do what you want at Ashworth. But there are two rules you'll need to follow. The Duval lineage can never be questioned; I will not raise a bastard. And for God's sake, no politics. You're going to be a duchess. I know you're American, but can't you see that?"

Louisa leaned forward. She kept her voice soft. She was determined to make him understand. "Henry. Forget me for a moment. Think about Marthe. Wouldn't you rather women like Marthe were not dependent, solely, on the whims of wealthy men? Wouldn't you rather that they could have other opportunities? Surely, I could use my position as a duchess to further the interests of women like your friend! You saw what was going on in Montmartre. You know what is happening in the street. For every Marthe de Florian, there are a hundred starving, desperate women who have no hope at all.

"As your wife," Louisa went on, "I am in a position to do something to help. And with your support, with your weight as a future duke, behind the cause...Henry, quite frankly, you have millions of pounds at your disposal. You'll have a position in the House of Lords, should you wish to take it. Surely, you would not want any daughter of yours to end up—"

Henry uncrossed his legs and stood up. "Louisa." He held out a hand. "You are quite delightful when you are passionate about such matters, but I'm afraid it simply won't work. You will have to deal with the forces of Ashworth. I couldn't. I left. Don't you see?

"You are welcome to stay here in Paris. I really don't mind if you do. Or you can go back after a time, but you are not going to be able to conduct any sort of political activity as the wife of the heir to one of the greatest estates in England. And I'm afraid that while my father, who is in good health, remains a duke and as close to the royal family as one could possibly be, you are better off staying here with me, or going back and playing your role to perfection, than you would be trying to take some radical position that will only be regarded as shameful. They will stop you. You won't be able to do it. Louisa, I know this from experience. When I spoke to my father about my hopes for a life in the theater—for a life working with Shakespeare, with Chekhov—he told me to grow up. He told me that if I mentioned such a thing once more in the house, he would disown me and leave everything to Charles."

Louisa found herself pressing her lips together in order to stop the flood of words that wanted to come out.

"But the irony is that we all have to act, my dear," he said. "I do so every day. It's just that I act in my life, not on the stage. Me, Marthe, you. You can't choose what role you want to play, because you are married to me. I'm sorry, but you made your choice. You decided to marry me. As I said, you are not stupid. Presumably you thought the entire thing through."

Louisa folded her arms. Anything she did or said right now would not be to her immediate advantage. She remained silent.

"I have an engagement in the Bois de Boulogne now." Henry adjusted his sleeves, checked his hair in the mirror, and moved toward the entrance hall. "Tonight, Louisa, I have tickets for us both to the ballet."

Louisa felt her breath coming in shudders.

"I will see you at eight," he said. "It's important you come. People need to see that you are accompanying me as my wife."

He nodded at her, almost bowed, and then there was only the sound of his heels clicking on the hard, patterned tiles before the front door shut with a thud.

"Damn you," Louisa whispered to herself.

Once again, that rhetorical question shouted in her ear. What was the difference between the web in which she was caught and the one in which the courtesan found herself? And that begged another question—who was better off?

Louisa chose to wear black to the ballet. This was deliberate. She hoped that the color was formidable. She stared straight ahead once she was in the carriage with Henry, but her thoughts spun in whirls. She simply could not stop. This afternoon, she had asked the footman to take her to the Louvre, where she had wandered around. She had begun with the idea of looking at art as a means of distraction from life, but she had finished filled with inspiration to forge ahead instead. She had stared long and hard at Delacroix's *Liberty Leading the People*, taking in every aspect of the artist's noble, resolute woman who spurred men to final victory.

And now, as she sat in the carriage next to her husband, Louisa reminded herself that she had never wanted to exclude Henry from her plans. Having a husband who was sympathetic toward her desire to make things better was something she had wanted and something she had hoped to find. Her failing was that she had misjudged Henry, and now, she had to carry on by herself.

Once they were seated in the Duval family box at the Opéra Garnier, with its soft velvet seats, gilt columns, and rich red walls, Henry's reasons for choosing to bring her to the ballet became even more telling. The Opéra was the place to show off to society, a place where Henry could appear as a respectable married man.

No one was looking at the stage.

As Louisa gazed around the theater, it was clear that the ethereal beauty of *Les Sylphides* was lost on this audience. The crowd spent the evening peering at each other through their lorgnettes. A constant stream of people came in and out of the Duval family box to meet Louisa and to chat with Henry as if oblivious to the ballet that was being performed on stage.

At intermission, Henry leapt out of his seat without even a glance at Louisa, but when Louisa went to follow him, he told her to stay where she was. He insisted that she speak with the *Comtesse de Laigne*, a woman who had appeared right on cue with a waiter bearing two glasses of champagne.

Louisa turned to her new companion, a splendidly dressed, short woman whose beady eyes looked Louisa up and down before she leaned in and spoke.

"You know where the men have all gone, don't you, my dear?"

Louisa shook her head. Smoking in the lobby?

"They are in the Foyer de la Danse." The *comtesse* spoke as if she were sharing some great confidence. She spoke as if Louisa should be flattered that she had chosen to share this information with her. "Wives and male dancers are not allowed to enter the room."

Louisa sipped her champagne, its fizzy sweetness tingling on her tongue. The older woman seemed to want to shock her. Louisa wanted to roll her eyes in return.

"And what happens in this Foyer de la Danse?" she asked, keeping her voice deliberately even.

"Your husband gets a season ticket to the famous Foyer along with his box," the woman said. Her bosom was powdered. Her curls bobbed. She fairly burst with the superiority of her knowledge. "The Foyer was built for the express purpose of facilitating encounters between the ballerinas and gentlemen ticket holders. It is a sort of club, where noblemen and industrialists alike linger with the dancers and watch them limber up."

Louisa stared straight ahead.

Of course. Why else would everyone come to the ballet?

"As one would expect, the dancers seek gentlemen with enough clout to advance their careers. Most of the girls arrive here at the Opéra starving. Most of them are young, perhaps fourteen or so?"

Louisa closed her eyes. Yet another brothel. "How interesting." She was aware that her voice had as much life in it as a painted doll.

She picked up her own opera glasses and peered around the room. Perhaps if she ignored the *comtesse*, the woman would find someone better to impress.

After a few moments, predictably, her companion began to shriek at a passing parade of friends who were promenading in the hallway.

"Do excuse me," the woman said to Louisa, patting her on the arm. Louisa nodded. *With joy,* she thought.

When Henry returned, Louisa felt more resignation than anything else. What an education Paris had turned out to be. What on earth could be done was the question. The challenge had to be squarely met.

"You should go home now, Louisa," Henry announced once the performance was over. He sauntered back down the famous Opéra staircase to the crowded street, leaving Louisa to trail behind him.

Carriages drew up, one by one. Theatergoers drifted down the boulevard. Supper after the Opéra was famous in Paris.

"Where are you going next?" Louisa asked. She was determined not to be left walking behind him.

"The circus," he said.

Louisa stopped. "You are joking, aren't you, Henry?"

"Would you keep moving, please?" Henry took her arm in his. "Do not make a scene in the street."

"The circus!"

"Louisa. While it is perfectly acceptable for you to attend the ballet—"

"Apart from certain rooms, it seems," Louisa muttered under her breath.

Henry went on. "The circus in Montmartre is only for men. Strictly. That's it."

"It seems to me that there is more segregation here in Paris than anywhere else I have been. Women in certain places, men in others, and then women are divided into two strict groups. I cannot believe that you said Paris was free."

"Good night, Louisa." He handed her over to the footman.

Louisa took one last glance down at him and settled herself in the carriage. She wondered if she would have more luck changing society itself than altering her husband.

Three days later, Louisa was on her way to Ashworth.

Henry had come to her the night before, and the night before that. She had suffered it. Just.

But now, enough was enough. It was time to do something. Plans were forming in her head.

Chapter Fourteen

Paris, 2015

Ashworth, 1895

My dear Marthe,

I confess that I endured a round of robust internal discussion before I found the courage to pick up my pen and write. But, I was so moved after the discussions that we had the last time I was in Paris, that I wanted to continue them. I don't want them to stop. I feel that our understanding grows deeper each time we meet, that there is some magic in place every time that we talk. I am drawn to you, hopelessly, and so I must write.

Indeed, when I imagine you, elegant in your Parisian salon, you are reading this with an arch of that perfect auburn eyebrow (forgive me) while at the same time, selecting those communications that you will preserve and dismissing those which you decide are not worthy of your attentions. I hope this letter will be of more interest than those which simply ask for an afternoon of your company.

You know I value you far more than that.

I wonder what criteria you will adopt when making such monumental decisions as to what correspondence you will read and what you will not? Will it be your heart that chooses which poor men will be "taken on" or must you base your decisions on protocol: on who is worthy of your attention, and who is not?

I suspect that the latter method must govern every choice you make. Society defines us, no matter how much we may pretend that it does not, right down to whom we must love—if we are allowed to do such a thing, which is questionable. I acknowledge that we are both surrounded by gilt, but is it worth it if we have no freedom of choice?

It could be argued that you chose your position in the world, that you have created yourself out of this very society which we both laugh at and abhor. That you have beaten it at its own game, as it were.

It is harder for me to do so, I fear. But that is not to say that I am not determined.

You must know how deeply I value the connection that I have with you. I know that you understand me, and I you. It is as simple as that. It is as if you are ahead of everything, cutting edge, so to speak, in every single way, and yet caught up in a world where your station at birth must still define your station in life.

We both know who we are, but we cannot be ourselves in the world as it is now.

It is a strange and wonderful relationship that you and I have. It is as if we are kindred spirits, were I to believe in the existence of such things.

And as for society, were I to attempt to understand that, I would say one thing: it is fear that drives our world, Marthe, fear of everything that is strange and uncomfortable and different and independent.

Society has set up structures with rigid boundaries to keep the great "other" out of its pale little version of life, and it is a pale version. Polite society, in denying us who we are, denies the human spirit. It denies us all the truth.

And there are two factions opposing this society that has been set up. One is the world that you and I inhabit. We escape, to a place of fantasy and artifice and illusion. We pretend that our world is the real world. But at the same time, we both know that it is not.

I cannot be who I am in the real world, so I must create a new one.

But there is another fight, one that I find unattractive, unappealing, and base. This is the world of my wife. It is ironic, do you not think, that Louisa finds my world unattractive? And yet these two opposing forces are two sides of one coin—two methods of rebellion, I suppose. Louisa lives for politics and reform. I live, simply, to be able to live as myself. And I see life in Montmartre. Montmartre is life. It is true to the body and the soul of a person. It reviles all those niceties that society constructs. And you, you embody this, and so do all the others—the poets, the writers, the dancers, the actors. I ache to be one of you. I ache not to be who I am.

I fear that my wife's way will lead to straight-out, head-on fighting, to death, to destruction. Men are not going to give up their positions, simply hand them to women. And the upper classes are not going to give up their role of leadership to the rising working class without some monumental fight.

I battle with the outcome of Louisa's ideas. Is it because she is my wife? Can you see how, possibly, any of this could change without fighting? Do you know why it is that so many people seem content with convention? They insist on preserving it as if they are some sort of moral force!

A self-created police force for the status quo. Is that all society is?

It is freedom that you and I seek in a way that will not harm others. It is true liberation that we want—the need for expression of our own humanity, not to be put upon or dictated to by anyone else. We both want to make our own choices. We both want to run our own lives.

But I fear that our kings who rule with the scepter of religion could only be replaced with much worse. I fear that the uprising that is going to have to happen, that is bounding around underground in politics, will only be pushed down by stronger forces of convention in the name of something else once we are done with our protesting. I have no doubt that we humans will find yet another form of repression to which we will expect those souls who do not fit in to submit to, because ultimately most of our species are scared of what might happen should those with too much independent thought rise up.

My dear Marthe, I cannot talk to anyone else of such matters, because you alone know who I am, and I, in turn, know you. The problem is, what is one supposed to do?

For me, Paris is the answer. And for me, you are the inspiration. If there is a real world, and a fantasy of my own creation, then I prefer the latter. And I prefer to share it with you.

For me, you hold the answer.
Au revoir, until I am in Paris,
Henry

Sarah laid the letter aside on her unmade bed. She had read Henry Duval's words over and over again before falling asleep sometime in the wee hours, the sense of warmth after her evening with Laurent and his friends distilling itself through her system. Was this how Henry felt when he was with Marthe de Florian? Clearly, he had a sense of being his true self and of freedom and encouragement when he was around her. Sarah, in turn, had not wanted to let go of the evening she had spent with Laurent. She had not wanted to fall asleep, because the night had been delicious—perfect. And being in Paris had made it seem even more magical.

She had woken with the light still on in her room. Now, the sun streamed into Isabelle de Florian's old bedroom, and here she was with a letter written to Isabelle's grandmother, a letter that said much, and nothing, about Louisa, Henry, and Marthe de Florian.

Sarah stood up, went over to the bookshelf where she had picked up the copy of *Tender Is the Night*, wondered how lacking in tenderness Louisa's life had been, and ran her fingers over the other novels. Their cardboard spines etched with gilt contained the words of those writers, of Hemingway and Proust and Stein and Pound.

Sarah turned away from the shelf. She had to decide what to do next.

Laurent was making sounds in the room next door. Sarah was used to hearing him in the mornings—it was companionable having him, in many ways, so close. When he knocked on her own door, Sarah went over to it, wrapping the tie of her white bathrobe around her waist.

Laurent stood in a blue-and-white striped shirt and jeans. He handed her a cup of coffee. He had been painting. The scent of oil paint drifted through the open door, and his hands were dabbed with spots of color. Even though his chin was lined again with a telltale shadow of stubble—had he slept at all?—his face was animated and awake.

Sarah thanked him for the coffee.

And, silently, handed him Henry's letter.

A frown ran across Laurent's face as he took the old paper, but when he read, it was clear that he was utterly absorbed.

"I can't imagine it," he said.

He had understood.

"It is hard."

"It's only raised more questions."

"Yes."

"To live like that, at every level of your life, a lie..." his words trailed off.

Sarah moved over to the bookshelf. "It's funny. Being here, talking to you last night..." She didn't steal a glance at him, but plowed on instead. "All of this has made me realize how you have to find your own truth. I know it sounds old-fashioned, but you have to be true to yourself. Henry and Louisa were trying to do that, I think. I have conflicted feelings about Marthe!"

Laurent was behind her. "You do have to find your own truth. Marthe was just trying to survive, I suspect," he said, his words soft.

"You're right," she said. "Of course she was. It's just that..." She turned to Laurent. "I don't know what her role was in relation to Henry and Louisa. I don't want to sound like an awful judge..." Sarah picked up a copy of *Brave New World*, searching its pages, but gently, with respect.

"You're not sounding judgmental." Laurent had wandered over to the books. "You found the letter in the bookshelf."

She turned back to him. "I was looking for something to read."

"Of course you were. And you chose Fitzgerald." He picked up the book that lay on her bed.

"The letter just fell out."

"As things like that do."

She chuckled and picked up the coffee. Sipped it. It was good.

"I take it you're going to search the rest of the shelf, right here, right now?" A twinkle appeared in his eyes.

"Yes," she laughed.

"Do you want me to help?"

She nodded. "Yes. That too."

He caught her eye and smiled.

"And let's not do it in order," Sarah said. The wonderful coffee was waking her up.

"Let's definitely not do anything in order, Sarah. In fact, I have been thinking about the merits of doing things backward most of the night."

Sarah sensed Laurent's eyes on her. She focused on the bookshelf. It was a safe bet. Tentatively, she reached for *The Sun Also Rises*. The book's pages were bound tight, as if they were stuck to each other, as if they had been that way for a long time. But there were no letters tucked inside Hemingway's song to the lost generation.

Laurent pulled a book out of the middle of the shelf.

An hour later, they were done. Piles of books sat on the pretty antique table in the corner of the room. Not one of them held another letter from Henry.

And yet, they had found these things: a list from 1934 about a trip to Lake Geneva in what Sarah now recognized as Marthe's confident handwriting—what to take, what to do, where to stay—a note from Isabelle de Florian to her grandmother, informing her that she was going shopping for the afternoon in Galeries Lafayette, and a ticket to the opera. All of these were from the 1930s. There was nothing from the Belle Époque.

Sarah surveyed the empty shelves. Dark marks ran across the wood where the books had been removed, but there were no other pieces of paper to be seen.

"Thoughts?" Laurent asked, his head tilted to one side.

Sarah looked at the stacks of books. "It's all getting more complicated, as things tend to."

"But Henry's confirmed that Louisa had other interests outside the marriage," Laurent said. "If Henry's relationship with Marthe was deeper than mere friendship, then that could have rattled Louisa, of course. But enough to drive her to commit suicide? Enough to take her own life?"

Sarah nodded. "Exactly. I need a time machine, Laurent. If only I could get inside Louisa's head. I do think Louisa could well have felt left out of what was clearly a close, understanding, and instinctive relationship between Marthe and Henry, that would be reasonable enough."

Laurent caught her eye. "A kindred spirit bond. She could have well felt very left out."

Sarah didn't look away. She nodded. For some reason, it was hard to know what to say.

After a few moments, Laurent took a step toward the door. "I better get back to work. And you need to keep going. That's all you have to do right now. We just have to work out the next step. That's all."

Sarah nodded. "I'll call Loic, and tell him about the letter."

Laurent paused in the doorway, looked as if he were considering what to say. "I enjoyed talking to you last night," he said after a while. "No matter what the outcome, no matter what your family story turns out to be, no matter what your stupid ex-husband did, you have your own choices now. You make your own decisions from here on, Sarah, decisions that are best for you."

She nodded. She agreed. If that path sounded a little lonely, she was not going to mention that now.

He spoke in that hushed voice again. "If Henry and Marthe did have a soul-mate connection, then they were lucky, weren't they?" he asked.

Sarah felt her mouth curve into a smile.

Laurent turned then, and went back out of the room.

Chapter Fifteen

Ashworth, 1894

Yellow autumn leaves were strewn along the driveway to Ashworth. Mist hung about, and the air was pregnant with earthy freshness. Louisa leaned out the window a little way, allowing the country air to revive her. The journey from Paris had been long, but peaceful. The stillness of the countryside seeped into her bones, and she closed her eyes as the carriage rolled toward the palace.

Two people had propelled her back to England: Charlie—she had allowed herself to think hopeful thoughts about the prospect of talking with her brother-in-law again—and Emmeline Pankhurst. Louisa was determined to make arrangements to visit the woman in Russell Square.

It was Charlie who greeted her at the entrance to the great house. There was no formal arrival party from the servants, and for this, Louisa was thankful. Charlie helped her out of the carriage, issuing orders to the footmen about how to deal with her luggage.

"My parents are out for the afternoon," he said, taking her hand and kissing it. "I'm afraid you will have to be content with me. But they will be home for dinner. They will want to talk to you about what you are doing back here."

"That sounds like a warning."

"Not at all." Charlie let go of her hand. He stood still and looked at her. "It all went wrong, didn't it?"

Louisa laughed. "Hello—it all went wrong? What a wonderful greeting."

But Charlie didn't budge. "You're going to have to tell me."

Louisa watched the carriage move back toward the coach house. They stood just inside the open front door of the palace. The mist falling outside seemed to create a feeling of closeness in the air. Charlie felt close too. And she felt safe, and more full of possibilities than she should, she realized, given everything.

"Nothing is wrong," she said, softer now. "Nothing you can fix." And regretted her last words.

"Something has affected your spirit."

"I'm tired, that's all."

"Would you like to rest?"

She knew she had not fooled Charlie. She knew that putting on the famous English stiff upper lip would not work with him.

"I have been sitting in carriages and on trains for hours, having been confined in a boat before that. I'd like to go for a walk."

"Of course you would," he laughed lightly. He was quiet for a moment. "Would you like some company?"

Louisa nodded. She had tired of her own presence and her own interminable thoughts. She didn't want to admit to the quickening of her heart at the thought of walking with Charlie. After a refresh upstairs, Louisa met him on the front steps. She gathered her favorite green cloak about her, pulling up its hood against the mist as they stepped out onto the driveway.

Charlie paused for a moment, reaching forward and tucking a tendril of hair behind her ear. "You do look tired."

"Fresh air solves more ills than anything else," Louisa said, attempting to put brightness into her voice. Aware that she sounded like her mother and had failed to convince herself of the veracity of her own words.

They walked away from the house in silence.

Charlie was the one to break it. "How bad was it?"

They turned right, following the driveway to the edge of the park, until they came to a path that was sheltered on one side by the forest, while affording a view of the serenity of the park.

"It was interesting."

"Interesting is a useful word. It covers everything and nothing."

"It is the word of diplomats."

"You found yourself in a position where you needed to be diplomatic?" His tone held a mixture of resignation and irritation.

They came to a fork in the path. One trail led directly into the forest. Damp yellow leaves were set into the rich earth. Louisa wanted the coolness of the forest.

"I suppose you can imagine what happened in Paris. And do not tell me you warned me—I cannot stand to hear that now." She marched into the denseness of the forest, her boots sinking occasionally into the soft bed of leaves. "I was not going to listen. I do not blame anyone except myself. It is what it is."

She was hardly the first woman to find herself in such a predicament, but still...

"Henry spent his entire time in the company of those people in Montmartre, didn't he? On your honeymoon. Excellent."

"I don't suppose he can help it," Louisa said, her words half-sincere. She felt exhausted all of a sudden.

"Oh, he can help it. Anyone can help it. It's a matter of doing the right thing. It's called marriage. But Henry chooses the opposite." Charlie stopped, picked up a stray stick from among the sodden leaves on the edge of the path, and then broke it in two, throwing half away into the forest and frowning at the other half as if it were the cause of all ills.

"I thought, the first time that I met him, that he and I might have something in common," Louisa said, her voice tight and drained. "And then, I admit, I enjoyed his company. I was flattered when he afforded me such special attention. Then, when it looked as if he were about to propose, I knew that I would be mad to turn him down. I'm afraid that I thought I didn't have any choice. And I thought I could play a role here at Ashworth, make a difference. Now, I'm not sure what to do."

Charlie stopped again, turned on the spot so that he was facing her. His dark hair was dampened by the mist that fell through the canopy of trees. "I know him," Charlie growled. "He can be extremely charming. I don't know how to say this without sounding cruel, but he saw you as a willing supplicant, Louisa. It's all about pleasing the parents on the one hand, while doing exactly as he pleases on the other. He knows they will turn a blind eye to his antics. He knows they will do anything to avoid having a scandalous son. That's partly why he goes to Paris, rather than London, to play up."

"That, and the fact there is a certain courtesan there," Louisa said.

Charlie reached out, touched her arm. "I know. Marthe de Florian." His tone was whisper-soft, and his words seemed to float in the forest.

"I'm sorry, this is a mess," she whispered. "I can sort it. There's no need for the family to become involved."

Charlie took her hand, placing it in his own and holding it for a moment before he spoke. "It's not your fault. I'm sorry, Louisa. You can file for divorce, if you can't stand it. But you'd have to prove cruelty as well as adultery."

Louisa nodded. "I know. I'm aware of the law."

He was quiet for a moment. "You're not sure that you want a divorce, are you?"

Louisa had to force herself to stop the wry smile that was forming on her lips. A divorce? Of course the possibility had crossed her mind. But there were a million other complications churning in her head, and right at the front of her thoughts was this: She did not want to abandon her burgeoning friendship with Charlie. Something almost beyond her control pulled her toward him.

She knew that was irrational, and completely ridiculous under the circumstances. But there it was. She had wanted to come back to Ashworth because she wanted to see him, although she did want to go to London as well.

How could she abandon the opportunities that she might have as part of the powerful Duval family, no matter what Henry said? She knew that Charlie would support her aims for women's rights.

She had married the wrong brother.

She had the sinking feeling that she was falling in love, but it was too late. Charlie treated her as an individual. Henry treated her as something to suit him.

Charlie was looking at her directly, his brown eyes honest—dark, but clear.

A bird called. It was close. Then the sound of wings flapped away through the trees.

"I'm here for you," he said. "Always."

Louisa wrapped her cloak tighter around her body. "I don't want to burden you."

"Believe me, you're not." Charlie turned then, started striding back to the path that edged the forest. His voice was clear in the silence. "We just have to take it step-by-step. But you need support."

They came to the entrance to the forest. A slight breeze had stirred—leaves fell, yellow, random, onto the wide path that edged it. Ashworth came into view. A smart carriage made its way around toward the main entrance of the house.

"My parents are back. Just carry on a normal conversation with them—don't give anything away. We need to sort things out, but we must use our heads."

Louisa closed her eyes. The irony was that she had thought she was using her head when she married Henry. It had seemed the best idea. And yet, while they walked, one question kept repeating itself in her head. How could she have gotten every fundamental thing about her decision to marry him so hopelessly, utterly wrong?

Chapter Sixteen

Ashworth, 1894

Three hours later, Louisa sat in the great dining room with the duke, the duchess, and Charlie. Flowers spilled over the tops of silver vases on the vast mahogany table. Ancestral portraits looked down from the deep red walls, and the heavy velvet curtains that lined the great windows were closed against the darkness outside.

Louisa had chosen dark green silk. She wore a diamond necklace that the duchess, Helena, had given her the day she had become engaged—she didn't know whether she had chosen to wear the piece tonight out of guilt or out of some last-ditch desire to please. And yet what was alluring was the way Charlie had looked at both the necklace and her tonight.

She was having trouble managing her own odd thoughts.

"I think you should take Louisa to the village fair tomorrow, Charlie. She needs to familiarize herself with how things work." Helena had carried on a round of practical conversations since they had met for drinks in the library. For this, Louisa had been grateful. The woman did not appear to want to dissect Louisa's reasons for returning to Ashworth, and Louisa did not want to be dissected in any way at all.

She did not allow herself to bristle at the fact that her mother-in-law had referred to her in the third person. She had noticed Helena doing so since the engagement—it was as if she were a thing, something to be shuffled about, and she sensed Charlie's irritation at his mother's rudeness toward her. Now he caught her eye and raised his brow.

"I can take you to the fair, Louisa," he said, addressing her directly. "I'll introduce you to people. It's always a fun day."

Helena sat up a little taller in her seat and coughed.

"Splendid idea," Lord Aubrey said. He appeared to be oblivious to the subtle politics that were playing themselves out at the table. "You need to show Louisa how things are done."

"I think you are capable of making your own decisions," Charlie said, looking straight at her.

Louisa laid her fork on her plate. "You have a beautiful apartment in Paris."

"The third duchess decorated it," Lord Aubrey said. "She was madly creative—needed some sort of outlet, apparently."

"Every woman is entitled to an outlet," Louisa said. And smiled.

There was a silence.

"They are." Charlie's words hung in the air.

"Women need to keep themselves amused in some manner," Lord Aubrey muttered. "And why not by decorating and opening fairs."

"Louisa will become familiar with the routines of Ashworth soon enough," the duchess added. She raised her white napkin to her still-beautiful lips.

"I'm sure you can make your own decisions, Louisa," Charlie repeated.

Helena diverted the conversation toward the flower-arranging competition at the fair.

Once they had finished their meal—an elaborate affair of pheasant and heavy caramel puddings—the duchess finally addressed Louisa directly. Louisa couldn't help but catch Charlie's twinkling eye. "Louisa, your duties will be of a philanthropic nature. Everything else is taken care of on the estate."

Louisa sensed Charlie bristling. But she also felt that he had decided to bide his time with his parents. And suddenly, she knew that she and Charlie were stronger as a team than either of them was alone.

Once dinner was done, Louisa excused herself. She was exhausted.

She would return for round two in the morning.

Louisa dressed in a white shirt and camel-colored skirt for the fair.

The duchess wore white muslin and lace.

"We wear white for the fair, and take parasols. You must follow protocol where these things are concerned." The duchess did not go as far as to say that Louisa must look like one of them—her tone implied it well enough.

But Louisa was used to looking the part, used to looking as if she fit in, while feeling utterly different. She had made an art form of it when living with her mother.

It was just that she had hoped that she would not have to do such a thing here at Ashworth.

A half hour later, dressed in the white ensemble that her mother-in-law had insisted upon, she decided she would choose her battles with care when it came to Helena.

Louisa stood with the older woman on the driveway and frowned at the carriage in front of her. "Surely we can walk to the fair, ma'am?"

The duchess raised her beautiful chin and looked down at Louisa. And it was at that moment that Louisa saw what she had feared was the truth. There was nothing in the older woman's eyes that spoke of kindness. And she knew, right then, that she was dealing with coldness to the core. But how had Helena come to be this way? Had she, too, been a bride with high expectations who had been shuffled aside by the machinations of Ashworth?

Louisa shuddered and looked out at the picture-perfect park. The weather was perfect, and the entire situation, like so many marriages, could seem to be perfect—if one didn't tap at the shell with any force at all.

Helena made a business of adjusting her hat.

Louisa curbed her response. Were she to displease her mother-in-law entirely, she would only make things worse. Far worse, she suspected. Because she had come to think that Helena, like so many married women of her class, was simply part of an institution. Her marriage was who she was. She had lost any sense of individuality that she may have ever had. The woman was a warning of what she, Louisa, must not allow herself to become, but it was hard not to feel some empathy for the older woman.

The ride in the carriage was strained at first. Louisa was determined to carry on a conversation, and she began to receive something of a response once they approached the village green.

Charlie was at the door to the carriage as soon as they arrived at the fair, and he opened it before the footman could alight from his post. The morning air suited Charlie's complexion. Louisa felt herself break into a smile at the sight of him, and his own boyish smile lit up his handsome features.

The duchess was gathered up by a group of friends.

Charlie's mood was so different from when they had walked in the forest that Louisa had to adjust herself and adapt to it. When he took Louisa's arm, even his step was light. He greeted nearly everyone they passed with a smile and a pat on the back. Every now and then, he stopped to introduce Louisa to people and had a chat, taking care to say hello to children as well as adults.

He seemed to know everybody. Of course he did, he looked after all the tenant farms. But his manner was far more country squire than lord of the manor. There was nothing pretentious about him at all.

"Come and play quoits," he said after a while. He had a playful look upon his face.

"Very well," Louisa laughed.

They stopped at a wooden skittle stall. Then they watched while a group of villagers threw quoits and cheered each other on.

Charlie became involved in their game, and when it was finished, he handed Louisa a set.

"Ready, Louisa?" he asked, the challenge clear in his eyes.

"I am."

She threw her first round, doing rather well, settling four woven quoits onto the wooden poles. Charlie got five. After three rounds, they were evenly matched. He was in fine spirits at the coconut stall, then marched across to play roller balls, with Louisa rolling more balls into higher-scoring arches than Charlie.

"I think we are in need of tea," he announced after that. "I am quite happy to concede that you are a fine shot at the fair, Louisa, but I want to talk to you now." His tone had changed, but his voice was gentle.

He chose a table near the cricket scoreboard, under which countless county matches had no doubt been played on other, summery days. When the tea arrived in a delicate china pot, served by Jess, she seemed delighted to see them both.

"It is lovely to see you again, Louisa," she said, holding out a slim hand. She served them with a plate of scones and delicate watercress sandwiches.

"I have enjoyed a lively morning," Louisa said, taking the pot and pouring for herself and Charlie. "If you weren't working, I would love you to join us. It is good to see you again, Jess."

"Most generous of you, but I will be in terrible trouble with the duchess if I break the order of things," Jess said to Louisa, catching her eye.

The sense that she had found a kindred spirit in the older woman strengthened, and Louisa found herself wondering if Jess might be sympathetic to improving women's lot.

"Tell me something, Charlie," Louisa said, once Jess had gone to help at another table. A villager started a round of running races for the local children—girls scooted along the grass with the boys, hair flying, pinafores flapping as they ran. "Does Henry spend nearly all of his time in Paris?"

"He does," Charlie said, his voice sounding intimate now, as if they were not in a field full of people at all, but alone in a quiet room.

"I should like to go to London myself," Louisa said, still staring at the children. Another race had started. A small crowd watched.

"The London house is in Knightsbridge. I go there often myself for meetings in relation to the estates."

"I contacted Emmeline Pankhurst," she confided, all of a sudden.

"Good." His tone was low.

"I would like to go to one of her meetings in Russell Square."

"You need to do that," he said. His hand lay on the tablecloth, and she found herself looking at it.

And at that moment, Charlie did something she had not expected. For one tiny second, he flicked his own hand over and lay it on top of hers.

Louisa started, took in a sharp breath. As quickly as he had laid it there, Charlie drew his hand away, and Louisa turned back to the race. One of the girls slowed, right at the end, her eyes looking to the side, to the boy who ran slightly behind her. She let the boy win.

Louisa sensed Charlie noticing it too. She saw the slight shake of his head.

"Shall we enjoy the fair a little while longer, and then make arrangements to contact Mrs. Pankhurst and go up to London?" he said, his eyes still on the oval.

"Yes." Louisa smiled. "I would like that very much."

Two mornings later, Louisa sat next to Charlie in one of the family carriages for the journey to London. The previous day had flown. She couldn't stand being idle, so she had ridden out with Charlie while he worked. He had her horse ready for her early in the morning, and the day had passed in bliss. He had introduced her to the estate manager, explained the fields' systems to her, and shown her how the working farms were run. Clearly, he was willing and strong enough to work around his mother. And this gave Louisa a monumental sense of hope.

They had lunched at the estate manager's house, on cheese and thick slices of bread, and the two men had included her in all aspects of their conversation. Louisa felt that she was enjoying herself more than she had since Samuel had left, and that she had the same sense that she did when she was with him, of easy companionship and mutual respect.

It was exactly what she missed and exactly what she desired.

She felt drawn to Charlie. On a certain level she understood why—he was good, kind, and as interested in her as she was in him—but she had never had the feelings that were beginning to surface for any man before, so why did they have to be for the one man she could never have?

She had, of course, felt drawn to Henry before the wedding. But her feelings for Charlie were quite different, no matter how hard she tried to fight them. Louisa realized that in some ways, she had seen Henry as something of a novelty—he was a diversion from the other, earnest young men. The fact that he was entertaining had amused her. The fact that he had seemed unique in his outlook had drawn her in. But now, she knew that one thing had been missing in her relationship with Henry.

And that one thing gave vitality to her relationship with Charlie. That one thing made things exciting every single time she was with him. Passion. She had never felt it before. Now, she was certain that she was in love with Charlie. But she was also certain it was hopeless. She was married to Henry. There was nothing she could do.

Louisa gazed out the carriage window at the glorious Hampshire countryside, swathed in golden autumn leaves, replete with green fields and villages that looked as if they had not changed in centuries. The idea of outward perfection had started to bother her again. If only life could be simple, but it seemed it never was.

"Was he always so . . . taciturn about his role at the estate?" The conversation had reverted to Henry. A new charge had come into the confines of the carriage. An intensity, a synchronicity that only grew every time she was with Charlie.

Charlie's voice came, but Louisa didn't look at him. It was enough to listen. If she caught his eye she knew exactly what she would see mirrored back. "Henry's skills are not regular, are not what you would call manly, or traditional," he said.

"Was he an accomplished child?" Louisa asked. The carriage slowed as they entered a narrow lane. They passed a small church. The gravestones beside it were lopsided, ancient—beautiful in a strange sort of way. Louisa was reminded of the old churchyard near Jess's house. She averted her eyes to the road.

"If he had been allowed to develop his interests, he could have been accomplished," Charlie said.

"That's what I suspected."

"He was good at the sorts of things that my mother felt were useless—drawing, music, writing poetry. He used to write plays, until he was found out."

"Such a shame," Louisa said.

"He was sent away to school. He suffered there, as so many do. You see, there's no getting away from it here. There's no getting away from your birth."

The carriage went over a bridge. The sound of its wheels clattered on the wooden surface.

"He's not developing his talents now, though; he has squashed them in a different manner himself," Charlie went on, his voice quiet, intimate. "Montmartre is full of comedy, of burlesque, but this comedy has its roots in anger, anger at the status quo. It laughs at it. And that is all Henry is doing. He is, in the end, angry."

"He is angry," Louisa said. She sat up a little. Charlie was right. Montmartre relied on satire. Its weapon was, in fact, wit. The courtesan was a mockery of a lady. Montmartre was a frame of mind; it was anti-establishment, and there was nothing wrong with that. But it was its approach that bothered Louisa—performances in Montmartre were full of irreverence. And this had somehow become a magnet for crime, pimp-making, and prostitution. It seemed that once again, it was women who were losing out.

"But the point is, Henry's not doing anything productive with his feelings. He is angry, and he is wasting his life. He has not stood up for himself here at home. He avoids everything. He runs away, to his own great detriment," Charlie said.

Louisa was silent for a moment. Charlie was right. But one question bothered her. One question had to be asked. She looked out the window when she spoke. "And you?" she said. "Are you leading a fulfilling life?"

There was a silence.

"Yes, for now. Henry and I have come to an arrangement. Unspoken, but it works for us both. I have a wonderful life running the estate." He sounded intimately close now. "By rights, I should go into the church, or to India, as the second-born son. But at the moment I'm in exactly the right place, even though it's conventionally wrong."

And then he turned to her. "And I think you might be in exactly the same position."

She turned then, and looked at him. And he held her gaze for a while. The carriage rolled on toward London, its wheels keeping a steady beat below.

Charlie seemed to come to life in a different way in the city. He was full of surprises, and fun, and Louisa found she had never laughed so much in her life. On their third evening, she wanted to catch up with some people whom she had befriended while doing the season in London. He organized for them to go out for dinner together to a smart restaurant in Mayfair.

The table was full of easy conversation and laughter. After dinner, there was dancing at a club. Louisa found herself, naturally, in Charlie's arms. Everyone accepted that she would be here with her brother-in-law. Everyone knew that Henry Duval spent his time in Paris. But as the orchestra played Strauss and they danced around the room, utterly in sync with each other, Louisa became even more aware of one thing. She wished she had met Charlie first.

Dancing was not helping. When she looked up, somehow irresistibly drawn to doing so, her eyes met his, and she saw exactly what she feared and hoped to see in his eyes. He did not have to say anything at all. When he drew her in a little closer, she rested her head on his shoulder.

As they walked up the stairs to the London house afterward, a footman held the door open for them both, but as they went to their bedrooms, Louisa was hit with the unthinkable. Charlie would have to get married. Charlie would fall in love with someone else.

The footman, having inquired if there was anything they wanted, disappeared, and they were alone, quite alone, and it was late. Charlie stood across the hall from her, once they were at the top of the stairs. The expression in his eyes could not have been more naked.

"I should go to sleep," she whispered.

He took a step toward her, then stopped.

"What do you want?" he asked, his voice more intimate than she had thought possible in the world that she had lived in, so far.

"Sleep," she lied. "But I will dream." She added this, and looked down at the floor.

He leaned forward, ran a hand over her hair. And then he held her for a moment, dropped a kiss on the top of her head.

She took one last look at his eyes, which she knew that she would be able to read for the rest of her life, and moved away from him, avoiding that last look that would end one thing and start everything else that they both knew was impossible. She went alone to her room.

*

Louisa could contain neither her excitement nor her trepidation as she traveled in the Duvals' London carriage toward Mrs. Pankhurst's apartment in Bloomsbury the following morning. She tried to focus outwardly, taking in the goings-on outside the window of her carriage as a distraction from her own agitated thoughts. But Louisa couldn't help but contrast the streets of Bloomsbury with those of Montmartre, and she couldn't begin to contain her sense of excitement about what she saw in this delightfully bohemian part of London. A sense of avant-gardism was in the air, and the stylish women who walked on these sidewalks clearly cultivated artistic awareness in their dress.

Once the carriage entered Russell Square, Louisa's nervousness only increased at the sight of the well-established gardens that were overlooked by rows of handsome terrace houses. The driver pulled up at number eight.

It was difficult not to feel intimidated as he held the door open. Louisa found herself suddenly worried that Mrs. Pankhurst might know a little of Henry, that she might think Louisa's choice of a husband was ridiculous. After all, Louisa's governess had also impressed upon her that Mrs. Pankhurst had been a woman who, it seemed, would only give herself to an important man.

After the young Emmeline Goulden's return from Paris, where she had attended finishing school, she had met Richard Pankhurst—a lawyer, a committed socialist, and a strong advocate of women's suffrage. He had drafted the married women's property bill in 1870, and the Pankhursts' home was a center for gatherings of the Fabian Society as well as the Women's Franchise League. Louisa couldn't help but wonder what Mrs. Pankhurst would make of Louisa's choice.

But as she was led into the front hallway, Louisa felt the tightness in her upper back release a little when Mrs. Pankhurst appeared, telling her servant kindly that she wanted to take Mrs. Duval, as she called Louisa, into the drawing room herself. Louisa was also immediately drawn to the tall, slender woman, with her unusually beautiful deep blue eyes and her raven-black hair.

Once they were seated and had exchanged brief formalities, Louisa decided to listen. She was not here to talk.

"We hope to run conferences all over England under the auspices of the Women's Franchise League," Mrs. Pankhurst said. "Our aim is simple, Mrs. Duval. We want to secure the vote for women in local elections all over the country. We want to arrange for speakers to visit each county. I feel that this is the ideal manner in which to inspire local women. I think there is interest, but women in villages may not be aware of our movement here in London. We need to create awareness, open up minds to thought. You would be in an ideal position to help. If you could gather up enthusiasm, then I can send speakers out to talk."

Mrs. Pankhurst's gaze was so direct that Louisa believed she would be convinced of the older woman's convictions no matter what she had to say.

"There is no rational reason that women should be denied a say in who makes the laws. We are adult humans just the same as men. Why on earth should we accept being treated as anything less? By accepting that we are not allowed to vote, we are condoning the attitude that we are not equal to men. But I don't think women think this way. There are two problems: the manner in which we are raised, and the manner in which we are, or, to put it bluntly, are not educated. Everyone else must come before us women—the idea is ingrained in us from when we are too young to question it. Our needs, as women, are to come last. We are not encouraged to speak up, and when we do, we tend to apologize for ourselves."

Mrs. Pankhurst placed her elegant hands in her lap and leaned forward in her chair.

"If we keep our message simple, we can hope to inspire other women to think in a different way. Once women obtain the vote and realize they are worthy of having a say in who runs our country, interest will develop in such matters as funding toward changing our education, not to mention our rights as workers. You will know about the terrible conditions we suffer at present." Mrs. Pankhurst spoke in a clear, even voice.

Louisa simply wanted the woman to go on, to listen to her speaking words of common sense. The sorts of words that she had missed since her governess had been sacked by her mother, who had attempted to raise Louisa in exactly the manner that Mrs. Pankhurst was questioning. "Tell me what I can do," Louisa said. "At a local level, I am determined to rally women together."

Mrs. Pankhurst paused before she spoke. "I am fortunate that my husband is not only supportive, but an advocate of women's rights," she said.

Louisa turned and gazed out at Russell Square. The pressure to marry, the sense that she would be isolated, alone, if she did not, had influenced her more than she cared to admit. Now, married or not, she was determined to be true to her feelings about all women.

"I support your ideas for conferences around the country," she said. And stopped. Henry's position was complicated. He was in Paris, but he had made his views quite clear. But, then, he was not a political person. He was a person who did not, it seemed, want politics to interfere with his own freedom or his family. As long as he conducted his life away from them, he seemed to think he was doing no harm. But then, he was, of course, a man. The rules were completely different for him. So, it all came back to that.

Mrs. Pankhurst remained quiet. Clearly, she was waiting for Louisa to say more.

When Louisa spoke, her words came out in a rush. "I have been in Paris, in Montmartre with my husband, and what I saw there cemented my views about women's rights. Montmartre is supposed to be about liberation, or that is what I had been led to believe. And I suppose it is, in a way, but it seems to be about liberation—excuse me if I am shocking you—of men's flesh, while women are more repressed than ever. They are simply on display. The role of the courtesan, the prostitute, is rife. Women are turning to the streets in droves in desperation in Montmartre. The few who make it to the top turn pleasing men into an art form—they make a business out of selling themselves. And yet, the courtesan is the most powerful trendsetter in Paris."

Louisa clasped her hands together in her lap. What she was about to say next was not something she would care to admit to a man, but here, with Mrs. Pankhurst, it was exactly what needed to be said. "It is as if we have some sort of built-in need to please, as women. But why don't we ever consider taking care of ourselves?"

Mrs. Pankhurst poured tea. She watched Louisa.

Suddenly, Louisa wanted to talk. If she was going to work with Mrs. Pankhurst, perhaps, she needed to be frank. There was something about the older woman—intelligence, understanding, wit—that inspired confidence. Something Louisa had never felt with her own mother.

"I confess," she said, not stopping the words as they came out, "Paris affected me on a personal level. My husband appears to have formed an . . . intimate relationship with a courtesan."

Mrs. Pankhurst handed Louisa a teacup, still watching her. But she did not look shocked. "I went to school in Paris," she said. "I am aware of the situation there. I was fortunate, in that the school I attended had a director who believed that women's education should be quite as thorough as the education of boys. We studied chemistry and bookkeeping. We were also taught to speak up." She set her teacup down. "Paris had a somewhat different effect on me, Mrs. Duval. I learned to wear my hair and clothes like a Parisian, and I learned to value myself."

Louisa almost chuckled. How different had their experiences been in Paris, then! "I admit, even in my case, there is more to the situation than appears at first glance. You see, it is as if Henry values this particular courtesan for more than her attributes as a woman of the night. I have seen them together, only briefly, but they seemed... connected somehow. And this, in turn, caused me to see the courtesan more objectively, as a real person, if you will forgive me, please. Imagine if Marthe de Florian had been educated, instead of not? Because I sense that she is clever."

"Yes. So if she had been fortunate to receive my education, rather than her lack thereof... you see, this is where politics enters the fray, Louisa. This is where we need the vote. Not allowing us to vote, to have equal educational rights to men, is akin to treating us like beasts who are only valued for our bodies, not our minds. The demimondaine is an elegant incarnation of this idea. I grant you she is powerful, but look at how she has had to abase herself to gain it. The fact that she is a strong, independent woman is a wonderful thing, but she has gained this by giving her body to countless men."

How perfectly the woman put it. Louisa looked out the window again. Frustration at Henry hit her again. Couldn't he see that he was condoning something destructive?

Her carriage had pulled up in the street. The Ashworth coat of arms on the carriage door looked beautiful and, at the same time, commanding. Society was full of structures that controlled women. They were going to be nigh on impossible to break down. But somehow, talking to Mrs. Pankhurst gave one hope. Hope that if enough women felt the same way, there could be an agency for change.

Spreading the word was of utmost importance. Louisa would get straight to work.

Her time here had flown. "Please, write to me and tell me how I can become involved."

Mrs. Pankhurst stood up, her wine-colored dress falling elegantly to the floor. "I will synthesize my ideas and write to you. You will need a meeting place, and a method of attracting women to our cause. You will also need some allies. You will meet great opposition, I suspect, Mrs. Duval."

"I am becoming more used to opposition than ever before, now I am married." Louisa gathered her coat and pulled it on herself.

"We are in the face of opposition, constantly. It is meant to make us weak, but for many of us, opposition does the reverse. Opposition only gives us strength." She reached out a hand, took Louisa's, and held it for a moment.

Louisa, after a sudden thought, asked Mrs. Pankhurst to address her correspondence to Jess.

"Please, call me Emmeline," the older woman said, suddenly. She caught Louisa's eye then, and smiled at her. If Louisa had shared a common interest before this meeting with Mrs. Pankhurst, she now shared a common spark. "We stand united, but to no attention here."

Louisa held the older woman's gaze for a moment, before turning and moving out to her carriage. Perhaps opposition to fairness for women was only a threat if one viewed it as such.

Chapter Seventeen

Paris, 2015

Sarah stood by the window in Isabelle de Florian's old bedroom. Sarah's bedroom for a time. Late-afternoon sunlight flooded the old room and Sarah remained lost in her thoughts. Henry's letter had done two things. It had helped her see Marthe as a real person, but at the same time it had caused her confusion. Because Sarah knew she hadn't gotten to the bottom of any of it, not yet. She must reserve judgment about the past for now, and she must keep on searching, but she had to work out where to look for the answers she needed.

Laurent appeared in the doorway.

"Would you like to eat in tonight?" he asked. He still held a paintbrush in his hand.

Sarah looked up at him. If anything, she would say that he seemed nervous. She felt her own insides tense.

"I'd love to."

"Would you like to keep me company while I cook?" he asked.

She couldn't brush away the feeling that he seemed a little shy.

"Sure. I'm happy to help." She took a few steps toward the doorway. Movement seemed like a good idea.

Laurent stood aside for her to go through first. She started to thank him, then stopped talking and moving all at once. Now she was feeling shy herself. It was as if there was an allure surrounding him. If she walked close to him, she would be caught in whatever it was. Which was crazy, silly. What was wrong with her?

She forced herself to step forward. Paris must be getting to her. Sarah focused on where she was going instead.

But she found herself, almost with surprise, in Laurent's bedroom, which hardly was the thing to help. She passed the grand four-poster bed. For one absurd moment, she felt a compulsion to make a ridiculous joke. About Marthe. She took in a deep breath. Laurent was right behind her. She was acutely aware how close. Halfway across the room he caught up. It was as if they were doing some odd sort of dance.

They reached the next door together. "After you," he said.

Sarah nodded and frowned.

It wasn't until they were in the modern kitchen that she felt the muscles in her shoulders loosen up. Laurent busied himself opening a bottle of wine and offered Sarah a glass.

It was all she could do not to gulp the entire contents in one frantic swig.

Sarah focused on what Laurent was doing. He moved around the kitchen, pulling ingredients out of cupboards. By the time Sarah had found a perch on a bar stool and had attempted and failed to calm herself with a few sips of delicious wine, he was busy forming gnocchi with great care at the kitchen counter. Sarah was enchanted, for some reason, by the way he molded the small morsels into picture-perfect shapes with his hands. Artistic hands, she thought. The results of his efforts looked worthy of a photo in a magazine—*Vogue Entertaining and Travel*, perhaps?

"Can I do something?" she asked, wincing when she heard how husky her voice sounded.

"Do you feel like making a salad?" he said, sounding intimate himself. The awkwardness she had noticed in him earlier had flown away now. She sensed amusement in his eyes as he looked up from his work.

"Sure." Moving away from him to the fridge seemed a very good plan. Although sensible was not what Sarah felt. She wondered if Paris had turned her crazy. Steven and her life in Boston felt more and more like remnants from the distant past.

Even Louisa seemed closer than Boston now. Sarah stared at the contents of the fridge. She picked up a strand of small, ruby tomatoes, their green tops intertwined with a slender stem. Several fat bocconcini rounds sat ready in a clear plastic tub next to a bunch of vibrant basil. Sarah clutched at these as if they were the only normal things in the house.

"Did you go food shopping today?" she asked, holding up the artisanal mozzarella to make sure he was happy for her to use it. It was an expensive ingredient, and not one that she would assume was there for her.

"Go ahead, use it," he said. "Yes. I did go to the Marché Anvers today." He dipped the shapes into boiling salted water. "I haven't been to the markets for a while," he added, and there was something whimsical in his tone.

"No?"

"I haven't cooked in ages either," he said. "I'm enjoying doing this right now."

"That's good." Once Sarah had made her tomato salad, she moved a little closer to him, watching over his shoulder while he pulled the gnocchi out of the boiling water, popping them into hot olive oil, rendering them crisp and delicately brown on the outside, then tossing spinach, pine nuts, and broad beans through the morsels.

"If you like cooking, then cook," she said, and he made a tiny sound. She knew, by instinct, that he agreed with her.

Loic and Cat's smart designer plates were the perfect backdrop for his final production, over which he grated Parmesan cheese and sprinkled chopped green basil. The artistically presented platter was worthy of a perfect still life.

"Have you decided what your next step will be?" he asked, as they sat down at the table. "Would you like to help yourself?" He handed her the large plate.

"Thank you." Sarah realized she was starving. It seemed like an age since the ham and cheese baguette she had eaten for lunch.

"I was thinking something this afternoon," he said.

Sarah tilted her head to one side.

"It's almost as if you have to find beauty again in your life, Sarah. After everything you've been through. And you know what?"

"What?" She looked up at him, and it was as if her eyes wanted to dance. "Tell me," she said.

"This reminds me of Botticelli," he said, and his words were very soft. "Sorry, I can't help but say it."

"What?" she said. "Why?"

But it was as if they were sharing some intimate joke now. The awkwardness turned to tension had turned to fun.

"Because," he said, leaning forward in his seat and holding his fork in the air, "like Venus, I think you've been covering yourself up."

"What?" Sarah was laughing now. "Laurent!"

"No." He had a real sparkle in his eye. "Listen. I mean it in the nicest possible way."

Sarah had to stop herself from giggling.

"I know I'm French, but..."

"Stop!" But she couldn't hold back her mirth.

Laurent blended his own amusement with sincerity and leaned forward as he spoke. "No. Listen. In the painting, the wind caresses Venus and showers her with roses, giving beauty back to her life. She has been shy until now, not really fulfilled. I sense that Paris is doing exactly that for you, Sarah. And this is good. It's a good thing. Let the city's beauty wake you up. I think that you're doing a good job of bringing yourself back to life too. Just coming here, getting away, was a positive step to take. It was a good thing to do."

Laurent held her gaze. "It's funny," he said. "Having gone out for dinner with Loic, and Cat, and...you. Seeing Cat and Loic together made me wonder what the hell I'm up to. I don't know what I've been doing. You weren't alone in being lost, Sarah. It's just that you need to find something new."

He put down his fork for a moment.

Now, Sarah knew it was she who felt shy. She wasn't sure whether she was glad of his next question or not, when it came. In some ways, she had to admit that she didn't want him to change tack.

"What's your next plan with your . . . investigations?" he asked.

Sarah reined her thoughts back to Louisa. "I need to tell Loic and Cat about the letter."

"True, but after that?"

She took the last bite of her gnocchi and wondered if it were the most delicious meal she had ever had. "It's getting more complex, and that only makes any possible answer more elusive still. Perhaps it's nothing. Perhaps there is no answer. Perhaps only Louisa, Henry, and Marthe will ever know what happened that night."

"You have to promise me that you're going to follow this through, though."

"I've done just about everything I can."

"In Paris," he said.

She frowned.

"Don't you see?" Laurent tapped his plate with his fork. "You have to go to Ashworth. They'll have family archives. It's the next step. You know that, don't you?"

But Sarah shook her head. "I'm hardly going to be welcome back at their family estate. Louisa's memory was most likely pushed under the Aubusson carpets faster than you could say her name. The way my father told it, they wanted nothing to do with the Wests after Louisa's 'suicide.' The Duvals were paranoid about any media exposure. I'm sure they expressed sympathy, but they weren't going to go any further than that."

"There's nothing stopping you from giving them a call."

"You make it sound so simple!"

"Yup. I don't see why it can't be that way." He leaned forward. "You have the opportunity to go to Ashworth right now. You might not have the chance again. My sense is that if you don't go now, you'll never do it. You said the family hushed it up. I say that could mean there was something to hush."

Sarah looked across at him. And she had the odd thought that it seemed as if he knew what she really wanted, or needed, with more intensity than she was able to feel herself.

But why?

"You really think I could just contact the Duval family and go to see them?"

"Yes."

"Really?"

"Why not?"

Sarah sat back. She didn't know why the idea of going to Ashworth seemed so hard. Did she fear that this noble family would look down on her? But Laurent was right, they were the people she needed to confront.

She sighed. "You know," she said, "in some ways, they owe us an explanation. They must have records of it. You're right."

Laurent held out his wineglass, and Sarah clinked hers with his right back.

Chapter Eighteen

London, 1894

Louisa sat bolt upright in bed. She had been half-awake, ideas floating about in her head like dreamy phantoms. She knew she should go to sleep, but she couldn't help forming plans about how to galvanize the local women at Ashworth. At the same time, strange worries nagged at her. Her situation was precarious. Her relationship with Henry had all but broken down in Paris. Henry's lack of support, his lack of any recognition for her as a person, had overwhelmed her. It was only natural that she would throw herself into her passion for women's rights—goodness knew she needed something to sustain her. And goodness knew, she wanted so much to give something to society. But now, in the cold, dim hours, doubts struck the same repetitive notes.

What if the duchess and Henry were to find out about her plans to form a branch of the Women's Franchise League? The fact that her husband and his mother loomed together as some indomitable force was hardly reassuring. They had caused her to feel less welcome in their family than a stray cat. Unless she fit in with them, she was going to be driven out into the cold. If Charlie were not around, quite frankly, she did not know what she would do. She lit the oil lamp by her bed. A clattering had begun downstairs.

Louisa reached for her silk dressing gown and edged her feet over the side of the bed. Her heart hammered. Louisa knew the noises that were coming from below; she had become familiar with the sounds in Paris.

Henry.

A few moments later, Louisa heard him climb the grand staircase. He was coming toward her room.

"Louisa," he said, from right outside her bedroom door.

The last thing she wanted was for Charlie or the servants to hear them having a row.

But what she also wanted more than anything was for Charlie to appear and get rid of Henry.

"Open the door, for God's sake," Henry said. "I'm not going to wake the rest of the house."

Quietly, she picked up her lamp and went to unlock the door.

"My mother told me that you were here," he whispered. "I trust you have come up to shop."

"You know I'm not here to shop," Louisa said. "You know I take interest in other things."

He looked at her.

Instinctively, she pushed the door toward him.

He moved closer again, put his foot in the door. And suddenly, bitter thoughts swirled in her head. He was here out of duty. He had come to see her in order to pay lip service to the role he was supposed to play. The fact that he wanted to be an actor was ironic. He could act one part with her, another with Marthe, another with his parents, another with all the houseguests and the friends he must have in Montmartre. But where was the true Henry? Louisa looked at him and thought that he was nowhere to be found. And if he ever was, he was not going to be revealed to Louisa. It would be Marthe who would see the real person.

And for now, what Louisa wished was that he would simply be honest. If only he would stand up to his parents, tell them he did not want the title, and allow Charlie to have it. Then Charlie could do what he was clearly born to do. Henry would be free to go to Paris. Act on the stage.

But life, like the stage, was not as simple as that.

Louisa sighed.

Henry was watching her. Half-bored, half-intent.

She didn't know which was worse—her husband looking at her as if she were a piece of prey, or the air of boredom with which he regarded her. One thing was clear. He didn't care a jot about her. And most likely, he never would.

"I am tired," she said. Her voice was strained, a collapsed version of itself. She must gather herself together. She never used to be prone to moods. "The hour, Henry."

"May I remind you of your duty," Henry whispered. "I have come all the way to London, because you are here. You will have to let me in, Louisa. If not tonight, then sometime. We both have expectations placed upon us. We have no choice but to fulfill them. I will try to make things as easy as I can for you."

Louisa closed her eyes. In Paris, she had latched onto any slight consideration he might show toward her. Now, she knew better. There was no warmth in his feelings toward her.

"I thank you," she said. "But I am sleepy now. I also," she added, "understand what you say."

Henry nodded. With a slight hop in his gait, he turned around and made his way back down the hallway.

Louisa closed the door. And leaned against it, sliding her body down against the hard wooden frame. And closed her eyes. And thought, not of Henry, but of Charlie.

After a few weeks back at Ashworth, things became at once clearer and far more complex. Snow lay on the vast lawns the morning after the Duval family doctor had been to visit Louisa in her private rooms; white flakes fell on the raked driveway, and freezing air blew in smoky tendrils from her cold lips as she ran in the only direction that she wanted to go. She rushed, in the early-morning stillness, when she knew no one else would be awake, right toward the stables. Because if she did not see Charlie, if she did not tell him, she did not know what on earth she would do.

"Charlie." She stopped, almost skidding on the ice in the courtyard.

He was already on his horse, but he swung the strong animal about and dismounted. She could tell instantly that he understood the urgency in her voice.

"What is it?" He took a step toward her and reached out, as if to touch her cheek, but then pulled back again, his eyes darting about the stables.

He glanced around again. "You need to talk. We need to go somewhere private. I know where to take you."

In one instant, he was down on one knee, making a step with his hands so that she could climb onto the horse. And then she was in the saddle, in front of him. His arms were around her waist. She almost closed her eyes with the sense of his closeness, but he nudged the horse on. The animal was so sensitive to Charlie's touch that it took off fast onto the wide path that led into the woods.

Gray, skeletal trees sat in silence on either side of the empty track. The air was still and snow covered much of the forest floor.

When Charlie pulled up at Jess's cottage, Louisa was breathing in great, hard gulps. She turned slightly toward Charlie and he reached out, ran his hand across her temple, down over her cheek, his eyes burning into hers. He jumped off the horse, but still he didn't speak. He handed Louisa down. She landed right next to him, looking up at his face. Not wanting to move.

He took her hand. With his other hand, he held his horse's reins. "Jess has a stable behind the house," he said, his voice resonating through the silent, still morning. "We'll leave the horse there. There's food, warmth for him. I wouldn't leave a squirrel out in this cold."

"I know you wouldn't," Louisa said.

He held her hand a little tighter. "Once we're inside I want you to promise to talk to me."

Jess was in her kitchen. A warm tray of freshly baked scones sat on the bench. Charlie had simply entered through the back door and marched straight into the warm room, having waved at Jess through the window as he passed with the horse. Jess turned, seeing the expression on Louisa's face, and in an instant, Louisa sensed that the older woman had made a quick decision.

"I'm going across to the village now," she said.

Charlie started to protest, but Jess waved him away. She gathered her cloak. "It is a five-minute walk, Charlie. The road has been cleared this morning."

Louisa's hands shook but she smiled. Thank goodness for Jess, for Charlie. It was as if the time spent with them, particularly here in the warmth of Jess's cottage, was her real life, even though the opposite was true.

Charlie rubbed his hands together. "Louisa, come and stand by the oven. And Jess, promise me you'll visit with someone."

"I have errands to run. And yes, there are always women who are keen for a cup of tea." Jess smiled. Her intelligent eyes passed from Charlie to Louisa. She slipped out into the wintery silence.

"You should eat something," Charlie said, reaching into a cupboard, pulling out a plate, then finding a knife in one of Jess's wooden drawers. He buttered a scone, put a dab of jam next to it on the plate, handed it to Louisa.

She dipped the knife into the strawberry jam, running the preserves over the warm scone.

"Have some tea." He moved past her to the range, and as he did so, his arm brushed hers. She resisted the impulse to lean her head on his shoulder as he passed.

Charlie poured two mugs of hot tea and handed her one in silence.

"Charlie," she whispered. The tea was strong and hot and good and the sweetness of the scone fortified her.

He was next to her in the flash of a second, standing close, his hand under her chin. "You don't have to tell me. I know. When is the baby due?"

"June," she said.

"I see."

The full stop at the end of his word seemed to resonate through the empty cottage. And suddenly, Louisa felt cold again. She put her tea on the bench and turned away from him.

"You must marry," Louisa whispered, even though she could hardly contain her impulses as she said the words. It was the hardest thing to say, and yet it was the thing that must be said. As she spoke, every part of her wanted to reach up, to put her arms around his neck, to nestle in and feel safe and secure and yet unutterably alive. But she would never hold him back. She could not do that.

Charlie pulled her close to his chest. He had taken off his great-coat, and it hung on a chair. If Louisa were to close her eyes, she could almost imagine that they were some simple couple living right here with scones on the table, a warm pot of tea, and a child on the way.

"You must know I have no desire to marry anyone else," he said. He lifted her chin up, his face so close to hers that she felt as if they were breathing the same breath, as if they were more as one than she had ever imagined possible. She closed her eyes.

"I am past hope," she whispered.

"What if we could persuade Henry to give you a divorce? You could marry me, and to hell with my parents," Charlie said. "And you know, Louisa, the thing is, they need me. They need me to run the estate. I would love your child as if it were mine. You know that."

He rested his forehead against her own for a moment. It was as if the thing that had always hovered between them—unsaid, unspoken, unreal—was insisting on being heard. But its kind, loving warmth had its own corollary sin—impossibility.

Louisa shook her head. Determination of a practical sort kicked in, and when she spoke, it was as if she were propelled by something outside of herself. She certainly did not agree with what she was saying. But she did feel that she had no choice but to speak. "Your parents would never accept us. I cannot bear to think of you losing your work, the work that you love, were they to cast you out, or, more likely, were Henry to send you away. Because he could. I couldn't bear to see you separated from Ashworth."

"None of them can run the estate without me. And you, you are just what this whole area needs. You would further the education of our local women, usher them into life in the new century. It is happening in London; you are right. I can run the farm, I can modernize and keep Ashworth going—and God knows that is going to be a risky prospect. I can keep jobs for our tenants, help support their families, and you, you can make a real difference. You could work with the schools, run conferences. You have so much potential…"

"Henry would stifle all of this," she murmured.

"No," Charlie growled. "I have never been scared of him. We would face him together, and he couldn't stop us."

Louisa took a tiny step back, but she was still in the circle of his arms. She gazed into his face. "I love you," she whispered.

He leaned down then, and just before his lips touched hers, he whispered exactly what she wanted to hear, what she knew even if he had never said it in his life, back at her. "We'll work it out," he said. "We'll get there."

Louisa reached up while he kissed her, and for a moment, she forgot that there was any need to think at all.

Chapter Nineteen

Ashworth, 2015

Sarah paid the taxi driver and stood at the entrance to Ashworth. Even though she had seen photographs of the palace, even though she had done her research, nothing had prepared her for what was in front of her right now. It was astonishing to think that her ancestor, a girl from Boston, had lived in such a place.

Sarah's communication with the Duval family had been odd—an email, a brief, uncomfortable phone call. The duchess, Olivia, was polite and formal, but not, Sarah suspected, keen. She sensed that an invitation had been given out of a built-in politeness.

"That old story," the duchess had half laughed after Sarah had explained herself with great hesitation from a written script. "I don't know the particulars. Apparently she jumped out of a window. Depression. Terribly sad."

Sarah had stumbled through the rest of the call.

Now, she stood in front of the palace. Rows of symmetrical grand windows overlooked the immaculate park. Everything spoke of order, of success, perhaps, of intimidation. There had not been an offer to pick her up at the train station. There had been a vague instruction to take a cab.

Sarah dragged her suitcase up the wide flight of steps that led to the front door. On one side of it, there was a large brass doorbell. She pressed it, and heard a great ringing throughout the vast house. A few moments passed. Nothing. Then, as she was about to press it a second time, footsteps sounded on hard floors.

The door opened. And there stood Lord Jeremy—Sarah had seen pictures of him on the official palace website. He was the eldest of the current duke and duchess's three children. She had done her homework. He was around the same age as Sarah.

"Hello," he said. Jeremy's dark hair flopped over to one side of his face, and he ran a hand through it as he spoke, his brown eyes appraising her, pleasantly enough. He did not look particularly affected to see her. If Sarah had to sum him up after one glance, she would say he looked a mild type of man.

Sarah introduced herself and held out a hand. He shook it; his handshake was limp. She stood there awkwardly for a moment.

"My parents had to go out for the afternoon," he said, holding the front door open. "They had forgotten that they had plans."

"You ended up on long-lost-relative duty." Sarah smiled.

As if on cue, a man with gray hair and a tweed suit appeared and took the suitcase.

"Empress of India room, Burrell," Jeremy said. "We still keep a butler," he went on, as if this were some sort of normal conversation that anyone would have. "But these days, there are only fourteen staff in the house. Much of it is closed up. We used to have hundreds of staff living here. In your ancestor's day."

Sarah took in the vast entrance hall, with its endless black-and-white tiles. A hallway led to the left, and to the right, she saw a glimpse of a magnificent room overlooked by high balconies with elaborate balustrades. It seemed to be under the great tower that she had admired from the taxi.

Jeremy was moving toward the vast space. "Come into the salon," he said.

An elaborate wooden staircase wound its way down into the enormous room. Two large wolfhounds lay in front of a fireplace, and paintings of hunting scenes lined the walls.

"This is a spectacular room," Sarah said. "It's very kind of you to have me here."

Jeremy pulled on an old-fashioned bellpull. "I expect you'd like tea?"

A woman appeared, wearing an A-line skirt, sensible shoes. Jeremy ordered tea, along with cake. He asked Sarah to sit down.

She perched on an enormous velvet sofa and tried her best not to gape. She had seen great wealth in her line of work before, of course she had. But this was something else.

"Your ancestor's story was very sad. We were surprised, to be honest, that you'd want to come back to Ashworth."

Sarah had decided to play the part of the interested descendant, one who was just hoping to see where her great-great-aunt had lived. The last thing she wanted to do was get off on the wrong foot. "I was curious about her time in England. I was in Paris, so—"

"Her suicide was tragic." He sounded firm.

Sarah bit back obvious questions while the middle-aged woman in sensible shoes returned with a trolley. She poured tea and gave each of them a thin slice of sultana cake. It was buttered, and the butter layer was thin too.

Sarah was glad for the interruption. She tried to think how to play this.

"Must have been jolly hard for all those American girls, coming to a new country, settling in. Impossible to imagine, really."

"I'm sure they were made to feel welcome." She stirred her tea.

"Of course."

"And Louisa had the most beautiful place to live, here."

"She did."

Sarah put down her teacup. She was going to have to think. If the famous British stiff upper lip was anything to go by, she could be having endless monosyllabic conversations and then it would be time to go home.

Jeremy stood up suddenly. Clearly tea was at an end. "You'll want to go up and rest. We meet in the library at eight for drinks. It will just be mother, father, myself, and you. No need for formal dress."

"Oh, well, that's good." Suddenly, she was aware of her leather jacket. She had considered not wearing it, and then, for some odd reason had put it on at the last minute.

"Oh, and one thing," Jeremy said. "Father likes to keep things on time. He gets upset if people are running late."

Sarah suppressed a shudder as they moved out of the salon. This did not bode well as far as the duke was concerned, but she would not allow herself to be swayed by irrational comparisons to her ex-husband.

Jeremy moved from the hallway into the first room on their right. This was one of the most enchanting spaces Sarah had seen. She felt the tension that had gathered in her body dissipate. Bookshelves lined the room. Wooden ladders were arranged around the walls at perfectly even spaces, as if the distances had been measured. And Sarah suddenly wondered how much reading went on in here, if the ladders were only placed for effect. A newspaper—today's, a tabloid—lay on a coffee table between two high-backed deep sofas. Plush cushions were scattered over these. A tall fireplace. Several windows overlooked the park.

"Heaven," Sarah breathed.

"Beyond this is the dining room, then the breakfast room, and a sitting room. You can come and sit in any of these while you're here. I'll show you up to your own room now."

"Thank you. It's very kind of you. It will be good to talk to your parents." She was determined not to feel awkward and utterly out of place.

Jeremy moved back into the salon, stopping at the foot of the great wooden staircase. "I'm not sure that…anyway." He shook his head and moved up the stairs.

Sarah rested her hand on the polished wood banister. She was going to have to come up with a plan, and fast.

The late-afternoon sun beamed down through the huge stained-glass window on the landing above them. The family crest decorated the glass—two stags and a shield with a Latin inscription.

"Never give up," Jeremy said. "The family motto."

"I like it." Sarah smiled. Something in that restored a little buoyancy to her flagging spirits.

He led her up the stairs and she followed him, half taking every detail in, half thinking up a strategy in her head.

Sarah was precisely on time for drinks. She had chosen one of her little black dresses, one that she loved to wear under that leather jacket, but tonight, she had decided to skip that, even though it was a bit chilly in the palace. Her hair was behaving, at least, swinging at its glossy black best.

Sarah glanced at the portraits that lined walls above the beautifully carved staircase as she went down to the library. The women were consistently beautiful, and every one of the men seemed to have strong dark features. She stopped and looked at the portrait of Henry Duval. Henry looked as if he were brooding.

Sarah moved on.

The sound of voices rang out into the hallway from the library. Laughter, short comments. Everything came in short bursts.

Sarah took in a breath and went inside. The room was lit with soft lamps that cast an intimacy while sending shadows onto the myriad books.

Lady Olivia sat on one of the two dark sofas. Her hair was bottle blond and pulled back into a chignon. Her skin was tanned, either by a lotion or a lamp. Sarah had to stop herself from smiling at this.

The duke, Theodore, seemed to be watching Sarah just as she was taking in everything in sight. His face was not what Sarah would describe as friendly. She detected a narrow calculation in his eyes.

Jeremy took a step forward from where he and his father stood in front of the mantelpiece.

"Father, Mother, this is Sarah West."

Sarah moved forward and extended her hand.

After Sarah had consumed a sherry, which was the only thing offered, and eaten a few olives along with some plain rice crackers and French onion dip, Olivia announced that it was time to go in for dinner.

Sarah checked her watch. Half past eight, on the dot.

The duke and Jeremy began a conversation about farm management, and Sarah found herself next to the duchess as they made their way down the wide hallway, past elegant side tables scattered with objects that Sarah knew must all have their own stories to tell.

Portraits lined the walls in the dining room. Charles II overlooked the head of the vast mahogany table. The table was laid at one end for four, with porcelain plates and crystal glasses.

The duke poured for them from a decanter of red wine, and Sarah reminded herself that she must keep her head were she to have any hope of steering the conversation.

After a few minutes, it became clear that the duke was not going to let down his guard. There was a round of polite chat with the duchess in which questions were asked about Sarah's life in Boston, her family, who they were, whom she knew, and where she lived. There was also an attempt to make a connection between the people the duchess knew in Boston, and possibly the entire United States, with Sarah's acquaintances and family back home.

The duke did not address her at all.

Sarah regarded him over her roast beef and decided to make the most of a pause in the duchess's conversation.

"I am interested in my ancestor's life here," she said, looking directly at the older man. "I have just come from Paris." And waited.

The duke put down his fork. "You know, I think all I can say about Louisa West is one thing, Sarah: your ancestor was not a very good choice for Henry."

Sarah took in a sharp breath. "I do know that my ancestor was interested in women's causes." Sarah threw that idea out softly. "That may have been difficult for the family."

"The family has always held liberal views about women." The duke brought his white linen napkin up to his mouth. "But there's no going around the facts. Louisa was depressed. She killed herself. It is something the family deeply regrets. But she was unstable. That is quite well known, Sarah."

Sarah glanced at the duchess. She appeared to have zoned out of the conversation entirely.

"Louisa not only had this strong interest in women's rights, but by all accounts, from my side of the family, she was a happy, intelligent young woman who was not given to bouts of depression," Sarah said. She knew she was pushing things; knew, even, that she was possibly extending the boundaries of her own knowledge, but something told her that the veneer needed to be broken. If she didn't press harder, she would be shut out of the truth for good.

The duke seemed to be watching her, and for a ridiculous moment, Sarah had the idea that she had met her match.

"Sarah, you do know that Louisa had a baby. She did not connect with her son. I don't want to spell out the idea of postnatal depression. I'm sure I don't have to in this day and age."

Sarah felt as if she had been hit in the chest. Why on earth did she not know of a baby? The duke had thrown her, but she kept her chin up.

"Louisa went to Paris, ran away from her responsibilities here, and killed herself at a party. As I said, our family took a sympathetic tone, but one has to admit—"

"Father," Jeremy interjected.

But the duke waved Jeremy away. "Yes, Jeremy, we know that Henry was hardly the ideal husband, off in Paris for much of the time." His tone was that of dismissal toward his son, and Jeremy looked back down.

Sarah was going to have to ensure that the duke did not use such a strategy on her. But she also knew that she must not upset the duke too much if she wanted to be able to see out her visit. She would have to bide her time.

Dessert appeared. Sarah's half-eaten main course was whisked away without question. She looked at the plate in front of her. A crème brûlée.

"Henry didn't want to run the estate," Jeremy said, all of a sudden. "He was, apparently, a talented actor."

"Yes," Sarah said. "I did know that. That would have been incredibly difficult for him."

"And the person he married couldn't let him be who he was." The duke seemed to want to blame Louisa—he was not going to allow for any role the Duval family might have played in Louisa's tragedy.

Why was he so adamant? Surely he couldn't be worried that Sarah might go to the media.

She picked up her spoon, poised it above the crème brûlée, and then put it back down again. She had two days. "Do you really think Louisa was to blame for Henry's...problems?" she asked, casual sounding. That was what she needed to be.

"Who is dining with us tomorrow night, Olivia?" The duke turned to his wife. "Or are we going out?"

Sarah raised a brow.

The duke talked quite firmly about other matters until the uncomfortable meal was done.

Sarah was left with a persisting question that forced itself to the front of her mind: had Louisa been seen as a person or as a commodity by this family? No wonder she had become passionate about women's rights.

When Sarah climbed the grand staircase to her guest suite, other ideas kept biting into her thoughts. Why had Sarah's Boston family never mentioned a baby? And what had happened to the child?

Sarah lay in the darkness in the vast bedroom in the vast old family estate. She was the only person sleeping in the guest wing. Were she in a Gothic novel, she would get up and search the house.

In the early hours of the morning, Sarah was still wide awake. She was going to have to ask more probing questions tomorrow. But searching the house was entirely against her character. Searching the house was something that rational, logical, strategic Sarah would never do.

But had that girl disappeared the moment she arrived in Paris? Or had it been a gradual shift?

After a few more minutes of lying in complete indecision, Sarah was unable to wait anymore. She had her feet over the side of the four-poster bed and her dressing gown wrapped around her body before she could think any more. No analysis. She was going to have a look around the house.

She tiptoed across her room toward the solid bedroom door. When she opened it, no sound upset the silence in the vast guest wing. Not that anyone would be listening.

Would they?

No.

Logic had its uses sometimes.

Sarah made her way down the silent passageway. The corridor was narrow. She had her phone, which had a flashlight app, but she dared not turn it on for fear of being caught.

As she reached the end of the long, still hallway, she stopped for a moment. She was at the edge of the main staircase. The vast stained-glass window that ran three stories down the length of the tower was blanked out in darkness.

Sarah moved onto the stairs, one hand on the banister. It would not do to slip and send noise crashing through the house.

Sarah stopped at the next floor down and frowned. She must be careful now. She knew that the family's bedrooms were on this floor, because the duchess had waved in a certain vague direction as they had been going upstairs to bed.

She moved, as silently as possible, toward the library. That was going to have to be her first scene of investigation. The oak-paneled door was open. Moonlight shone through the vast windows, sending smooth shafts of light onto the bookshelves. Sarah moved to the middle of the room.

The thing was to work out how the collection was organized.

Henry had lived until 1943.

What she needed was a family Bible.

Sarah closed the library door. Then she slipped her phone light on and scanned the shelves, starting at the bottom, moving around the room in an orderly fashion, checking each gold-leaf spine for any hint of the Duval name. Once she had searched the entire bottom shelf, she stood back and counted—fifteen shelves to the top. And ladders.

Her phone buzzed. She stopped dead.

Sarah frowned and turned around quickly. She would hear footsteps, she would hear a door handle turning, she told herself, if her phone had disturbed anyone in the house.

She checked the text. It was Laurent. *"You're probably asleep,"* he wrote. *"Sorry I haven't been in touch yet. What's happening? What have they said?"* She smiled, thought for a moment. Then texted back: *"They aren't going to budge. I'm searching the library in the middle of the night."* He responded, and his words on the screen caused Sarah to smile. *"Would you like a chat? Some company while you sleuth? I'm working anyway."*

Of course he was. Sarah reminded herself how big the palace was, how quiet she would be on the phone in here, how unlikely it was that she would wake anyone up, and called him. Whispering, she moved around the shelves. Her eyes had adjusted to the darkness. She could read the spines of the books using moonlight. Shelley, Byron, Keats...

"What's happening?" he asked.

"The family has a stock story. Louisa committed suicide, no discussions. When I tried to probe, the duke cut me off. They described her as a 'bad choice.' That didn't impress me much. What was she? A commodity?"

Laurent was quiet.

"But I have learned something." Sarah ran her eyes over Tennyson. First editions, she could tell.

"Yes?"

"Louisa had a baby, apparently. The duke says she suffered from postpartum depression, hence the suicide. But why didn't my family know about a baby?"

"Keep pushing on," he said. "The baby, for a start, confirms that there is more to it than you thought."

Sarah stopped. End of row two. "True," she said.

She started another round.

She stopped and frowned at the books in front of her.

Not one family Bible. Not just one. There were at least ten.

"Laurent?" she whispered.

"Yup."

"I have to go. I've found something."

"Don't hesitate to call anytime."

"Thank you," she said.

And hung up.

The Bibles were all in perfect order.

She picked up the one dated 1870–1900. And moved to the window, sitting on the wide windowsill to read.

Chapter Twenty

Ashworth, 1895

Louisa had taken to visiting Jess in the afternoons once the older woman had finished her duties at the school. Their friendship had blossomed into an understanding, and a complicity of sorts. Jess was helping to set up a branch of the Women's Franchise League. And Louisa spent her evenings with Charlie. She had come to a sort of truce with herself whereby she could almost pretend that Henry did not exist. The only problem was, he did.

"I have spoken with nearly every woman in the village now," Jess said while she cut Louisa a slice of cake. "Some of them had heard of Mrs. Pankhurst's activities. There was a bit of resistance—antipathy, and also outright damnation from some quarters—but I say those women simply needn't come. I have five women who will. That is a good start."

"Mrs. Pankhurst is determined that the promotion of women's rights should be attained in a peaceful manner. We are not going to alienate those who do not wish to join us," Louisa said. "Although, having said that, I find it difficult to imagine why women would not want to be liberated from their lot." She sipped at Jess's tea in its floral china cup. "I have a list of speakers from Mrs. Pankhurst who will come down and address our meetings. We need to work out a place in which to gather. Jess—"

"My house, for a start."

"Thank you."

There was a silence for a moment, before Jess spoke. "Louisa, I don't know how to bring this up without sounding jolly negative. But, how will you deal with the duchess?"

Louisa put her pretty teacup down. "I confess, I have been putting the idea off and contemplating not telling her, or Lord Aubrey, at all."

"The duke will think it is beneath him, ridiculous and a waste of time. But he could put a stop to it if he feels it will threaten stability in the village," Jess said. "He would argue quite rationally with you. I think it would be better to keep it quiet at first. After all, if there are only seven of us, we are hardly starting a revolution on the estate."

Louisa was beginning to think that her plans for a local Women's Franchise League were the only rational thing in her life. The tumult of feelings that she had for Charlie were beginning to drive her to distraction. She had come to realize that the way she felt for him was beyond her control.

And the fact that she was carrying Henry's child only confused her even more. Why had she fallen in love with Charlie? What on earth use was that? Why could she have not loved his brother? Why had she met Henry first? Why had she agreed to marry him? And why, in turn, did Henry have to be the person he was? If these questions kept her awake at night, the knowledge that she was about to bring a child into this complicated mess only made things a hundredfold worse.

As for the Women's Franchise League, Jess's plan to stay silent about their activities seemed the only sensible option for now.

More silence. The duke and duchess never commented on Henry's absence. She and Charlie could not say a thing about their feelings to a soul. And as for Henry, he never said anything to anyone about whatever was going on with Marthe de Florian.

She took one last bite of Jess's delicious cake. "I think we should keep our meetings confidential to start with, at the very least, Jess.

When the time comes that we must talk with the duke and duchess about the League, it would be better to have some local support. Then the duke will have to think twice about stopping his villagers from an activity that is established."

Jess's brown eyes caught Louisa's own. "You are beginning to think like a strategist."

Louisa stood up then and held her friend's hand for a moment. She was going out with Charlie this afternoon. He had organized the carriage to take them to visit a tenant farm.

Louisa loved working with him, and it meant so much to her that he had stuck to the promise he'd made on the very first day he had taken her around the estate. He included her in his work whenever possible. And it was something that Louisa valued more and more every day.

Henry arrived at Ashworth at the beginning of summer. Paris was relatively deserted for the season, so he said. People escaped the city, and it was the perfect opportunity for him to come home.

The duke and duchess were excited about Henry's return. Louisa sensed that they still hoped, in some ways, that he would get over his predilection for Paris and come home for good, especially with an heir of his own on the way.

Charlie drove Louisa to the Women's Franchise League meetings now that the date of Louisa's confinement was nearing. Louisa had grown the number of regular attendees at Jess's house to ten with the help of Mrs. Pankhurst's pamphlets and a visit from one speaker. The ten women who did attend had sworn secrecy about their activities.

But the League was spreading its wings around the country. It was becoming clear that women wanted change. It was becoming clear that many women wanted the same rights as men. And this was exciting.

Louisa felt her upper back stiffen at the sight of Henry's carriage on the drive. She had a perfect view of his approach from where she sat on the terrace, and now she eased herself out of her wicker chair and gripped the handle of her white parasol.

The carriage rounded the corner to the front of the house. As Louisa glimpsed Henry inside it, he turned to face her. He looked at her, but he did not wave.

Louisa took up the letters that she had been writing to her mother and to Samuel. The one to her mother was brief. But she had no idea what to say to Samuel. She had always been open with him, but she could hardly reveal the truth about her complex feelings for Charlie. Louisa's life had turned into something that she knew was beyond what her younger brother would understand.

Henry's footsteps sounded clear on the hard tiles in the entrance hall. Louisa moved through the open French doors into the ladies' sitting room, then out into the corridor, turning left toward the secondary staircase that wound its way upstairs. She wanted to be alone in her rooms.

But Charlie came out of his office as she approached the back stairs.

"You're letting Henry's arrival upset you, and I don't know why," he said, stopping her right there outside his office. He took her arm. "Talk to me."

Louisa shook her head. "I would rather go upstairs."

Gently, Charlie led her into his office.

Everything in the room was neat—papers were stacked in piles on Charlie's large wooden desk. His shelves were stocked with farming manuals and books on the running of estates. A set of double doors was open to the farm manager's office. The man worked alongside Charlie. Louisa knew that they both understood the importance of being innovative with farming methods on the family's vast estates.

Louisa glanced out through the open door. Henry had moved into the library. She could hear him talking with his father. Laughter resonated up the hallway.

"Don't let him get to you," Charlie said, his voice low and deep. "You know what to expect from him, so why worry? Enjoy the baby, when he or she arrives."

Something caught in his voice as he said the last words.

Louisa forced herself to move away from him, even though her entire body was willing her to move closer. Instead, she walked over to the open French doors. His office overlooked a walled garden. A bird played in the fountain that was built into the back wall, its wings flapping, spraying up water onto its body, reveling in it.

Charlie stood behind her, reached out, ran his hand down her arm for a moment.

She turned and looked up at him.

It was even more impossible and even more real when their eyes met. But she could not expect him to go on like this. She just didn't want to do it to him, and yet the thought of losing him . . .

"I'm glad that you and Jess have become friends. I'm glad that you are working together. If you can keep going, you will make a real difference in how the local women think. I have every faith in you, you know that."

He ran a hand over her cheek.

She closed her eyes and imagined his hand running down to her waist.

But he stopped at her chin, holding it between his thumb and forefinger.

She opened her eyes. There were his again. There was such truth in them—too much truth. She almost could not bear it.

"How do you feel about me now?" he asked, suddenly, his voice so intimate that Louisa thought she might not breathe.

She felt her lips tighten for a moment, then open, just slightly. "You know," she whispered.

He tilted his head, shaking it a little, still holding her gaze. "And you know I'm never going to marry anyone else."

"But you must."

"No, I mustn't."

He leaned down, his lips brushing hers for one tender moment. And she reached up, she couldn't help it, her arms wound around his neck, her baby was between them, and she felt that it was more his child than anyone else's, and he opened her lips with his own, exploring, deeper, until Louisa felt she might explode.

He stopped first, running a hand over her hair, kissing the top of her head. "Go and rest, darling," he said. "You are so close. You have done so well. And everything is going to be all right. The most important thing is your health right now—one day at a time."

He still held her hand.

"Rest," he whispered. "And for God's sake, don't upset yourself over Henry. Think of the baby too."

She nodded.

But she did worry that every time he kissed her, it would be the last.

A week later, Louisa held her baby, Evelyn, in her arms. Henry had appeared after the birth, white, shaken, a diminished version of his usually confident self. Louisa was to rest for three weeks. A wet nurse had been called in. The baby spent most of the day in the nursery, and all this did was afford Louisa too much time to think.

Because when Louisa lay alone in her room, tears would fall silently out of her eyes; she stared out the window at the glorious weather that was a mirror of what it had been when she first arrived in England.

A naïve young girl.

She would change everything if she could.

Chapter Twenty-One

Ashworth, 2015

The morning after her secret mission in the library, the words inscribed in the family Bible wound themselves through Sarah's mind like threads on an endless spool. The book was filled with countless family trees, intricate diagrams decorating page after page, illustrating cousins and branches of the family that spread all over the world. Were Sarah not on a mission, she could easily have spent hours reading stories about certain characters in the book. Some family members, who were clearly regarded as unique, had paragraphs devoted to them. Sarah had read several such books back in Boston, and she was able to locate Louisa at first glance using the well-documented hand-written index.

Louisa had been accorded an entry, which was both a surprise and a comfort to Sarah. The odd thing was that Louisa's entry described a woman who was nothing like the "bad choice" whom the current duke had dismissed. In the Bible, Louisa was described as a family member with a keen interest in furthering women's rights. She was instrumental in the formation of a branch of the Women's Franchise League at Ashworth. She had known and corresponded with the now famous suffragette Emmeline Pankhurst. Furthermore, the Women's Franchise League had spread around the country as a result of the efforts of such women as Louisa Duval. Their achievement had been the gaining of the vote for women in local elections. Louisa had died, tragically, in Paris, in 1895.

But it was the next part that intrigued Sarah. Louisa had planned a four-day conference of the Women's Franchise League at Ashworth village after her return from Paris. The conference had been postponed after Louisa's death, but her supporters had held it in her honor at a later date, and her tireless efforts in arranging it were acknowledged. Had she lived, there was no doubt that her achievements would have been remarkable.

In fact, Louisa had inspired local women so much that the Ashworth branch of the League had gone on to become one of the most active in the country. Louisa was remembered for her determination, her love of life, and her intelligent approach.

The more Sarah delved into Louisa's story, the more she sensed that Louisa herself would never have given up. The fact that Louisa had a conference organized on her return from Paris stood out in Sarah's mind like a red flag.

Now, she gazed out of her bedroom window at the park. A gardener, an elderly man, swept the terrace in front of the house in the early-morning sunshine, his broom moving in slow, rhythmic strokes. Sarah frowned and turned back to her bedroom.

She gathered an outfit together—a black linen dress, black patent sandals, a silver necklace—and packed the rest of her clothes away into her suitcase.

Her phone rang.

Glad of the distraction from her thoughts about what she was to do next, Sarah picked it up. There was a pause before she heard Laurent's voice come through.

"Hello," he said, sounding tentative.

Sarah suddenly realized that she didn't want him to be that way.

"Morning, Laurent," she said, aware that her own voice was brightening the moment she spoke to him.

"I just thought I'd check how things were," he said.

Sarah looked at her clothes on the upholstered chair by the window. "I'm not sure what to do," she said. She told him, briefly, about the entry.

"You're going to push on," he said.

"I suppose I am." She knew her voice sounded absent.

"The family is spinning you a complete line."

"You sound confident."

"My instincts. Your logic. Together, they make a formidable team."

Sarah felt as close to him as ever. She didn't say that the only thing she had left was her own instincts and that it was he who sounded more logical then she felt. And yet, she felt such a connection to Laurent right now that if someone had told her he was right there in the room with her rather than in Paris, she would have had no trouble believing them.

"Sarah," he said. "Have you thought about asking whether there are any of Louisa's things left in the palace, or Henry's? Did they keep anything? Letters, you know what I mean. Diaries, journals? So many people recorded things back then. You found that letter here in the apartment. I just wonder if you should ask. Say that you'd love to take her things back to your family, or something innocuous like that."

Sarah allowed the smile that was forming on her face to develop into a grin. "You know, you're quite good at this," she said.

"What?"

"Strategy," she chuckled, knowing her voice had dropped. "Thank you. I'll ask Jeremy. He's the most approachable. I won't get anywhere with the duke. And as for the duchess…"

"Go and get on with it," he said, his voice firm, but there was humor underneath. "And Sarah…"

"Yes."

"Don't let Jeremy fob you off. Sounds like he's under his parents' thumb to me."

Sarah found herself grinning again. She didn't want to hang up.

"Go, Sarah," he said.

"Have a good day." She was still smiling as she stepped toward the shower.

The rest of the family appeared to have finished breakfast by the time Sarah came down. Silver platters held hot food, and the coffee was blessedly good.

Jeremy popped his head in the door while Sarah was eating. A yellow scarf was tied around the neck of his shirt. Sarah couldn't help thinking that this was rather sweet—it was as if he were expressing himself, and this seemed to be a good thing for him to do.

"Jeremy, I wanted to ask you something."

"Yes?" Mild again.

Sarah couldn't get around the word.

She put down her empty coffee cup. "I was wondering if you might have any of Louisa's things here on the estate, whether the family kept any mementos that I could see? Letters, anything like that?" She almost held her breath while she waited.

Jeremy tugged at his scarf, pulling the yellow silk down into one continuous smooth run. He stood there, and sighed.

"I'm not sure if I should tell you this..." His voice trailed off. "But I've been thinking about it ever since you arrived. My father can be...well. I can't see how it would hurt, were I to tell you..."

Sarah stopped moving, her glass of orange juice halfway to her mouth.

"You see, the thing is, the wing of the house where Louisa and Henry lived, where that generation lived, has been left exactly as it was. My father hasn't said anything about not letting you see it all, but..."

Sarah put the glass down.

Jeremy waited a moment. "You see, both Henry and his younger brother Charles died almost straight after the Second World War. Huge sections of the house were closed off in 1946. The estate had lost nearly all its workers—servants were no longer easy to find, of course, and their wages had gone up, so my grandfather shut huge sections of the house off. What else could he do? But what that means is that all Henry's clothes, and so forth, are still there.

Along with Henry's younger brother's belongings. My parents never got around to tidying it up either. It's all just sitting there."

Sarah had to take in a long breath.

"Jeremy." She would revert to curator mode. She had to keep her head. "Please, I'd really like to see their rooms. It would mean a lot to me to be able to see the wing where Louisa lived, where she spent her last years. It might help lay her ghost to rest, if that makes sense."

Jeremy nodded, but as he leaned against the mantelpiece, looking, oddly, half like a pale version of the lord of the manor, and half like a confused young man, Sarah suddenly wondered how comfortable he was with the idea of inheriting this vast estate himself.

"Would you like to come with me?" she asked.

Jeremy tilted his head to one side. "Yes," he said. "Yes. I would. Shall we meet once you have finished your breakfast, say in about fifteen minutes?"

Sarah nodded. She sat still for a few moments once he had gone, unable to eat any more. So she went to her room, brushed her hair in a vague sort of way, cleaned her teeth, put on lipstick. Was this too good to be true?

When she followed Jeremy up the grand staircase, up through the beautiful tower, sunlight lit up the family crest. Sarah's nerves sang their own odd tune in her stomach.

Jeremy kept up some banter, but his voice was shaky too.

Sarah wondered if he had ever gone against his father's wishes before.

He stopped once they reached the third floor. A closed door with glass panels led to a long corridor beyond. "You see, the thing is that neither my father nor my grandfather like complications. They both believe in keeping things simple," he said. "If things are too hard, they tend to shut them off."

"Well, I, for one, am grateful that they did not remove my ancestor's possessions," Sarah said.

Jeremy paused. "You're ready?" he asked.

Sarah nodded, feeling quiet all of a sudden.

Jeremy turned the handle of the glass door and they entered the long, cold hallway. Rows of closed doors lined either side of the seemingly endless space. The floorboards were bare, but the wood was darkened where, once, a rug had run down its center. The smell was of must, of age. Sarah took deep breaths to calm herself down.

They came to another landing. A circular staircase wound up from some other part of the house—a back staircase, a private family one, perhaps. Sarah imagined Louisa tripping up it, up to her bedroom. How had she felt? What had gone wrong?

Light danced into the space through large picture windows, the brightness seeming to mock them, Sarah thought. Once, there had been life here. Now, there was not.

She wrapped her arms around herself.

"How long has it been since anyone has been up here?" she asked.

"I don't know." Jeremy sounded far away now. Several doors led off the large landing.

Which one led to Louisa's room?

Silence cloaked the strange, empty space, and dust motes floated in the air. A round table sat bare against one wall. Paintings hung, still and ghostly on the walls, but these were frosted with dust too, their frames housing thick blankets of gray residue.

Jeremy moved toward one of the doors. "I'm not exactly sure which room is which. Haven't been up here since I was a teenager, to be honest, and I can't remember. It's all been shut off. It's strange being back up here."

He turned the brass handle of the closed door, and when she followed him into the room, she could not help but gasp.

A four-poster bed sat, resplendent, in the middle of the room. Dust formed layers of filth on the green counterpane. A tennis racket leaned at an angle against the wall next to the bed, and a green crystal glass sat on the bedside table, next to a photograph in a silver frame.

Jeremy picked it up. "Henry," he said.

Sarah moved across the room to look over Jeremy's shoulder.

Henry Duval stared out at them as a young man, just as Louisa would have known him. He wore a striped jacket and his trousers were white against the background of the photograph. He wore a boater hat. He was good-looking, Sarah thought, and there was something rakish in his smile.

He stood out on the terrace at Ashworth, which was clearly recognizable, and behind him a group of people was draped, as if for effect, in wicker chairs around a table. Drinks were laid out, and the women wore white dresses and held parasols. It was a particularly charming scene, an English scene, and it all looked perfect.

If only people knew.

Jeremy moved to the window and pulled the curtains open, bathing the room in yellow light. More photos in silver frames sat atop an old chest of drawers, glinting in the sun now through the grime. Henry was in every one. An old pair of silver cufflinks sat near the photos, embedded in layers of dust. A tall mirror in a wooden frame sat on the other side of the wall, next to a wooden rack for hanging men's suit jackets. A freestanding wardrobe completed the picture.

Sarah's eyes kept returning to the wardrobe.

She thought for a moment about what to say. "One thing I've learned in my line of work is that men often keep odd things in their suit jackets. They don't seem to clean them out unless they need to."

Jeremy seemed to consider this, but his eyes did not narrow. There was nothing suspicious in his looks. "Is there anything in particular that you are looking for?" he asked.

Sarah knew she would have to be careful answering that question. "I'm wondering about letters," she said.

Jeremy seemed to consider this. "My father's worried about you opening things up again. From the past." He hesitated for a moment. "Sarah, you would never go off to the media about Louisa's death, would you?"

So, she had been right. "I promise you that I will never go to the media."

Jeremy smiled then, and something almost whimsical passed across his face. "If you find a letter from Louisa to Henry, then you can keep it. It's just an old story, but I can see that it's more to you. Go on. Have a look."

Sarah walked over to the cupboard. It stuck slightly but she prized the doors apart. Inside, there were only a few suit jackets, a couple of shirts, and a few pairs of trousers. Perhaps Henry, too, had died in Paris.

Sarah reached into the pockets. She was familiar with the intricacies of 1930s clothes. Knew to search for hidden crevices in suit jackets. A waistcoat had fallen to the floor of the wardrobe. It lay crumpled in the dust. Sarah turned up a bill for cigarettes, a cigarette case, and a couple of handkerchiefs, both monogrammed with Henry's initials. This touched her, for some strange reason. She had not thought of Henry as a man with handkerchiefs.

Jeremy turned them over in his hands, seeming fascinated too.

She reached into the depths of a checked jacket, rather smart. Jauntier than the others. Perhaps he wore it in Paris.

And pulled out an envelope.

Jeremy stopped dead still. "Do you want to read it now, or take it downstairs once we've looked in Louisa's and Charles's rooms?"

Sarah glanced around the dust-laden old bedroom. "I think we should read it downstairs."

Jeremy smiled at her, whimsical again. "Louisa's room first?" he asked.

She nodded. She was finding it hard to know what to say. If this letter was as revelatory as the last one she had found, she wanted to read it somewhere quiet. Sarah followed Jeremy through the open door, back out to the strange, wide landing. It felt permeated with ghosts. She turned the old envelope over in her hands and stopped when she read the name of the sender.

Marthe de Florian, Rue Blanche, Paris.

Jeremy opened two more doors, peered in, shook his head.

"This one," he said at the third.

He stood there.

It was her room.

Louisa's bedroom was dustier, with a more archaic feel than Henry's space. Only one thing sat on the table beside the pretty, floral-covered bed. And that was a fading photograph of Louisa. Even though the image had started to break up with stains, Sarah knew it was her. She had one photo of Louisa at home herself.

Louisa looked determined. The photograph was only of her face and her shoulders, and yet it was clear that her bearing was confident. She looked as if she were dressed for the evening. Gauzy material floated around her décolletage.

Jeremy pulled the curtains open. Sarah turned the photograph over in her hands, rubbing at the glass with her forefinger and her thumb, smoothing away layers of dust until Louisa looked straight back at her.

What happened to you? Sarah asked silently. What went wrong?

Jeremy opened the wardrobe. A few dresses hung, along with several old coats—a green hooded cloak and a shawl. Several pairs of shoes were lined up along the bottom of the old armoire, their silken tops barely visible through layers of thick dust, and in the drawers, there was a selection of satin gloves. Moths had made a feast of Louisa's corsets and undergarments.

A pair of silver-backed brushes lay on the dressing table, which was fancy with elaborate wooden scrolls. Sarah felt a shiver as she caught a glimpse of herself through the dark stains on the old mirror. Other than that, Louisa's drawers contained empty perfume bottles. Sarah did a quick check, her professional self fighting with the urge to stay here, to clean everything up. To care for Louisa's things the way they deserved. But after a quick look, it was clear that Louisa had not kept any correspondence in her sleeping quarters. Of course, Sarah reasoned, maids would have been in here daily, and she still suspected that the family may have taken issue with Louisa's intents.

The urge to go downstairs, to open Marthe's correspondence to Henry, was great. But at the same time, Sarah wanted to linger in this half-haunted space.

"There is one more room," Jeremy said.

"Henry's younger brother?" What, if anything, was known about him?

And it struck her then, right here in that space, how little is left when we are gone. How insignificant we all are. This was, she thought, both liberating and sad. In some ways, she realized now, she had taken her life so seriously in the past. How much did it matter? Up in these old rooms, everything looked like a dream.

Jeremy moved out toward the corridor and held open Louisa's bedroom door.

Sarah turned back one last time to look. She had to stop herself from saying good-bye out loud. Instead, she walked out the door, and Jeremy closed it with a soft but final thud.

Charles's room was neat, organized—the mood was completely different. Sarah felt the slight twinge of guilt that sometimes passed over her before she searched through other people's things. There was far more of a sense of someone in this orderly, yet dusty and aged space. Sarah explored Charlie's suit pockets and found some old pens, a farm manual. On his chest of drawers, there were only books about estate management, and a pamphlet on shipping lines to the Far East.

Nothing else.

When Jeremy closed the door, she nodded at him. She followed him back down the stairs, as if on automatic pilot.

Back to the splendor of the lived-in rooms. But something, some part of her, was still up there, in those empty, yet utterly full rooms. It had all gone. But the mystery surrounding Louisa's death remained intact. Would Sarah ever find the answer she sought?

And yet the past was all, every bit of it, still up there in those silent bedrooms and corridors.

Paris, 1939

My dear Henry,

I know that I am not long for this life. I know that this will be my final letter to you. And, indeed, I admit that I struggle to put my pen to the page, but as always, I feel so drawn to you and I cannot leave without saying good-bye.

But, before I depart this life, whatever it is, I want to ask you something, Henry. Can you do this for me? This might be a strange request, but when you think of me, I want you to promise to remember me as I was.

I know that our friendship is timeless. I know we were in love, or at least, I was. But I never told you, did I! I thought of you most days; goodness knew, I thought of you most nights.

I think that I didn't want to risk things, does that make sense? I knew that we could never be together, me a courtesan, you the son of a duke. I was always on the periphery of your gilded world. Always on the outside. I was never going to fit in or be accepted as Louisa was. And yet, in some ways, darling Henry, we were together, weren't we?

Because we both just knew. We did. And that was enough.

I think there is love that is tragic, there is love that is real and warm and lasting, and then, there is love that is left unspoken and yet understood by both the parties. Ours was the last type of love. And it mattered to me, so very much.

The air was charged with something that I have never felt anywhere else except with you. And that was enough too. That bond between us made up for all the cold transactions and the falseness of everything else in my life. It made up for everything that happened with every other man I knew. I wasn't married as you were. Instead of one cold-hearted deal, I had to face hundreds, Henry. And I, too, had to face them in order to survive.

But even we courtesans knew how we felt.

And you treated me so very well.

You were the one man I wanted. The one man I couldn't have.

You had your responsibilities—you had your role to play. And I was forced into mine. But, my dear Henry, what fun we had! And what a friendship was formed in spite of everything. I don't know, to be frank, what I would have done without you as my friend to sustain me over the long years in Paris. You, at home at Ashworth, coming to Paris when you could, me here with my dear Isabelle, who provided me with such delight as she grew up.

But now, the shadows of war hang over us yet again. And I don't know that I want to live through another one of these foul shows—they are the very worst things that we humans can conjure.

And I find myself thinking strange and odd thoughts. Apart from my darling Isabelle, what will happen to all my beautiful things? What if, as they say, this is worse than the last awful episode? The last war was the end of our beautiful, complex Belle Époque, but where will this next war lead us?

We can never have the past back, but it will always remain as part of us, as part of who we were. The future is not in our hands. This is not our time anymore, Henry. For that reason, it is easier for me to depart.

Henry, I am dying. I suspect I will not be here in a month. I want to write this before this foul pneumonia takes over completely and I am gone.

I want to say good-bye, then. And yet I know it is not the end. I know that you will always be there, will always be with me, no matter what. You have never belonged to me, nor I to you. We have always let each other live as we wished. And yet, every time we were together, we knew. We knew that we loved each other.

It was better that way, better, perhaps, than anything else could have been.

It was everything.

Thank you.
Yours, with my greatest affection, and love,
M—

Chapter Twenty-Two

Ashworth, 1895

Louisa wondered if the only answer was to leave Ashworth. It was, quite simply, becoming too difficult to be there. The idea of going to Paris with Henry was perhaps her only option. At least in Paris she would not suffer the exquisite pain of being in close proximity to the man she loved. And yet, the idea of being apart from Charlie seemed even worse than staying at home. Until Lady Anne Devon appeared at Ashworth.

Lady Anne was the daughter of an old friend of the duke. The duchess invited her to stay for the remainder of the summer. The young woman had recently completed finishing school in Switzerland. She was charming, elegant, and well read, just as Louisa was. In some ways, Louisa saw a younger version of herself in Lady Anne—without all the opinions, without the complications with Henry, and without any of the regrets that lingered in Louisa's head. What was more, Lady Anne showed a strong interest in Charlie's farming methods.

Lady Anne was always up early with Louisa and Charlie. She first asked about the home farms at breakfast one morning, following an evening of dancing in the salon. A string quartet was in residence at Ashworth, and the duchess had arranged for a small dinner party the night before—forty guests—in honor of Lady Anne's visit.

Louisa smiled and smiled through the dancing. Charlie danced with her, too, he had even rested his head on her shoulder for a brief second, but when he danced with Lady Anne, when Louisa watched him laughing with the girl and grinning as if he had not a care in his life, she found herself twisting her hands around and around in her lap. She wanted to stand up, to walk out, or to run to him. She was sure of his feelings for her. And yet, she had told him over and over again that their being together was impossible.

So what did she expect?

But could she bear to stand by and watch this? If only her feelings for him were not so strong!

Charlie's invitation to take Anne out for the day was, unfortunately, too much. Louisa put her teacup down on its saucer with a resounding clang as soon as he uttered the words. She felt her breathing quicken, her forehead crinkling into a frown.

"I must go and check on Evelyn," she said, her words coming out in a terrible rush. Louisa ran up the back stairs to the family wing, pausing on the landing in the sun. She must compose herself before visiting the wet nurse and baby, but her breath was coming in hard, solid gasps.

Her thoughts had turned to a panic. Would Charlie leave Ashworth and live on one of the other, smaller estates? Would Henry return and take over the estate? What would become of her work with Jess and Mrs. Pankhurst?

Louisa ran a hand down her skirt, smoothing the white muslin. She lifted her chin and went to see Evelyn. Louisa did not know whether she could remain at Ashworth and watch Charlie and Lady Anne play out the thing she dreaded most. Equally, she knew that she could not stop Charlie from marrying, that she should not and would not stop his finding happiness were he to develop real feelings for their visitor.

She might just have to bear what she could hardly think of at all.

But as she walked into the nursery, moved across to the window, and leaned over the baby's cradle, she saw Charlie and Anne outside on the driveway, walking off to the stables, she keeping pace beside him. An answer jumped into her head.

"I am going up to London for a time," she told the nurse all of a sudden, picking up her child. She stated it before she could begin to think. London was her best escape. It was the perfect distraction.

"Yes, madam," the girl said.

Irritation at the girl's compliance bit into Louisa's mind. The young nurse's acceptance of her role, her place, the hopelessness of what would be her life annoyed Louisa, even though she was aware that this thought was unkind. She knew that the girl had absolutely no choice.

One thing was certain—Louisa's choices might be limited, but she knew she was not going to give up on herself.

She sat down; Evelyn wrapped one tiny hand around Louisa's forefinger, clutching it.

She needed to be strong. She would miss Evelyn, but her role as a mother was limited. She was only required to visit at certain times. All the work was done for her. Goodness knew what she would amuse herself with if she did not have her interests. She would return and spend time with her child as soon as it was tenable. Having an answer about Charlie and Anne would be preferable to the agony of being here and not knowing exactly what was going on between them.

She would entertain herself with visits to Mrs. Pankhurst in Russell Square. Meetings there were exactly what she needed. Stimulation, discussion. She had written to the woman about the possibility of organizing a proper conference here at Ashworth. What if she were to talk about that with Mrs. Pankhurst face-to-face? It was just what she needed to do. It was productive. Positive. Within her control.

That afternoon Louisa sorted a carriage.

She came out of her bedroom in perfect time to leave. She wore a light traveling coat, her favorite pale blue, which she knew suited her and highlighted her blue eyes.

But Charlie was in the hall, right outside their bedrooms in the private family wing. He held a childhood photograph of Henry, turning it over in his hands. He almost jumped when Louisa appeared.

She stopped.

He marched toward her.

She remained frozen. Their fate was sealed. Everything was going to keep them apart. There was nothing to be done. So she stood there.

When he took her in his arms, running his hands over her hair, kissing the top of her head, she stood impassive, like a limp rag doll.

How was she supposed to be in the same place he was when he was with someone else? They could put on the pretense of a friendship, of some pale form of acquaintance that would never satisfy either of them. That would never work.

What she wanted was a fantasy, a dream. She had to give it up.

"I love you," he said, his words muffled by her hair.

She relented, rested her head on his shoulder. It would be impossible to speak and not tell him the truth. She loved every part of him, at every level. Sometimes she wondered why she did, and other times, she knew that the answer was obvious. She loved him for his kindness, his steadfastness, his loyalty. These were all logical reasons, but deeper things came into play too.

She had come, through Charlie, to believe in love, and also to know that she had to make a difference in the world. These two things, love and work, could coexist in perfect harmony, as long as they were both right. As long as both worked as they should, then things would fall into place.

But the opposite was going to happen. That was the only thing that was clear.

And the carriage would be ready to take her to London. She must not keep it waiting.

"I have to go." She whispered the words.

"You don't have to leave."

"We both know I do," she said. And gently, she pulled herself back from Charlie and wrapped her arms around her own body.

He reached forward, touched her arm.

She took his hand in hers for one brief, tiny second.

And then she shook her head, held it up, and moved down the hallway to the waiting carriage.

Chapter Twenty-Three

Ashworth, 2015

Sarah placed Marthe's farewell letter to Henry on a small side table in the library. Jeremy, in a thoughtful way, had given her time to read Marthe's correspondence by herself. The woman who worked for the family appeared with tea—that traditional English balm—and biscuits, delicate-looking cookies arranged in a fan shape on a pale green porcelain plate. Sarah waited while the woman poured out tea, knowing that if she offered to do so herself, she would upset the balance that Ashworth seemed to rest upon.

And that was it. Neither Henry, Louisa, nor Marthe, it seemed, had wanted to accept the way that things were run. They had all been young. They had all had ideals, she suspected, hopes for themselves that could not be borne to fruition, and that had sent them spiraling into a tragic triple mess.

But one thing had changed, and this sat well with Sarah: now she saw Marthe as a person, not a villain. Sarah admitted that she had probably viewed the woman's life in a judgmental manner. How easy it had been to jump to conclusions. And now, here Sarah was, having to admit that Marthe's letter to Henry was one of the most moving things she had ever read. Marthe's letter had tweaked Sarah's heart. Clearly, their relationship transcended friendship and was born of trust, akin to that of soul mates. Perhaps it held equality and mutual respect that were well in advance of their time.

Sarah finished the last sip of her strong tea. She moved to the window and lingered next to the tall bookshelves. At least she had shuffled a ladder a bit while she was here. No one had noticed. Or if they had, they hadn't said anything.

She looked out at the park and the trees that spread their beautiful branches, resplendent with green leaves, over the grass. As if they were protective. As if everything was somehow right.

For the past dreadful months, Sarah had fought relentlessly every foul occurrence in her life. Everything, every part of it, seemed utterly wrong. She had wanted the past back, her life back to the way it was, to the way that it should have been.

But now, as she looked out onto the garden that Louisa must have gazed out at too, over one hundred years ago, Sarah asked herself if she would swap the experiences she had in Paris, the time she had spent with Laurent, and the knowledge and understanding she had gained about Marthe and her complex relationship with Henry while staying here at Ashworth for the old life she had lost. Her parents' tragic deaths aside, would she swap her time in Paris for years spent with Steven, living out their lives in the way they had always done?

Marthe's letter had forced her to confront the nature of relationships, even to consider the woman for whom Steven had left her. Sarah realized now that if she did not move on from this, if she did not let go, then she would be allowing her past to control her for the rest of her life.

While Ashworth had been enlightening in more ways than Sarah had hoped, she still had not found what she came here to find. Was the labyrinth of twisted truths surrounding Louisa's death going to remain intact? Had Louisa really been both suicidal and strong at the same time? Desperate enough to kill herself, yet capable and motivated in equal measure? It still made no sense at all.

Sarah's suitcase sat by the front door in the hallway. Her invitation expired today. Home, her apartment, her job. All these things awaited her. Was there any point in returning to Paris for the rest of the summer as she had planned? She had done all she could there. Boston was where she lived. There was no use running away anymore. She would just have to leave Louisa to rest.

She moved out of the library, across to the front door. The old man who swept the driveway each morning stopped at the bottom of the front steps. He surveyed his handiwork, looking as if he were admiring the neat, circular marks that were left by his soft rake in the pale gravel. He moved toward the small electric cart that he drove around the estate.

Sarah frowned. Suddenly, as if on some insane impulse, she picked up her phone and dialed Laurent. She wanted to talk to him.

"This is going to sound crazy," she said.

"Fire away."

"What do you think about approaching an old servant? Someone who has been working here for years, by the looks of it?"

Laurent chuckled then. "What are you waiting for? Go on. You've only got the morning. Don't stand there talking to me. It's an excellent idea."

"Thought you'd say that." Sarah hung up the phone and watched the old man.

What if she was risking the duke's wrath by approaching the groundskeeper, an estate employee? As she looked at him, her mind whirled on. He must be in his eighties. That would mean he was born in the 1930s, wouldn't it?

Pushing away the logic that told her she was mad, crazy as a snake, Sarah moved down the wide steps to the driveway below.

She came to a shuddering halt. The old man simply stood there. And looked at her.

"Hello," she said. Inane, but what else could she say?

"Aye." He nodded.

Sarah looked at him and considered that odd sort of stepping between two questions—should she reveal herself, or not? Strategy would advise her not. Of course.

Sarah pushed that right out of her head.

She felt her shoulders drop, as if they were shedding some burden. Laurent was right. She should just go ahead. "Look. I know this sounds odd, but I was wondering. I was wondering if you had worked here a long time, and whether, perhaps, you might have heard of Louisa West. And Henry Duval. Whether you might know anything about them. They were members of this family, once."

The man stood stock-still, but he didn't shake his head.

Sarah went on. "Louisa was my ancestor. I came back here to find out more about her. I'm from Boston. My name is Sarah. West. Sarah West. But I'm sorry. You don't know anything, do you? It was a long shot. And I'm about to leave."

Silly. To trust those instincts. She should have known better.

The old man leaned on his rake. "Miss West, is it," he said. He cleared his throat and looked out, over toward the forest that bordered the park. And it was as if, Sarah thought, he was staring out at the past. And at that moment, hope sprang in her. And at that moment, he turned back to her and nodded his head.

"I'm leaving, this morning. I only have a couple of hours," she said.

"You are Miss West, you say?"

Silently, Sarah reached into her handbag, and she held her passport out to him.

The old man glanced at it. He set his old mouth in a firm line. He was quiet for a few moments before he spoke. "I think it would be worth us having a chat, Miss West. I'll be finishing up here in ten minutes. But it would be best if you came to my cottage. We could talk there and make sure that you are back here in time for you to leave. My house is only a few minutes' walk."

Sarah's legs felt about as stable as two pins holding up a bridge, but she listened to the old man's directions. Walk past the family chapel, he told her. It is just beyond the woods. He would drive his cart, but it was piled up with all his rakes and tools. She would find it a squeeze sitting next to him. And she would enjoy, he said, the walk that edged the forest. The old gardener made a point of insisting she must stop and look at the family chapel. His cottage was a short distance beyond that. He told her she would see Louisa's grave in the old chapel garden.

Sarah nodded. She started to walk, putting one leg in front of the other, but found it hard to think that anything might come of talking with the gardener. Heat emanated from the gravel underneath her feet. A strip of unwieldy grass divided the path that edged the forest into two. A small lake appeared in the clearing ahead, beyond the line of trees. Willows hung over the water, their long branches reflected in its depths.

Beyond this, there was a garden, a strange, half-tended thing. It was an old-fashioned garden full of old-fashioned plants. Agapanthus stood upright, their handsome purple heads standing proud against the sky.

Sarah stopped at another clearing.

A chapel stood right in the middle of the space, a small, stone building. An old sign was stuck to its wooden front door. Services, it said, were held once a month.

Sarah pushed on the door—nothing. Next, she tried the handle. It didn't budge. She rounded the side of the building. Heat shimmered up from the graves that were scattered about on the ramshackle lawn; the graves were ramshackle too, poking out of the ground at odd angles as if they had been placed, Sarah thought, for effect. Some of them were grand, their headstones elaborate, surrounded by handsome railings. Many were tiny—children, then. Sarah felt a stab to her stomach as she wandered among the old Ashworth stones. Louisa's grave was separated from the others. She rested by herself in a corner by the old wire fence, under the shade of a gnarled tree.

The inscription on the headstone was simple. Louisa West, beloved wife of Henry Duval, died in Paris in 1895. Sarah wished that she had some flowers. Anything to place on the grave. Instead, she leaned forward, touched the headstone, and moved away.

Henry's tomb rested in the heart of the family plot, right next to that of his brother, Charles.

Surrounded by the dead, Sarah felt two things. She wanted to move away from this old family site, but at the same time, there was a sense of peace here, peace with the distant past. And what Sarah realized, now, was that perhaps her search for truth about the past was more a search for peace within herself.

She turned back and looked at the chapel. She realized that the stabbing pain that she had learned to live with during these last hard, hard months was loosening its grip now. Perhaps this had happened gradually, perhaps coming to Europe had sped the process up. But one thing was clear to her. And it was important. She had stopped loving Steven. Her feelings for him had faded away.

He had not behaved well toward her. That was the simple truth. It was time for her to move on.

Sarah smiled to herself because now she had one new problem—if one could call it such a thing—she had certainly developed feelings for Laurent. There was no hiding from the fact. Sarah took one last look at the old graveyard, shook her head, and followed the path back out.

The sound of slow, uneven footsteps crunched on the gravel around the chapel.

"Hello," she said to the old man, who appeared from the opposite direction. She realized that she had been so busy gabbing on about herself that he hadn't told her his name.

He leaned heavily on the wooden gate, with its pretty curved archway, at the entrance to the graveyard. As Sarah approached him, he held out his leathery old hand.

"Frank," he said. "Frank Moore." His blue eyes remained clear and he held her gaze. "I never knew that you'd come back here. I never realized that you would be interested, you see. But, I've thought it through while I rode back to my house, Miss West. Aye, in fact, it is a good thing that you've come."

Chapter Twenty-Four

Paris, 1895

Louisa had developed a sort of forced routine since her arrival in Paris. The main thing, she decided, was to avoid thinking too much. If her thoughts slipped to Charlie, and Ashworth, and her baby, she would simply make herself change tack. Henry seemed neither pleased nor concerned at her arrival. He carried on just as he desired. Louisa busied herself in Paris, looking at art and walking in the parks.

Today, though, she had decided to accompany Henry to the Longchamp Racecourse. She had become tired of her own company. She stood next to him on the side of the racetrack in the Bois de Boulogne. The horses thundered past, eyes bulging, sweat flowing down their necks. She hated the races. Hated the way men bet on the animals she loved. But she stood next to her husband as if, for all the world to see, she was the perfect wife.

After several weeks in London, Louisa had started to feel as if she were hanging about. She met with Mrs. Pankhurst. They arranged a conference at Ashworth by correspondence with Jess. But once that was done, Louisa reached a point where she needed to move on. She sensed that Mrs. Pankhurst was not a woman who approved of lounging about. The idea of returning to Ashworth left her with complicated thoughts. She felt guilt over her relationship with Charlie and missed her baby, although she realized that she was not of much help in that direction at this stage. She also had the sense that she should not overdo her work with the local women; she must keep the balance right. But the awful truth was that she could not bear to be near Charlie when he was so obviously infatuated with someone else.

She hardly knew what she was thinking now in Paris—did she hope that she and Henry might be able to come to some form of truce? Perhaps it was the only option left.

This morning, Louisa smiled and chatted with the group of upper-class friends whom Henry had arranged to bring in a steamboat down the Seine to Longchamp. They had all wandered freely into the Royal Box.

Louisa had seen the courtesan almost every day these past two weeks. The woman moved freely within Henry's circle—she was ubiquitous, Louisa felt. Marthe made her entrance late today, in a carriage, resplendent in diamonds and accompanied by her burly bodyguards. It was as if every appearance the courtesan made was to be treated as a special event.

Henry marched straight over to Marthe, taking her arm and leading her through the Royal Box. Louisa was unsure of what she felt as she stared at Henry and Marthe. Their intimacy stared straight back at her.

This morning, Henry, like Marthe, wore makeup. It was a foppish custom among his arty set. Louisa stood on the edge of the group. Suddenly, finding standing alone unsupportable, she maneuvered her way out of the box, into the vast crowd that lined the racetrack, working her way through the well-dressed Parisians. She had to get some space.

Until someone took her elbow. "Louisa."

She stopped and stared upward. She would know his voice if she were in a jungle full of screaming apes.

"Come with me," Charlie said, gently. "I saw you from a distance. I'd spot you anywhere."

"I hate to ask the obvious question," she said.

"I heard you were in Paris. I came as soon as I found out."

Louisa felt a half-hardened laugh escape from her throat. Her mind darted forward, jumping to the reasons for him to come. He was going to tell her that he was engaged.

She could sense it.

She did not want to have the conversation.

Charlie made his way through the crowds, leading her to a quiet spot behind a grand white marquee. The sounds of laughter and French conversation filtered out into the hot morning. Louisa fanned her face with her free hand.

"How are you?" he said, but there was an urgency in his voice.

"Very well." She steeled herself. Thought about responses. Congratulations? What else was there to say?

"I don't want to live a life that is not real." Charlie turned her toward him and looked straight into her eyes.

Louisa shook her head, diverting her own glance off to the side, anywhere but toward him. "Of course," she said. "You don't have to tell me what I already know. I . . . congratulations, if that is in order."

"Marry me, ridiculous girl," he said, all of a sudden. "Darling, you could do exactly what you want if you were with me. Divorce Henry. I can deal with my parents."

She looked up at him, and confusion obfuscated her thoughts. This was not real. What he was saying simply could not be true. "But you are to marry Lady Anne, surely that is what you are here to say," she said, her voice sounding hoarse.

"No." He stood so close to her that Louisa could hardly bear it. But for some reason, she was unable to take in what he said. Surely she wasn't about to be happy! She had given up on the very thought.

But Charlie seemed determined, no matter how hard it was to take in what he said. "We have to tell Henry the truth. I think we should do it tonight. We are all adults. We sit down and we talk this through and we tell him that we want to work things out. He doesn't love you. I'm sorry. But it's the truth. I adore you. I want to marry you, I love you. I want to be with you for the rest of my life. It doesn't have to be difficult. Who cares what society thinks? In any case, society will get over it. So will Henry, and so will my parents. But this is our chance. It's our future. And that's what matters."

Louisa folded her arms around her waist. This was not game playing. If she had accepted Henry in a daze—looking back, she could not understand what she had been thinking at the time of her engagement—now she knew that she needed absolute clarity if she were dealing with Charlie.

Because the situation was completely different. She was in love with him. The stakes simply had no end.

"Promise me you'll always be honest with me," she said.

And he promised.

Afterward, when he took her hand in his own and kissed her palm, she looked at him, and she told him yes. "I can't see that Henry will object. He will, after all, be free."

And she knew why she loved him. She knew why she loved Charlie. And she took his arm and she walked with him, away from the races, out into the open woodland.

Chapter Twenty-Five

Ashworth, 2015

A hot breeze picked up in the graveyard, flattening the grass into flowing green waves. Sarah turned to the old man standing at the gate.

"Did you find her?" Frank Moore asked.

Sarah gathered herself before she spoke. "Yes," she said. "I found her." She thought for a moment. "How long have you worked here, Mr. Moore?"

"I was born here. I've worked here since I was fourteen," he said, and he started to walk down the path through the garden. And then he stopped, turning to face her instead. "Everybody calls me Frank. Would you like to come into my house for a cup of tea?" As if it were the most common question in the world in circumstances such as these.

"Thank you." Sarah's heart rate scaled up.

He indicated the direction with a slight incline of his white-haired head. Sarah walked beside him, past those old graves that would sit there, for centuries, after such relatively brief lives.

But then Frank stopped beside the church.

"There is another grave," he said, as if he were making an announcement.

Sarah was quiet as he started to move back into the graveyard again. The sound of his slow footsteps resonated in the silent morning air. When he stopped at a tiny grave not far from Henry's, Sarah drew in a breath.

Evelyn Duval, born 1895, died 1895, she read. Beloved child of Louisa and Henry Duval.

"I missed it altogether." Sarah breathed out the words. It was impossible not to feel even more saddened at the sight of this tiny gravestone, for Louisa, for what she had given up, in many ways, to marry Henry. And then, her baby had died.

Frank stayed quiet next to her for a few moments, but when Sarah turned away from the little grave, he didn't follow her.

"There's nothing in the baby's grave." His voice seemed to travel through the air behind her, lingering among the headstones.

She turned to him.

But the old man moved away. He inclined his head at Sarah and walked back past the church to the gate.

"We need to have a chat," he said. "My cottage is right next door."

Sarah opened her mouth, then closed it again. Frank had already started walking.

Sarah took in a long breath.

Paris, 1895

Louisa's stomach tingled and spiraled with anticipation, hope, and dread, were she honest, as she and Henry stepped out of their carriage. Was Charlie really going to follow through this very night? She alighted on the sidewalk outside the house where the party was being held. The house looked elegant and Parisian and smart, but the scene outside in the street was typical Montmartre. The usual scrum of people flocked about vendors, who flogged their wares and hassled passersby in the street.

Louisa had spent extra time at her toilette, fussing over details, trying to control her thick, wavy hair, patting it into place. She had even experimented with rouge, then removed it. It was not who she wanted to be.

She hovered outside her carriage. Whenever she was with Charlie, it felt as if everything was possible and there were no limits. But if he wanted to open up discussion with Henry, wouldn't that ruin everything? Henry left her standing alone while he marched ahead.

Charlie had said that he wanted to approach his brother in a place where he was certain Henry would behave. If his friends were about, Henry was less likely to make a scene. While this had seemed logical earlier, now Louisa felt sickened at the thought of what might ensue.

The evening air was sharp on her cheeks as she made her way to the entrance of the corner house. The entire upper floor was lit up—lights beamed out onto the street, half in welcome, Louisa thought, and half showing off. Louisa gave her name to the servant who stood just inside the door.

The building's interior was marble and light and tall. A smart staircase wound its way to the top floor, curving in elegant curlicues. A great urn of sickly bright flowers sat at its base. Louisa ran her hand over the banister as she moved upward. Even through her glove, she could feel that the banister was cold.

But the farther she climbed, the warmer the air in the building became. Voices and the sound of raucous laughter rang down from the apartment upstairs. She paused at the top of the staircase.

The double doors were thrown open wide. Painted women and men smoking cigarettes in long holders spilled out onto the wide landing. The smell of tobacco was rank, along with a myriad of sweaty perfumes. It was hot, too hot. Louisa's instinct was to go back downstairs.

But Charlie would be here. She thought of him and made her way through the crowd, past tittering, chattering groups. No one greeted her, not at all. One woman reached out and stroked her hair. Louisa pulled away from the stench of alcohol that emanated from the other guest's body.

Double doors led to the next room, and more to the one after that. A raised platform was set up in one corner and a group of musicians sat on a dais nearby. Maids, their makeup overstated, cheeky smiles hovering on their masklike faces, flounced about under the grand chandeliers. But were they maids, or women of the night dressed up? It was always impossible to tell in Montmartre.

Louisa accepted a glass of champagne. And reminded herself that all of this, and Henry, and the high-class courtesans who decorated the room, were artifice. None of this was real. She raked the room for Charlie. She clung to the words that he had said. He wanted to live a real life. And so did she. So, dear God, did she.

The band struck up. Three women dressed in tailored men's suits appeared on the platform, crooning, while men in tails pushed past Louisa to see.

Then she spotted them. She spotted them both.

Charlie stood a good head taller than Henry. Louisa tried to push her way through to them. But she became stuck several times. In the end, she skirted her way around the edge of the crowd, took an undignified swig of her champagne, and placed it down on a side table.

Then she was right upon them. She stopped outside their peculiar little circle. Neither of them realized she was there. Their heads—brothers' heads, both cut from the same cloth—were close.

Louisa sensed something then, some unity between them, a brotherly conferring. And hope soared into her for a moment, and she dared not interrupt. Could they possibly work this out? Surely, Henry would see sense. Her feelings jumped, darting like sparks from a fire as she watched Charlie's expression, and then Henry's.

She was not part of their discussion.

Yet it had everything to do with her.

People pushed past her, constantly elbowing into her side, her back, almost toppling her off her feet several times. She wiped a hand across her forehead and started to feel faint.

And then it happened.

"How dare you," Henry growled. But his growl was not a low snarl. It was not something that only he and Charlie were going to hear. It was loud, and it resonated.

A hush fell over everyone nearby.

Someone laughed, a rushed, forced laugh, and the chatter resumed. A few snorts and snickers then. Louisa bit on her lip. Hard.

She caught Charlie's eye. The expression on Henry's face worried her. She took a step toward them both. But Charlie shook his head. He whispered something in Henry's ear.

"Go back to Ashworth. Get out," Henry said.

"Henry." She was unable to stand by and wait.

Henry turned toward her, swift as a snake, and his eyes looked like a snake's eyes too. He looked startled, though, as if he was in shock.

Louisa shot a side-glance at Charlie, and he caught her eye. That tiny motion told Louisa everything. It wasn't going to work. She had to become involved.

This was her life, her future.

And, quite frankly, she had had enough.

"Is there somewhere quiet we can go and talk?" Louisa addressed her words to Charlie. Her hands were damp.

Henry ran his own hand over his chin, leaving it there for a moment and closing his dark eyes. For an inexplicable, odd second, Louisa felt a wave of compassion toward him. And she knew she had to take advantage of that very moment, that second of vulnerability, because goodness only knew it was not going to last. Louisa leaned forward, took Henry's arm, and kept her voice whisper-soft.

"Let's go somewhere and talk this through. We can't leave things as they are. You know that. I know you do. Please, can we just talk?"

Henry looked at her as if she were someone he hardly knew. He looked like a hunted animal. He looked scared. And suddenly, Louisa understood. For the first time, she saw him for who he was.

He ran away from everything.

He wasn't strong.

But she was. Charlie was.

"Staircase. Go upstairs, Louisa." Charlie's voice came from right behind her. She loved the way he pronounced her name—there was such respect for her in his tone. It was something that she had never had from Henry.

Henry was so close to her that she sensed his tension, felt it herself as they made their way through the crowd. He opened his mouth a couple of times and pushed at her impatiently, like a child. And as she looked at him, she realized that his expression was childlike too—callow, obstinate, petulant. He had never had the chance to grow up. He was still, for all intents and purposes, a boy rather than a man.

Charlie was ahead of them now. Once they reached the top floor, he strode up a hallway that was lined with a series of firmly closed doors.

It was quieter up here, but it was still stifling hot. Louisa needed fresh air.

Elegant urns lined the hallway, all filled with miniature versions of the hideous bouquet that graced the entrance hall below. The parquet floor was covered with a dark runner, and the walls were lined with gaudy, vivid art. This was all part of the new world. The problem was that it clashed, violently, with the old.

Henry was caught between them both.

Charlie looked at her, a question in his eye. She nodded. They had become complicit now. It was as if they worked as a team. And this gave Louisa confidence, such confidence in the future and in his maturity and in their combined strength. She could see them, together, no matter what work they did. Charlie held open the door to an empty room.

It was a bedroom—tasteful, for this house. But a vase of wretchedly vivid flowers sat by the bed. Henry stood in the doorway, his arms folded, his feet spread wide apart.

Louisa moved across to the window.

"I need air," she told Charlie.

He nodded.

Henry glowered from where he stood.

She pulled the curtains open. French doors sat behind them. There was a small balcony outside with a balustrade—low decorative iron—such a pretty thing. Louisa threw the doors open. And she stood outside and breathed.

She lifted her face up to the clear sky. Fresh air embraced her, as if it were a cool, blessed shroud. Noises drifted up from the street. Laughter. Sounds of an accordion filtered into the air. Some old French tune.

Henry stood just inside the wide-open doors.

Charlie was a little farther into the room.

When Henry spoke, his voice emerged like a snarl. "I was always expected to be the sensible one, the damned heir. Paraded around the countryside as if I were some half-cocked hero. And then, women were paraded for me."

"Henry." Charlie's word was a warning.

"You had everything." Henry spat out the words. "Freedom, a life."

Louisa closed her eyes. Henry's words hit her like punches to her soul. Charlie had taken over Henry's role—he was covering for him. Why couldn't Henry see that?

"I know that our parents wished that you had been born first. I'm not stupid. I can see that."

Louisa shook her head. "I want to set you free, Henry. Charlie and I both want that. Can't you see?" She fought to control the tremors in her voice.

But Henry turned to her. His mouth was set in a fatal sneer. "You are tied to me until we are both dead and buried. And that, Louisa, is that."

Louisa gasped.

Charlie looked down at the floor.

"But forgive me," Henry said, adopting the light tone of a comic, changing tack, it seemed, faster than a tiger on the hunt. "Forgive me if I want Paris before I come back to my slow death. My father's death will be my own death, you see. Only then will I return to Ashworth. I'll assume the cloak that I damn well have no choice but to wear. But I swear, Louisa, I will not divorce you. I won't do that to the family. I have no idea how you could think I ever would. Are you fools? I'm going to be a duke, God damn it. You are both socially naïve."

Someone shouted in the street.

Louisa turned and leaned against the railing, her arms spread wide on the delicate wrought iron.

Chapter Twenty-Six

Ashworth, 2015

Frank Moore's front garden was resplendent with life. Tomatoes clung, lush and red and ripe, to wooden stakes in neat rows alongside lettuce, onions, and young carrot plants. Everything was orderly, everything looked to be in its place.

Sarah followed Frank up the pathway to his cottage, sensing that there was nothing she could say that was going to hurry him up. But she could not help conjuring up visions. Had someone dug up the baby's grave, Heathcliff and Cathy–like? What had happened to it?

Frank stopped on the narrow path that led to his house and Sarah nearly fell into him. "This garden gives me such joy. One of the young under-gardeners comes and does most of the work these days. I work alongside him as much as I can."

Sarah forced herself to concentrate on the new turn the old man's conversation appeared to have taken, while glancing at the roses that had been planted close to the cottage, the white petunias that tumbled out of terra-cotta pots. She stopped right behind him at the green-painted front door.

He turned the brass handle and led her through the small entrance into a tiny sitting room. She had to bend her neck so as not to hit her head on the top of the old wooden frame.

Exposed wooden beams lined the ceiling. Two small sofas were set up in front of a simple fireplace—a thick piece of wood did duty as a mantelpiece. Sarah thought how cozy this all was compared to Ashworth and its sense of grandeur, and she could not help but appreciate it after the iciness that nipped at her when she saw the graves.

"I'll put the kettle on. Do come with me into the kitchen, if you like."

Sarah followed him. Floral curtains made do for cupboard fronts. Frank took the kettle to the old sink and filled it before placing it on his Aga.

"This is lovely," Sarah said.

Frank busied himself with a pot, filling it with tea leaves, watching his kettle until it bubbled and steamed on the stovetop. He seemed intent on his task.

After Frank had given Sarah an old, thick mug, he led her back into the sitting room, opened the window wide, and secured the glass pane with a hook to the thick window frame. It was far cooler in the cottage than outside. Sarah sat down and sipped at the tea. Strong tea. And waited.

He regarded her for a moment. Then put down his mug.

Sarah found herself unable to speak.

Frank blew out an audible breath. "My great-aunt, Jess, was the governess for your ancestor's husband, Henry, and his younger brother, Charles, until they went off to boarding school. She was supposed to take care of Louisa's baby too, once she was finished with the nurse."

Sarah sat up. "I'm sorry? Did you say she?"

Frank seemed to chew at his teeth a little. He looked off to the side, and Sarah found herself staring at him, wanting answers. What was he talking about?

"Sorry—I'm confused, Frank. The family here told me Louisa had a boy."

"The Duval family was not going to give up a boy," Frank said, as if he were telling her an accepted fact.

"Give up?"

He looked at her, and sighed. "Sarah, you need to know that the story of the baby's death was fabricated by the family. Your Louisa's husband, Henry, was convinced that Louisa's baby had been fathered by his younger brother, Charles."

"What?" She had given up trying to keep up.

The old man shook his head. "They were in love. Your Louisa, and Henry's younger brother, Charles."

Sarah slumped back in her seat.

"Louisa's baby was a girl, Sarah. And she lived. Her name, my dear, was Evelyn."

"Then who are the family living here now descended from?"

"After Louisa's death, Henry claimed that Evelyn was not his. He refused to have anything to do with the little girl. What's more, he wanted his brother, Charles, out of Ashworth."

"Oh." Sarah reached forward and picked up her mug. Her hands were shaking now, fluttering. Fast.

"Charles, who could have turned himself to anything, so the story goes, went to Hong Kong, where he became successful in business in his own right. He took Evelyn with him. He did come back here to visit though. Charlie visited his parents, and he forged some sort of relationship with Henry in the end. But he didn't live here. Not after Louisa's death."

"Hong Kong?" Sarah shook her head.

"Henry's parents desperately wanted him to return home and run the estate. His absence was embarrassing," Frank said. "Henry was forced to come home. It was Charlie who had to go."

"How concerned they all seemed with appearances." But the sense Sarah had gotten of Henry and Marthe from their letters was that they were fighting against society's focus on what looked right all the time.

"Aye. Henry's parents knew that Evelyn would remind him of Charles and Louisa's betrayal, as he saw it. And Charles wasn't going to leave Louisa's daughter in the hands of his parents. The duke and duchess, in turn, didn't want any more of Louisa's scandal hanging about."

"Scandal again," Sarah murmured. She thought about how far the family had gone to get rid of any sort of taint surrounding Louisa. Sarah began to wonder if she might have become a suffragette herself, had she lived in the late nineteenth century.

"Henry finally saw that he had to take on his role here."

"Was he very good at it?" Sarah couldn't help but ask.

"He was fine. He escaped to Paris when he could. But apparently, he resigned himself to his lot. Determination to punish Charles and push him away for trying to take Louisa took over."

Sarah shook her head. "Extraordinary," she whispered.

Frank nodded. "Samuel, Louisa's younger brother, came here," Frank went on, "right after Louisa's death, and met Charles. Both loved Louisa—apparently they developed something of a bond. Since there was no future here for Charles, he went with Samuel to Hong Kong—and took Evelyn. Charles wanted to give Louisa's daughter the chances that Louisa never had. He wrote to my great-aunt Jess with regularity. It was much better for the lass than staying here at Ashworth would have been for her. I have no doubt about that."

"But Evelyn is even recorded as a boy in the family Bible." Sarah's thoughts were in a whirl. And she still had not been told the answer to her question. Did Frank know? Because she was absolutely going to ask.

"So you have been snooping about!"

Sarah couldn't stop her lips from forming a wry smile, but Frank smiled back at her.

"That entry in the Bible and that headstone in the churchyard are Henry's fabrications," he said. "Henry liked theater—part of him always loved to make things up. It sounded more dramatic if he said he'd lost his only son. He changed the family tree once his parents had died, and no one was going to question the Duke of Ashworth.

"Henry was not going to acknowledge the little girl and risk her coming back, claiming her rights as heir to the estate. Mind you, he knew that Evelyn probably wouldn't come back, not if she were anything like as stubborn as her mother. All she would want was freedom. Henry's false legacy lasted for generations. But now, you are here."

Sarah didn't want to keep on gasping. But she was not sure what else to do. "But hang on—what about the family who are here now? Henry died childless. And it looks like his heirs are cousins?"

"Aye, a cousin inherited after Henry died soon after the Second World War. He was the current duke's father." Frank regarded her and went on. "Charlie raised Evelyn in Hong Kong, where Charlie and Samuel worked together. Evelyn married and gave birth to a daughter, Alice, in 1922.

"During the Second World War, Charles, Evelyn, her husband, and Alice returned to England, but Evelyn's husband was killed in an air raid. Charles and Evelyn went back to Hong Kong, while young Alice chose to go to America in 1945. To Boston."

"To Boston?"

Frank continued, a determined expression on his face. "Alice took up a job in a bank. But in 1953, she became pregnant. She was unmarried. It was a quick affair. She found herself alone and lost."

Sarah felt herself blanch. Something landed, hard, in her stomach.

Frank stood up, easing his stiff legs straight, and Sarah did not know where to look. "Alice decided to give up the baby. She decided it should have a better life. The West family in Boston were relations. Edward and Elisabeth West were childless. Edward was—"

"Samuel's grandson." Sarah brought her hand up to her mouth. Her other hand shot out to the faded old armrest at her side.

"Edward had found the war very hard. He couldn't cope, like many men."

"I know. He struggled with illness all his life. The war affected him terribly. I think," she whispered, "his troubles couldn't help but affect my father..."

Frank regarded her now. He sat down and folded his hands to make a tent. "Not coping with the war was no disgrace."

"I know. Please, go on."

"Edward and Elisabeth adopted the baby. Alice kept out of it. She felt it was best. She ended up in New York, I believe. She stayed in America, worked all her life, was successful. But she didn't see her baby, Simon—"

Sarah's hands were shaking again. Her father's reticence about the past. Had he ever known who his mother was? Had he suspected? Had he been told? Was that why he had kept that letter locked away? It would have come from his birth mother. If Charlie had somehow gotten hold of it, he had probably given it to Evelyn and she would have passed it on to her daughter. Alice clearly thought it was important enough to be handed down to her son.

But had her father ever read it? Or had he decided, like his adopted father, that the past was simply too much? Had he bottled it away?

One link, one letter. What damage it could do—or was it damage? How much should we share with each other? It was impossible to tell.

Frank went on.

Sarah's mind flew backward, like a film reel in reverse.

"Simon was just what the West couple needed. They were childless, like I said."

Frank eyed her. "Secrets abounded around adoption back then, Sarah."

Sarah stood up.

Frank was quiet for a moment. When he spoke, he sounded as if he were trying to apply a balm. "The older I get, the more it astonishes me how little of ourselves we share with others," he said. "I think it depends on the nature of our relationships as to how open we are ourselves. If they are not good . . ." His voice trailed off.

"Yes, I suppose that's true," Sarah said, and she was aware that she sounded wistful now. She moved across to look out the window at the garden, at the bees and the flowers outside. And wondered: what legacy would she leave for future generations? Shrouded secrets? Or would she be open and share everything? She turned back to face the old man.

"My great-aunt, Jess, was very old when I was born," Frank said, his voice barely audible. "This story was so hidden, and yet of vital importance to Ashworth. Jess asked me to keep it safe."

"Thank you," she said. He had told her so much, had clearly kept all this information in his head for years, for the family's sake. His loyalty was touching.

She looked down at the old man as he continued to speak. "Charles and Evelyn kept in touch with Jess, then with my mother, over the years. And now, here you are." He paused for a moment. "Things turned in a full circle, in the end. As they tend to."

Sarah moved closer to him. "But the family here knows none of this. I wonder why it had to be kept such a secret from them?"

Frank eased himself back in his seat. Sarah waited. But she had a dreadful feeling that she knew exactly what he was going to say.

"The reason it had to be kept secret was because you, Sarah, are the true heir to the estate. There was never anything to say a woman couldn't inherit. The third duchess was the eldest daughter back in the mid-1800s. And she inherited. That was one of the reasons that Henry never wanted to see Evelyn, who he suspected was Charles and Louisa's, ever again. He had to obliterate her memory, so that she could never claim to be who she was—and neither, Sarah, could her descendants."

Sarah sat down opposite him with a thud.

Paris, 1895

A chill breeze picked up in Paris, sweeping cool shafts of air around the balcony that had become a refuge from the ghastly scene that was playing out inside the apartment. The coals that had simmered between Charlie and Henry for who knew how many years seemed about to turn into a roaming, windswept blaze. Louisa knew that she would be hard-pressed to stop it. It was as if the fireball needed to run its course.

Her breath was coming in hard, fast patterns. Half of her wanted to run, to get help, to shout out, but she also felt an overwhelming desire to step in, to calm things, to sort this out. But in the end, she knew Henry's animosity ran too deep.

"How dare you," Henry growled now, his voice barely recognizable.

Louisa took a step forward. Goodness knew, she would intervene if she had to. Charlie stood right in front of her. His body shielded the open doors.

Louisa could not pull her eyes away from her husband's face. His mouth was twisted into a distorted, strange shape. Louisa hated to think what it was going to spit out. She closed her eyes against nausea, but sadness filtered into her system too, for this whole situation, for the madness of its descent.

But then she started at the sound of movement. On instinct, she sensed herself at full alert.

She took a step toward Charlie, but Henry lunged at him, shoving Charlie into a side table against the wall.

Henry punched Charlie, hard, in the mouth. Charlie reeled backward, falling against the wall. Louisa moved nearer to him, but Henry blocked her path.

"And how dare you," he growled. He was breathing hard, like an animal on a hunt.

Louisa braced herself. She shot a glance at Charlie, but he was still slumped against the wall. Henry's hand was raised. In one split second, he dashed toward Louisa, stepping out onto the balcony, which seemed more like a cage than a relief now—all she wanted to do was to get to Charlie. Henry pointed his finger at her face as he spoke, forcing her closer to the low railings. The cold, sharp air hit her, and she glanced, desperate, toward Charlie, but she couldn't see past Henry. His hair blew in the wind, backward in streaks. His face, which was too close, was pale, and his mouth was drawn back in a contorted grimace.

"You betrayed me," he said. His voice was unutterably low. "With my brother. With my own brother?" His voice jumped up a few octaves on the last words.

"No." She had married him in good faith. She had not betrayed their marriage, even if she could no longer hide her love for Charlie.

He didn't love her. That was clear. So was it pride and vanity and ego that mattered now to him, the fact that she was his property? The fact that she was not behaving as his wife? The irony of his attitude astounded her.

"Henry," she said. "Calm down. You don't want me. You haven't wanted me…"

But he simply shook his head. "That's hardly the point."

Louisa couldn't stop the hollow laugh that escaped from her throat.

But then, movement. Henry turned around. In the flash of a whip, Charlie was on the tiny balcony too, next to her, his arm around her shoulders, firm between her and Henry. Louisa stood as close to him as she could.

"Your betrayal is complete," Henry growled again. "How the hell long has this been going on? Since before our marriage? Since the first night you met?"

Louisa closed her eyes at the sound of his hard, hostile voice. Her lips were frozen. She shook now, her whole body convulsed with rapid shudders that she could not control. It was all she could do to keep breathing; her chest rose and fell alongside the shivers of the wind.

Charlie moved his hand down and placed it in Louisa's.

Henry's head shook back and forth in a fast, clocklike rhythm. He was half on the balcony, half in the room. "Seeing you like this—"

"Henry." Charlie stood, quiet and still, but his breathing was hard and strong and real and he stroked Louisa's palm with his fingertips.

And right then, Henry looked down and saw it too. "I will never speak to either of you again." And he raised his hand at Charlie.

Louisa was next to Charlie on the balcony, but she was on the far side, right next to the low railing.

She stepped forward to protect Charlie from the blow. If she did so, she thought in that split second, perhaps she would stop him from being struck again. God knew, Henry would hurt him. Louisa thought fast. If she pushed Henry's arm away, toward the railing, he would strike the hard iron instead.

She tried to deflect Henry's hand before it struck.

But she underestimated his speed and his strength.

Henry pushed her arm away as if it were as slight as a stick in the forest, and she heard snapping, then felt harrowing pain as Henry's fist landed on her side instead of Charlie's. Louisa could not stop herself from keeling over backward, fast, faster, and Charlie was shouting, and she had lost her grip and she slipped over the small, hip-height railing, toppling and twisting, her body free-falling like a rag doll. For a moment she felt Charlie grabbing at her arm, but her hand was cold, clammy, slick.

And she realized, suddenly, that she was falling.

Louisa heard screams as she went down—she was aware of that. She was aware, strangely, of French accents and that smell again, that awful nauseating stink of cheap perfume and wine and cigarettes and bodies, heaped up. Were they underneath her, or above, was she upside down, or straight up? And her instincts moved her toward Charlie, and he was shouting, desperate, scared, his voice wrenching into the air. She reached up, instinctively, again toward him. She loved him so much and with such pure, honest force. But her head hit concrete. Another dreadful crack. Harder, more final this time. And her eyes flickered for a moment. Her baby—Evelyn—Jess, her work, Charlie?

Blood dripped out of her mouth; she felt her own red warmth on her lips. Her own blood. There was the fuzz of the crowding of strangers above her, words, random things—last things, she suspected—coming in rapid, urgent French. Shadows, stink. And then Charlie. She felt him by her side. His hands around her body. And he picked her up and he held her, close to his chest, and her aching, leaden head was against his heartbeat now.

"You'll be safe," he was whispering. "You'll be all right."

And she leaned in closer and her head pounded with something stronger and harder still. But it wasn't a life force. It wasn't that. She tried to tell him. But her mouth wouldn't open. Not now.

"I love you," he said. "I'm always here."

She tried, again, to nod, and focused what little there was left now on his heartbeat.

"I adore you," she managed to say. And she tried to reach up. "I always will."

And his head touched hers, and his arms cradled her body.

And then she had to close her eyes properly. They were too heavy now.

Just for a moment. Just for a rest.

Ashworth, 2015

Sarah picked up her empty mug, turning the old ceramic piece over in her hands, running her fingers over the thick china. It was still slightly warm from the tea.

"Frank," she said, "thank you so much for what you've said. The thing is, now I know all this, but you see, there was something else that I came here to find out. I guess the one thing that is haunting me is how Louisa died. Her mother did not cope, her parents' marriage crumbled, and her father lost his business after what happened in Paris. Cousins kept away. Now I have no family left. That moment on the balcony in Paris has lingered like a heavy rock at the bottom of a clouded pool in my family. I don't think that what happened to her is clear. There seemed to be so much subterfuge surrounding the circumstances. And a lot of determination to say that she killed herself. Too much, for my liking."

Frank leaned back on his seat. He paused for a moment, as if he was deciding whether to speak.

"My great-aunt told me what happened," he said, after a while. "Charles told her, but only her. You see, Louisa died trying to save Charles's life. Henry was about to hit him when they were on the balcony at the party in Paris. Henry had just found out about Louisa and Charlie. But you couldn't have the heir to one of the greatest estates in England arrested for trying to murder his brother and mistakenly killing his own wife instead, now could you?"

Sarah took in a sharp breath and nodded her head at him.

"Charles decided not to prosecute." Frank sounded firm. "There was little Evelyn to consider. How would the idea that her father had killed her mother affect her, even if it had been a terrible accident? Charlie didn't speak out in order to protect Louisa's daughter. He didn't want the shadow of foul play hanging over her for the rest of her life. But by protecting the present, he endangered the future. By not laying bare the truth, he left future generations in the dark. I don't know if he did the right thing. But I sometimes wonder what other choice he had."

Sarah nodded. What would she have done? It was impossible to imagine the turmoil that Charlie must have felt at the time—his ability to make rational decisions would have been wracked by grief and anger toward Henry. Had he had a choice, in the end, about any of it? About whom he fell in love with, about the outcome of that?

"The best thing Charles could do was take Evelyn away. Give her the freedom, the education, that Louisa always wanted," Frank said. "Charlie wrote up a piece in the family Bible for Louisa, which he made sure was kept faithful to her spirit and her character, but he never indicted his brother in her death. I think he understood, in some ways, what Henry's struggles were too." Frank looked thoughtful, but he was quiet.

So, it had been Charlie who had written about Louisa. The length of her entry had been a little enigmatic, given all the family had done to wipe the circumstances surrounding her death from history. But someone had respected her. Someone had believed in her and valued her. Was that, in the end, what mattered most?

She walked over to the window and looked out.

Frank cleared his throat.

Sarah was quiet for a moment. "Can you promise me something?" Her words came out as a whisper.

He looked at her, his old eyes steady.

"I don't want you to tell anyone that I'm the heir to this estate."

He smiled. "I knew that," he said, "which is why I told you. You'd have to live with the lot who are here now, anyway. Doubt they'd budge."

Sarah moved toward him and held out a hand. Frank stood up and held it for a moment. His hand was surprisingly soft, still warm with life.

"Thank you," she said. "Thank you for everything." She leaned forward on an impulse and gave him a hug.

She took one more look around the cottage. So, that was that.

It was done.

Now she knew.

Chapter Twenty-Seven

Ashworth, 2015

Half an hour later, Sarah climbed into the taxi that sat at the bottom of the front steps. Jeremy and his parents stood framed in the front doorway like any family waving off a cousin. And she waved back to them, as if everything were as normal as could be. She watched them turn around, returning into that great old house. They would take care of it, Sarah knew, just as Charlie would have wanted them to.

And one thing was certain—they wouldn't rattle any ghosts from the past. Was that a good thing?

As the car wound its way along the edge of the park, along a path that Louisa would have walked on countless times, Sarah found her thoughts turning to more practical matters.

She found herself thinking about where she was going next. She had been so caught up in Frank's story that she had pushed her deliberations about going back to Boston out of her mind. But it seemed inevitable that she would have to go home now. She leaned her hand against the car door, then moved it, pulled her phone out of her bag, and put it back.

She forced herself to concentrate on what was going on outside. They passed through the gatehouse, where pretty cottages were built into the stone walls. A family sat outside at a table in the garden. Sarah waved to them, and then frowned at her phone.

She should simply go home to Boston.

But she wanted to go to Paris. Laurent, who she thought was a Henry, had turned out to be a Charlie instead. Soon, Sarah had formed a record number of lists and rationales in her head.

But while all of this analysis had its merits, she returned, stubbornly, to the same conviction. She could not get on a train to London, then a flight home, without making one call. So she scrolled through her contacts list and found the number she needed.

"Sarah." Laurent picked up after the first couple of rings. "How are you?" He sounded friendly enough.

Sarah chewed on her lip. "Bonjour, Laurent. I'm well. And you?"

There was a pause. "Fine. Good. Merci."

She told him about Louisa. She told him what she had learned. Laurent worked out straightaway that this made her the heir to the estate.

"I'm not going to do anything about that!" She was surprised to hear the laughter in her own voice.

"I know you won't," he said, sounding as if he were next to her in the cab.

They arrived at the station in Alton, and the taxi driver pulled up in front. He popped the trunk of the car open. Sarah paid him and grabbed her luggage, but then she stood there on the sidewalk. She didn't even know which train she should catch.

"I'm just going to the ticket counter," she said to Laurent. And decided this was utterly inane.

"Have you thought about where you're going next?"

Sarah stood opposite the woman behind the glass counter.

"Where to?" the woman asked, looking bored.

Sarah fought the impulse to ask the attendant to make the decision. She was being ridiculous. She could hardly just go back to Paris.

She closed her eyes and took in a breath.

"Where to, please?" An indentation appeared between the woman's brows, and she peered past Sarah in a telling fashion at the queue that was forming behind her back.

Sarah clutched at her suitcase handle. And decided she must have completely lost her mind.

"You'd better give her an answer." Laurent sounded as if he were amused now, as if the thing were a huge joke.

Sarah stood stuck on the spot.

Had she ever done such a thing? No. She had let Steven find her. She had let Steven search her out. She had gone along with it. Why hadn't she ever taken her own destiny into her hands? What was that about?

"Do what you want to do, Sarah," Laurent said. "Just tell her where you want to go. It's your call. You can do what you like."

The woman stared at Sarah as if she were crazy. Okay, she had gone to Paris. Okay, that had been a risk. But she had been researching Louisa. It was about her family. Now she had the chance to make her life about what she wanted, perhaps for the first time ever. All that loss, all that sadness—but what she had left, what she had now, was herself.

"Paris," she said, finally, waiting for a reaction down the line.

The woman handed Sarah a pair of tickets. One to London. One to France. Asked for the next person to come forward in the queue. Sarah stepped aside.

"Great," Laurent said. "That's great," he repeated, and she smiled at his genuineness.

Sarah knew he meant what he said. That was the thing about Laurent. She took the tickets to Paris and wandered across to the platform opposite, where she stopped at a magazine stand. Perhaps she would buy something lovely to read on the way back. *Vogue*? She chuckled at the thought that Laurent's work would be in an issue not far off.

"What time do you get in?" Laurent asked, his voice still intimate.

"Four o'clock," she said. Paris at four? It sounded like the perfect idea. She picked up the magazine and paid for it, smiling at the old man behind the counter.

"I have to be at the Louvre all afternoon. Otherwise I'd pick you up. But why don't you drop your things at the apartment? Cat's there. She'll let you in. Then come to the Louvre, meet me. Would you like to go out for dinner, after that?"

"I'd love to," she said, not caring that a grin had spread onto her face. "See you later."

So she climbed onto the train and began her trip to Paris.

Sarah rested her head on the back of the seat and watched as the train moved past rolling green fields and through towns filled with half-timbered houses and old market squares. It was different here from Boston, and difference, Sarah knew, was what she needed in her life now. She had been percolating an idea for the past few days, having realized that in many ways, she didn't want to go back home to work just now. What if she made a suggestion to Amanda? What if she were to curate an exhibition, a collaboration between the museum in Boston and the Musée des Arts Décoratifs? She had even dreamed up a title: *Paris during the Belle Époque: The Lost World of the Courtesan.*

Because Marthe's world had been lost. The discovery of her apartment had been profound, in many ways. It was a remnant of the distant past, a past that had not been given much consideration once it was overshadowed by those two world wars.

When Sarah knocked on the door of Marthe de Florian's old apartment, Cat came straight to the door.

"Hey," Cat said, leaning forward and enveloping her in a hug. Sarah embraced the other girl back. And also hugged a baby, a dark-haired, brown-eyed little person wrapped in a gossamer shawl.

"Hello," Sarah said, unable to resist touching the baby's button nose.

"This is Isabelle." Cat smiled. "Isabelle, meet Sarah."

Sarah smiled at the baby, and the tiny girl looked back.

Cat adjusted her daughter in her arms. "Come in, Sarah. I've been up here to interview a photographer. Loic and I are going back down to Provence this evening. But Laurent's still in town. He's been asked to paint at the Louvre for a week. Students can go and watch him paint, so he's working on some of the Boldini projects there for now. I hope you enjoyed England? Come in. Let's have a coffee."

Sarah smiled at her. "Yes, yes, I did enjoy England…" Her voice trailed off.

Cat didn't ask awkward questions. That was a relief.

"I'm pleased," Cat said. "As for Laurent, he's inundated with students. Apparently, the entire final-year art history class at the Sorbonne was told to go and sit and watch him for a few days as part of their studies in current artistic trends. So they are, apparently. All of them."

Sarah wondered if she should interrupt. "But won't I just add to the crowds?"

Cat paused for a moment, and it was as if she was contemplating what to say next. "We had a bit of a chat with Laurent last night, Sarah. Loic got him to talk—he tends to be good at drawing people out."

Sarah waited for Cat to continue.

"Laurent wants to see you," she said, reaching forward and resting a hand on Sarah's arm. "He was lost, for a while. It seems that before he met you—well, he tells us that he's never felt anything so real in his life. He was so hoping that you'd come back. But he wasn't going to push you. He'd never do that. The bad boy thing really wasn't working. It wasn't him. But I suspect you knew that."

Sarah chuckled her agreement, but her mind latched onto one thing Cat had said. "He told you and Loic that he was hoping I'd come back to Paris?"

Cat nodded. "He did."

Sarah stood still. Ran a hand over her bob. And then she let it swell, that feeling, that sense that everything might at last be coming right. Was she now at the point of realizing that no matter how bad things got, no matter how dark it all seemed, there was also, in the end, light?

"I don't think I need that coffee," Sarah said. Suddenly, she wanted to rush to the Louvre.

Cat grinned back at her. "Just go and see him."

Sarah turned and went to the door, and then she stopped, because Cat was saying something else.

"Sarah," Cat said, "welcome to Paris."

Sarah managed to avoid the long queues outside the Louvre. She used her pass to the Museum of Fine Arts, which allowed her to go straight to the front of the queues. Soon she was wending her way to the room where Laurent was painting, having asked directions from someone at the information desks. If there was one thing she could do, it was to find her way through a crowded museum. She could do that like a pro.

Sarah stopped behind the large group of students that was hiding Laurent from view in one of the rooms off a wide corridor full of Italian art. Slowly, politely, she tried to make her way through the crowd so that she could see him.

Suddenly, a student stood up, taking his folding chair into his arms and holding it aside. He indicated that she go right on past. Sarah thanked him, with a smile, and then another student moved her seat out of the way. And another. Until there was a direct, smooth path that led to the front. This was so very polite that Sarah was enchanted.

French, perhaps?

Were students in Paris always this well-mannered?

Something stirred in the crowd. A murmur turned into something else. People were muttering, staring at her as she made her way through.

When Laurent looked up from his easel, his face broke into the smile that she knew she would always love.

"Hello," he said simply.

Sarah couldn't move.

The room was silent.

Laurent's eyes met hers. Right across the room. As if there were no one else there.

And slowly, Sarah moved farther up the aisle that the students had made for her. Until she stopped, awkward, at the front. And stared at the easel. And frowned. And bit her lip.

"This one's not for sale," he said, his head tilted to one side. "It's going in my apartment. After all, Marthe had a portrait of herself in her bedroom. I wanted one of you."

Sarah stared at the canvas in front of her. He had made her dark hair shine and her eyes and face were clear and her complexion was creamy and she smiled. Straight at the viewer. Confident in herself. She didn't look boring or reliable or in any way dull. Because he had captured her as she was now. Here. Not that shell of a girl who had been crippled by grief before she came to Paris.

Laurent had painted her in an evening dress. It was black, and she wore long black gloves. She wasn't adorned with diamonds or rubies at her throat, not like Marthe, perhaps, would have been. But on her dress, he had painted a brooch, on the left side, right in front of her heart, and she peered at it. On it was a tiny and exquisite portrait in itself.

It was Venus, coming out of her shell. A miniature rendition of the Botticelli. Sarah turned to him, shaking her head. Right now, she didn't care about the students or the crowds in the gallery. Laurent reached forward, tilting her chin up toward his face.

"Thank you," she said.

He leaned down and brushed his lips over hers, for one exquisite moment.

"No. It's I who have to thank you, Sarah."

And the audience started to applaud.

Author's Note

The premise of this book, while obviously linked with my previous novels, *Paris Time Capsule* and *The House by the Lake*, is inspired by an interesting story that I will share with you here. When I was young, my mother told me something that was probably fatal to share with a little girl who had a big imagination!

We would go for walks together around the old suburb of North Adelaide, in southern Australia where I grew up. The area is filled with beautiful colonial mansions, as well as cottages in some of the narrower streets.

My mother grew up in North Adelaide, and I remember her stopping outside one of the suburb's grand old homes and telling me about a party she was at during the 1930s when she was eighteen. I can still see the house, even though I have not walked past it for many years. I can picture the driveway, the balcony, and the sense of sadness that I projected onto the lovely old façade. I can still feel for the eighteen-year-old girl who jumped out of a window and fell to her death in the middle of the party.

I don't know how old I was when my mother told me this story—perhaps eight, an impressionable age. But this girl's tragedy informed the premise for *From a Paris Balcony*, and I would like to acknowledge here, in a small way, that young girl and the tragedy that surrounded her.

As many of you will know, Marthe de Florian was a courtesan during Belle Époque Paris. My characterization of her in this book is based entirely on my own imaginings, while the historical context surrounding her has all been, of course, researched. I wanted to delve into the courtesan as a person rather than thinking of her merely in relation to her role. I think this is the strength of historical fiction. Getting into someone's head gives us an entirely different perspective than reading a nonfiction book.

A Letter from Ella

Dear reader,

I want to say a huge thank you for choosing to read *From a Paris Balcony*. If you did enjoy it, and want to keep up to date with all my latest releases, just sign up at the following link. Your email address will never be shared and you can unsubscribe at any time.

ellacarey.com

I hope you loved *From a Paris Balcony* and if you did I would be very grateful if you could write a review. I'd love to hear what you think, and it makes such a difference helping new readers to discover one of my books for the first time.

I adore writing, and each of my characters are so special to me. I travel all over the world to research the settings for my books. It means so much to have walked in the places you've read about here—it's a privilege to be able to learn about other people, places, and times. Once I've traveled to research a book, I read and read about the time, place, and stories surrounding the real people who lived through the historical time period concerned. When I've interviewed those who know about the topics in the book, it is wonderful to find my characters and story evolving, almost as a simple tribute to those who have gone before us and who have lived through times that seem so different to our own—but, in many ways, there are always links, always ways to find empathy, always pathways to understand. I am a huge believer in the power of stories to connect us in the present and to help us understand the past.

I would love to share my future books with you, and would love it if you would like to join me and my readers on my Facebook page, through Twitter, Goodreads, or on my website, where we chat regularly, and where many of my loyal readers have become friends. It's always me at the other end!

With love,
Ella Carey

ellacareyauthor

@Ella_Carey

www.ellacarey.com

Acknowledgments

My thanks to the entire team at Grand Central Publishing, most especially to my wonderful editor, Kirsiah McNamara. Thanks to Elizabeth Connor for designing such a gorgeous cover. Huge thanks to my brilliant agent, Giles Milburn at the Madeleine Milburn Agency, for everything you do for my writing career, and also special thanks to foreign rights agent Liane-Louise Smith. *From a Paris Balcony* is a book that is very close to my heart, and I am hugely grateful to all the readers who have read, reviewed, and enjoyed the novel. I appreciate each and every one of you.